BROKEN *strings*

a
romance
novel

FRANCESCA FORBES

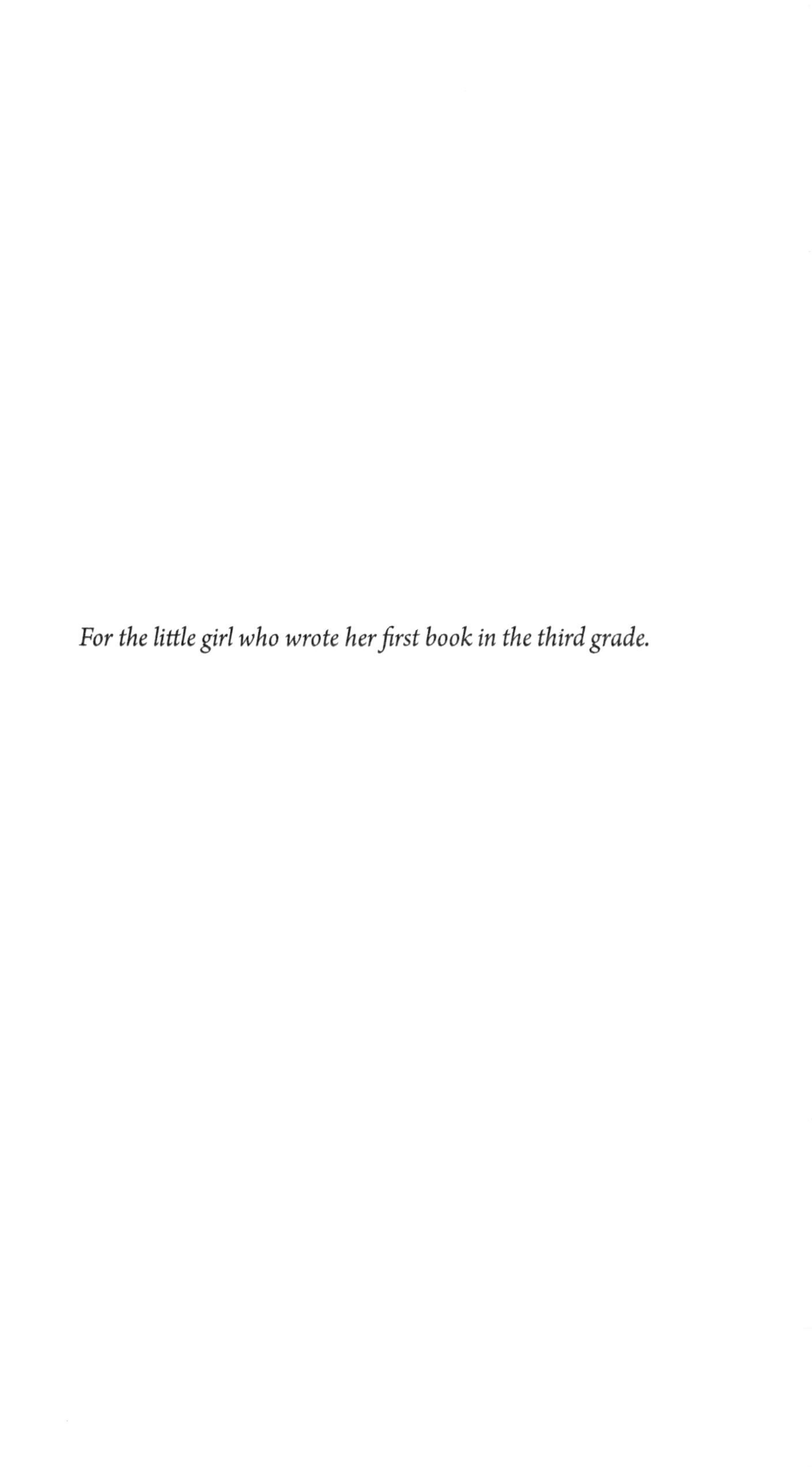

For the little girl who wrote her first book in the third grade.

BROKEN Strings

Chapter One

ASPEN

SHIT.

We were running late. Again.

Despite everyone's best efforts, we were running about an hour behind schedule.

At least according to Elissa, whose nose never came up from the iPad in front of her. She had counted off the exact time Lyle would need to get to the venue and go through rehearsals, plus every other tiny detail practically down to the second. So, making good time was especially crucial in her eyes.

I, like everyone else, only slightly acknowledged her continuous murmuring as I leaned back into the leather upholstered couch across from her. As the stoplight ahead turned red, the bus driver screeched to a halt as we all were jostled around in the front lounge of the tour bus.

"Do you mind?" Elissa yelled at the driver as she annoyingly brushed off the neatly ironed sleeves of her jacket and sat back upright. She immediately went back to tapping on the large iPad with that stylus of hers.

It was almost too stressful to watch Elissa operate on show days. She was so intense and demanding, that most people steered clear of her for fear of being on the receiving end of her wrath. Which was really her own way to ensure everything was going according to plan.

"Elissa, please. You're not dying. Get a grip," Clara quipped as she came out from the back of the bus already dressed in all black for the night.

"You know Clara, I'm the one who will have Lyle on stage and on time tonight, no thanks to you. Just leave me alone so I can work in peace," Elissa replied back snarkily.

Clara, who was entirely unbothered by her attitude, shook out her tight ebony curls in a perfectly rounded shape while looking in the mirror, and simply rolled her eyes. Elissa was the tour manager and had full control most days, but Lyle never would have made it so far without an agent like Clara. She was cutthroat, and pure dynamite in business deals.

She had also become a somewhat decent friend of mine.

Clara had joined us temporarily for our string of South Carolina shows to ensure the tour was going well and to report back to the label on how Lyle was doing overall. Elissa however had a tough time with sharing the 'boss' duties with Clara.

"I don't know how you put up with her on show days Aspen," Clara whispered as she slid in next to me on the couch. I stifled a laugh with Elissa so close by but just shrugged my shoulders in response. The last thing I needed was to upset her when we were this close to the venue.

"Come on ladies, let's all play nice," Lyle said walking out from the private bedroom at the back of the bus.

He was wearing black jeans and that gray pocket tee whose sleeves were deliciously tight around his biceps. *My favorite.*

"Right, Aspen?" he asked me, awaiting my backup. I knew he was expecting me to play fair and be the voice of reason, as per usual.

"Of course. We're in Charleston already and the weather's holding out so far. It's going to be a great show tonight," I tried to say optimistically.

Elissa laughed dryly at my cookie-cutter response. I bit my tongue to resist saying a remark back at her. It could wait.

Lyle kissed the top of my head and smoothed his hand over my back before taking a seat next to Elissa and looking over the schedule for the night.

I honestly couldn't fathom how he did it, the whole 'you be here this time and there this time' and the general micromanaging of his entire life. Being thrust into his wild level of fame so quickly and having to adapt to the transient lifestyle of a cross-country tour with all the chaos that came with it was not for the faint of heart. It still made my head spin, and I'd been with him since the beginning.

But as usual, he just nodded his head as Elissa explained everything and set alarms on his phone, so he'd know when he needed to get his ass in gear and move to the next thing. It had become second nature at that point. We all knew our place as part of the tour to make sure things went as smoothly as possible.

And I, being his loving girlfriend, would be in the background the whole time unseen. I'd watch the craziness ensue as show time dawned closer and I slowly got pushed out. There would suddenly be ten people surrounding us, all primping him and giving him instructions before disappearing into the shadows. Sure, being shoved out of sight sucked, but what was worse was cheering him on from afar. I used to be front row at every concert.

I'd never missed a single show of his. Even at his first gigs when no one showed up, I was always there. At first, it didn't matter how much his popularity rose; I would simply push my way to the front of the crowd and still be in his eyeline.

But then came the fame, the record deal, Clara, the album. It all happened so fast. Then there was the wonderful decision from his label that he could hold his own on a massive tour.

Which left me being at the front of his 'debut sold out tour,' out of the question.

So instead, I started to hang backstage with the crew and watch him from behind. With venues holding as many as 50,000 people, it was deemed to be in my 'best interest' to just stay backstage and wait for the show to be over before seeing Lyle again.

And I cooperated at every single show on the tour.

As much as it annoyed me, I would follow their rules like the loyal girlfriend I was.

Clara and I stood backstage at the Charleston show. "He sounds great tonight, Aspen. Don't you think so?" She was in awe of his stage presence, like everyone else who ever saw him perform.

"Yeah, he really does. This venue is amazing," I replied looking around at all the filled seats.

It was definitely one of the biggest arenas of the tour, and the sound system was incredible. Lyle was talented enough as it was, but having his voice magnified on the huge speakers made him sound even better.

He was about halfway into his set and had just paused to talk to the audience, taking a minute to rest as he slung his guitar back over his shoulder.

It was slightly unsettling seeing girls that couldn't be older than 13 crying their eyes out, screaming about how much they loved him in the front rows. But honestly, I was happy if they were. I was their age once. A concert like that would have been eagerly awaited, saving up money for merch and meticulously planning outfits.

It warmed my heart, not just because of Lyle's success, but because he made people *feel* something. I enjoyed seeing it firsthand, even if it was from backstage.

"What an amazing turnout. I'd love to come along to the next show, but I have a plane to catch in the morning. The label will be very happy that the tour is doing this well though," Clara said as she watched the crowd intently. "There's hardly any empty seats and Lyle seems to be handling the fame really well. I wish I could stay and see some more of his shows. It's like being a proud mother."

"In this business, he would've been eaten alive without you. But it is incredible being at a show like this one. Trust me, it's a mutual feeling," I laughed.

Clara would be sorely missed when she left for L.A. but deep down, I was aware that this was still all business for her even if we had grown close over time. But it sure was nice having her around.

"Well, in this industry it's a dog-eat-dog world. Luckily this top dog found him before someone else did. Just look at the result of it now."

We both looked around and it hit a lot harder realizing that the tour and the money and marketing behind it wouldn't even exist without Clara and many other people's support and backing.

"It is amazing, I agree. Now, don't work too hard out there. I know you, and you deserve a break every once in a while. Perhaps on a lavish beach on a beautiful island with a beautiful man," I laughed as we dodged one of the crew members coming through with equipment.

"Hey, a girl's gotta eat. Although I suppose I could spare a few days for a vacation with a pretty boy… in another year," she joked as she playfully shoved my arm. "And hey, look at you girl. Your life is like a permanent vacation now. Traveling across the U.S. with your famous boyfriend is a pretty sweet deal, Aspen. I'd certainly love to be in your place."

I laughed her off but didn't really feel like I was on a

permanent vacation. Or that I was living the dream. Certainly not *my* dream.

"What can I say, I'm a lucky girl."

I smiled as I said it, but I knew my smile didn't reach my eyes. I just hoped she wouldn't notice.

The show was only two hours long, so I knew I didn't have much longer before I had to head out. It was key that we left before the whole place became a real madhouse.

Not that the screaming audience knew, but backstage all the venue's crew members were hauling ass to start getting everything ready to take down as soon as the show ended. Our team was already preparing to head back on the bus as quickly as possible and get Lyle out without being seen by fans.

Or chased.

Being chased in cars or on the bus was one of the worst parts of his newfound fame. Some of the girls would tailgate us and follow the bus for miles and miles, screaming his name through the windows. Then there were the less successful fans, who just tried to chase after the bus on foot but couldn't keep up for long.

Anything more than that and I was sure I'd feel a lot differently about how amazing this tour and its massive audience was.

"Ladies, we're packing up! Let's move please. We have places to be," one of our staff called out to us as we gave him a thumbs up.

I checked my watch and realized how quickly the show had flown by. I had lost track of time watching Lyle perform. He was absolutely in his element when he was in front of big crowds like this, and I just loved seeing him so free on stage.

I walked to the tour bus parked around back. A few stagehands would direct Lyle over to the bus as soon as the show ended so I didn't have much to worry about for the rest of the night.

Except for the joy of a jam-packed bus.

Nighttime was the worst. There were six bunk beds in the middle of the bus, a queen size pullout in the front lounge hidden in one of the couches, and the bedroom in the back that Lyle and I shared.

Everyone was usually moving around during the day, so we weren't all piled up and right on top of each other. But at night, it was a very different story.

There would be a total of ten of us trying to sleep on the way to the next show, and I could not put into words how awful it was trying to sleep with them all.

Even being in a separate room with Lyle didn't help. I could *always* hear Harlow's snoring that sounded like a freight train, and Christian had insomnia which meant he was up at almost all hours of the night making noise.

I'd always thought I'd been a good sleeper until we went on the road. It was then I realized I was not only a light sleeper, but someone who needed sleep to truly function every day.

And for all those reasons, I really hated nights on the tour bus.

"Hey, doll!" Harlow yelled out to me as we ran into each other going back to the bus. "Can you please ask Lyle to shave tonight? I don't have time to deal with his stubble before every show because he's too lazy to fucking shave," she complained to me as she walked ahead and up the stairs.

Harlow was his lovely hair stylist who had a mouth on her like no one else I knew. She was a wild card, the kind of girl so confident that no one could touch her. It was admirable in some sense, and I personally envied the hell out of her for it.

Truthfully, I didn't know what was louder, her or her bright pink pixie-cut hair. Also covered in sleeves of tattoos, she was the one person onboard who never let anyone, or anything bother her. She dyed my hair every few weeks for free too, so I really couldn't complain about her attitude or boisterous personality. She was damn good at her job.

"Yes, Harlow. But you know as well as I do that he can't keep up with it to save his life."

She looked back at me and threw her hands up in frustration. "I swear that boy! A 24-year-old man should know how to keep up with shaving his face for Christ's sake. The label wants him clean-shaven, so that's just the way it is. Remind him of that tonight please, so he can keep this fancy tour."

Well, the label could kiss my ass. Who actually cared if his face was shaved or not? This was the kind of trivial stuff from the label that drove me insane.

We all filed up the stairs to the tour bus, one by one. It was nearing midnight, the inevitable tiredness kicking in after running around for a few hours. A couple of the band members made sandwiches for dinner for the night, and I grabbed a bag of chips from the cupboard to hold me over.

All we were missing now was Lyle, Elissa, and Christian, Lyle's personal assistant who bled into a best friend role.

"I need some wine. Ugh thank God I'm going back home tomorrow. You all are saints trying to survive this shit with no alcohol," Clara whined as she walked out of the bathroom in a satin robe for the night.

Her very limited time in the *one* bathroom aboard the bus was already up, unfortunately.

I didn't respond to her wine comment as she either didn't recall that I was only twenty or thought I could use the drink regardless. But a sober Lyle was one of the catches of a tour of this magnitude. Which meant we all had to be as well.

As one by one went and used the bathroom sparingly for the night, I looked at my watch and realized it was getting late. Each person took their turn in the tiny bus bathroom, and I started to worry about how late Lyle was.

He was *really* late.

Where was he?

The show had long past ended at that point and usually, there was someone moving like their ass was on fire to get Lyle aboard the bus as quickly as humanly possible without anyone seeing us.

Something was wrong.

Chapter Two

ASPEN

I MADE MY WAY PAST EVERYONE ONBOARD AND UP FRONT toward the bus driver who was settling in for the drive.

"Hey, you haven't seen Lyle yet, right?"

"Nope, not yet. We really need to get on the road too. We've got a long drive tonight."

Shit, where was he?

I thanked the bus driver and thought about asking Clara to come with me, but she was already getting ready for bed.

Going against my better judgment, I hopped off the bus alone and ran back into the backstage area in search of him and the others. I thought I caught a glimpse of Elissa's sleek black bob out of the corner of my eye, but there were so many of the venue's crew members coming in and out I could hardly get by them.

"Excuse me! Excuse me please," I tried to say politely, squeezing by them.

I tapped on Elissa's shoulder, and she swung around in pure panic.

"Aspen, oh thank God! *Please* tell me you've seen Lyle. The show ended thirty minutes ago, and I can't find him anywhere!"

"No, I just came back here to see what was going on. Where the hell did he go?" I yelled over all the noise.

"I have looked everywhere backstage. He has to be somewhere outside! He's with Christian."

"Outside? Shit, this is bad Elissa. We're way behind sched-ule. People are getting ready for bed already. Lyle needs to be on that bus!"

"Okay, okay, I'll go check and make sure we didn't just miss him and he's not already on the bus. You look for him and Christian around the venue. He better not be messing with me. I am not in the mood for this!"

As she stomped off back toward the bus, I tried to keep my nerves at bay. I was sure Lyle was just messing around but with how tight the schedule was, it was a really bad idea. And he had scared me shitless, which I also didn't appreciate.

I walked around aimlessly outside at first, not seeing any-where he could possibly be. But then I stumbled upon a heap of equipment by a stage door and saw a shoe poking out from around the pile.

"Lyle? Lyle, is that you?"

As I rounded around the corner, I saw Lyle and Christian sitting on the ground, passing a joint between them.

"Aspen! Hey, I was hoping to see you. You want a hit?" Lyle asked through a fit of giggles, holding it out to me.

Okay, just a little weed. It could be much worse.

"No, I don't want a hit," I sighed, grabbing the joint and throwing it in the bushes. "I swear to God Christian, I should kill you for smuggling this in. Do you know how worried every-one is? Elissa is freaking out!" I yelled, pulling Lyle up off the dirty asphalt.

"Whoa, whoa now. Let's take a chill pill, Aspen! Lyle just needed to blow off some steam, okay? He's fine, we can walk back to the bus in a minute," Christian tried to reason with me as Lyle started to play with my scarlet-colored hair.

I took slow deep breaths to try and not lose it on him with both men being high as a kite.

"Look, I was going to get some coke at first. We agree that

would've been way worse right? See, the weed really isn't all that bad!" Chris told me as he got up off the ground.

"Chris, you are not helping. Please go back to the bus and tell Elissa we're coming. She can kill you instead," I said with a fake smile plastered on.

"Okay, boss." He laughed to himself and started making his way back to where the bus was parked, which was quite a walk.

As he walked away, I turned Lyle's face toward me to see how bad it was. His eyes were bloodshot to hell and back, making his crystal blue irises stand out even more against all the bright blood vessels. But he seemed to be fine overall and could get his reprimand in the morning from everyone.

"Alright Lyle, let's go back to the bus where you can sleep it off for a while, okay? Come on," I said, interlocking our hands.

He got his footing after a second and gave me that goofy smile that always made me melt as we walked hand in hand together.

"You look very beautiful tonight, Pen. I was looking for you everywhere, why weren't you in the crowd?" he asked me sadly.

"You know they won't let me, Lyle. I wish I could still be out there right in front, but I'm always backstage supporting you. The label says it's where it's best for me to be right now."

"Oh right, I forgot about that. Maybe I should stop playing these big venues so you can still be in the crowd like old times. I miss that," he pouted.

"God Lyle, I'm going to pretend you didn't just say that. And you should be glad no one else heard that either. You're something else when you're high."

Lyle didn't say anything in response but looked at the stars above in a daze.

"I'm going to get yelled at, aren't I?" he sighed as we continued walking through the dark.

"Probably. You seriously scared us. You can't just wander off like that when we have to get on the road so soon after a show. I know you know that Ly."

"Yes but—"

"*Oh my god*, it's him! It's Lyle!" a girl squealed from behind us.

My neck almost snapped with how quickly I moved, turning to see a swarm of young girls all realizing that *the* Lyle Hawthorne was in front of them. The look in their eyes told me we had to get the hell out of there, and right that second.

"Fuck, Lyle. Run!"

The second we broke out into a sprint their screams followed us, and they instinctively followed in hot pursuit.

I was not a runner, not in the slightest but I'd be damned if I gave those girls the satisfaction of catching us. We had no time to spare for their pictures and autographs and whatever else they tried to throw at us. We had to get back to the bus *immediately*.

"I'm going to pass out, Aspen! Holy shit!" Lyle yelled through heavy panting breaths.

We had eyes on the bus, Elissa waving us in before the bus doors shut behind her.

So close, so close!

All of a sudden, someone's foot hit the back of my calf and my leg folded on impact.

Nearly in slow motion, I slammed down on the pavement, crushing my chin and skidding my elbows in the process as I failed to catch myself.

"Oh my god! Why did you do that?"

"Seriously? You know why!"

"Look, Lyle's still running. Come on we can catch up!"

All their voices blended together before disappearing and it was then that I realized Lyle had dropped my hand in the fall and continued on without me.

As I slowly raised myself up, I tried not to cry at how much my body hurt.

I hoisted myself up on my forearms, the shooting pain immediately telling me how bad I was banged up. I nervously swiped my palm across my chin and winced at the warm blood coating my hand.

Gross.

"Hey, are you okay? I saw what happened. I'm so sorry you got pushed," a kind girl said coming up to me who'd left the insane crowd.

"I think so? I can't tell how much I'm bleeding."

She grabbed my hands and helped me back up on my feet as I tried to get a better look at my scratched-up knees and elbows.

"Well, you're definitely bleeding on your chin, but I think you can get patched up okay. These people have no decency I swear," she said as she slyly wiped her hand off that now had my blood on it.

"Thank you for helping me. I really appreciate it."

"Of course, that was awful. I promise we're not all this crazy. Just don't check social media very often. People are kind of ruthless on there," she laughed.

"Right, because somehow the girlfriend who existed years before he got famous is the target somehow," I said under my breath.

I brushed myself off and tried not to focus on the stinging pain in my chin and knees.

"Right… Well, I'm sorry again. Best of luck!"

She waved and went on her way, so I was left alone again to figure out how to limp my way back to the tour bus.

It couldn't be that far away, right? I'd been so close before I fell.

I began making my way back around the side of the venue and had to urge my stomach to settle down. I hated the smell of blood, the feel of it. And because I had absolutely nothing to wipe myself off with, I was left letting it run down my body and subsequently, onto my clothes.

Pain seared through my jaw as I tried to find my way back through the darkness. I was cursing everyone out in my head, unable to restrain my hatred anymore for these "fans" of his that were completely unhinged.

The tour bus came into view, and I caught a glimpse of Lyle's bleach-blonde hair heading up the stairs.

At least he was okay…

I slowly, and painfully, finally made it to the bus steps and banged on the door with my bloody hand. As soon as the driver saw me, he gasped and immediately opened the door as quickly as he could.

"Aspen, what happened?" he asked as I ached the whole way up the three little measly stairs.

"Towels, I need towels," I cried out, unable to answer him.

I made my way to the bathroom as some of the band members tried to dodge my dripping blood.

"Oh my god, Aspen, oh my god!" Clara yelled after hearing my voice. "Harlow!"

She came running toward us, everything happening so quickly. We all squeezed into the tiny bathroom; towels being ripped off their holders as they simultaneously asked me questions.

"Aspen, there's so much blood. Are you okay, where does it hurt?" Harlow asked as she grabbed two bath towels and started patting at my knees.

"My chin and my knees. They look really bad. Lyle's okay though?"

"Yes, Pen he's fine, just winded. Someone get Lyle, for fucks sake, how did this even happen?" Clara yelled as she held another towel at my chin.

Almost as soon as she said it, Lyle came out from the bedroom still slightly high.

"Pen? Holy shit, that's a lot of blood," he said, staring wide-eyed at the sink where the blood from my chin had pooled.

"Are you a fucking moron? Yes, it's a lot of blood! What happened, Lyle?" Harlow yelled.

As he refused to answer, Harlow pulled my filthy hair into a ponytail and away from my bleeding face which was now practically the same color as my hair.

"Dudes take it easy. He's still riding out his high," Christian shouted out from his bunk.

"*High? High!*" Clara demanded.

Harlow smacked Lyle on the back of his head and he rubbed it half-heartedly. "Ow!"

"You will have your ass handed to you later. Tell me what happened and why she is bleeding this much!" Clara still persisted.

"We were chased by fans! They tripped her on accident I think, and we got separated. They ran me back around the venue before I lost them, but one still got kind of grabby before I lost her. I had no idea Aspen was this bad off, I swear!"

Elissa, who'd heard all the commotion, finally came into the bathroom and looked at me. She completely ignored Lyle's sorry excuses.

"Well, her knees are pretty scratched, but I think will be fine bandaged up. Elbows are mild too. How bad is her chin?" Elissa asked Clara.

"Uhhh," Clara stalled, taking the towel off my chin to check. "Bad. Like there's open flesh kind of bad. I think she might need stitches." With the towel absorbing so much blood, we were finally able to see how deep it went.

"Fucking hell. I'm going to murder them, both of them! But

first, Christian." Harlow left the bathroom and climbed up the ladder to where Christian's top bunk was.

"You got him the weed, didn't you, you little shit! I should have you thrown off the tour, you jeopardized all of us! This is my livelihood, this is Lyle's career!" she screamed, hitting his shoulder.

"Ow! Ow, stop hitting me Harlow! He needed to just chill out for one night, okay? And it wasn't even coke, so you seriously need to calm down. No one was going to know until Aspen showed up to drag him back here. It wasn't a big deal."

"Maybe because that's where he was supposed to be, and she knew we had to get on the road already! She's the one keeping his ass in line every day, not you! God, you're useless!"

Lyle came back out from hiding to defend Christian.

"Chill out Harlow, please. It's true, I asked him for coke originally and he brought me weed instead. Which was obviously a better decision, although I understand neither were great. But the only person you have to blame is me."

Harlow climbed down the stairs and got in Lyle's face. "No, I don't give a *fuck* what you asked for. What you are, is a goddamn idiot! The fact that you would not only put all of us at risk, but yourself too is mind-boggling. All for a night of fun? Really, Lyle? And why don't you look at your poor girlfriend and the state she's in all because she had to go find your sorry ass!"

"Harlow, you're being a bitch. Obviously, I didn't think it through but I never, ever meant for Aspen to get hurt. We were ambushed by a horde of fans, and they were relentless! I feel terrible about it, okay? I do! I'm sorry," Lyle finally apologized.

Harlow clenched her fists and then released them as she went and let the bus driver know we had to get to the closest hospital or urgent care center.

"Are you sure we can't just put a bandage on it, Clara? I don't want to delay us," I asked her genuinely, not paying any mind to the blowout between Lyle and Harlow.

I did *not* want to be held responsible for us possibly missing the next show.

"Aspen if I take this towel off and have you look in the mirror, that'll answer your question. You should feel lucky you still have your teeth after an impact that hard."

Maybe it was just the adrenaline, but the pain had actually subsided a lot since getting on the bus. I trusted Clara though and accepted that the safest thing to do was get fully checked out by a doctor.

The bus's engine turned on and the driver called out to us that there was a hospital only a few minutes away.

As Clara let out a sigh of relief that we were so close, she handed me the towel to continue pressing at my chin to control the bleeding. Elissa put two soft bandages on my knees and some ointment from the first aid kit to help them heal.

All patched up temporarily, I went to the back bedroom where Lyle had been hiding and sat down next to him on the bed.

"I don't blame you, Lyle. It wasn't your fault those girls came after us."

"Yes, yes it was. If I hadn't been out there and had just gone straight to the bus like I was supposed to, you never would've gotten hurt. I'm really sorry, Aspen."

He wrapped his arm around my waist, and I tenderly laid my head on his shoulder as we stayed in each other's embrace until the bus arrived at the hospital.

"I'm going to come with you, okay? This is my fault, so I want to know how bad it is."

I nodded my head and figured it would be okay with everyone else. Clara agreed to stay back and let the next venue in Virginia know about the tiny delay. She also decided to make some phone calls to the label about what happened after Elissa's insistence.

Harlow offered to come with me for support, but she was frankly still too angry at Lyle to be able to stay civil with him. I didn't blame her for that.

Ultimately, Elissa and Lyle ended up being the only ones who were going to come with me to the hospital, which I was perfectly fine with.

I was embarrassed enough as it was that it had turned into a whole ordeal that was going to hold everyone up. I was just hoping it wouldn't take too long and we could all be on our merry way.

The bus arrived after a few minutes and parked at the back. I cringed seeing how much blood had dripped on the floor.

We entered the emergency room with the blood-soaked towel still pressed against my face and walked up to the front desk.

"Hi, I need to have my chin looked at and possible stitches depending on how bad it is," I said with a somewhat pleasant smile.

"Look, is there any way we could be seen right now?" Elissa interrupted, always concerned about the fucking timing of everything.

"The wait right now for the E.R. is two hours ma'am, I'm sorry. We are only able to bring back serious cases for immediate medical needs," the lady at the front desk explained to Elissa.

"No listen, it's just stitches that she needs, that's it! Do we really have to wait two hours just for that?"

"Yes, everyone here also has something that they need taken care of. We will call you up when a doctor is available to assist, okay?"

"What about a nurse? An intern, or a resident? Anyone that

is below a doctor but could do stitches without maiming her?" Elissa started anxiously asking.

I tried not to laugh at how Elissa's demanding, type-A personality translated into the real world, especially since she was doing it on my behalf. But it was really hard not to when she was practically begging this lady for anyone who could get us in and out in less than the quoted time.

"I understand that you cannot seem to wait the estimated time, but the medical staff you listed all have tasks they need to attend to right now. The answer is no," the lady answered as nicely as possible.

"Look I'm Lyle Hawthorne, and this is my girlfriend who's only here thanks to me. Could you please just find someone that can do stitches?" Lyle shamelessly asked.

Name-dropping in a hospital… classy.

"Well Mr. Hawthorne, while I'm sure your platinum records get you some perks in life, a hospital does not operate that way. We will call you when there is someone available to help. Please go sit down and fill these out," she asked while putting some forms on a clipboard.

Lyle huffed as she handed me the clipboard. We went to the waiting room and sat down in worn fabric-covered chairs as I tried to ignore how upset they were. Elissa crossed her arms, clearly annoyed but was restraining herself to not show it as much. I grabbed the pen that was attached to the clipboard and started filling in all my information.

I just knew I was in for a long night.

Chapter Three

FTER JUST ABOUT AN HOUR AND A HALF, I STILL HAD not been called up to the front, much to the dismay of Lyle. He'd given enough passive aggressive sighs to last me a lifetime. Elissa had fallen asleep long ago and with how hard she worked all day; I didn't want to wake her.

"Aspen Reddick!"

Oh, thank god.

I stiffly got out of the horribly uncomfortable chair and met the nurse with the clipboard by the door. She smiled at me and confirmed the information I'd written down before motioning me to follow her. Lyle woke up Elissa and the two of them followed behind me as we were sent to a hospital bed in the corner.

I, not-so-gracefully, hopped up onto the bed as the nurse closed the curtain.

"Alright, Miss Reddick, what seems to have happened?" the nurse asked as she peeled my hand and towel away from my chin.

"To make a long story short, I tripped and fell on the pavement. I was told I might need stitches with how bad my chin looks, and how long it's bled."

"Hmm." She turned my chin side to side with her gloved hands. "It does look pretty deep. I'm surprised you don't have more damage honestly. It seems you got pretty lucky. I think you'll just need a few stitches and then you can be on your way."

I nodded my head, and she wrote something down on the form I'd handed her. "We'll have the doctor in right away to give you a numbing shot. It'll take a few minutes to take effect but then we can get started."

Lyle groaned and put his head in his hands as he realized the full extent of how bad it was.

Elissa called Clara to give her an update and let her know we'd be out as soon as possible. I was sure that most everyone on board had fallen asleep and I just cringed knowing how annoyed they'd be when we had to make up for lost time.

And to make matters worse, no one knew how bad I was with needles.

I swallowed roughly and wiped my sweaty palms on the bed's stiff sheet beneath me. My hands were tingling from nerves and my throat had gone dry. As much as I didn't want anyone to see, I knew I wouldn't be able to hide it for much longer.

"Pen, you okay? You look super pale," Lyle asked, rubbing my shoulder gently.

"Um, not so much. I'm not good with needles… like at all," I said.

The curtain to the room slid open as a doctor appeared with some medical supplies in his hand.

"Hello Miss Reddick, I'm Doctor Athem. I'm going to clean you up here first and then give you some lidocaine so you can be stitched up pain-free and on your way."

I nodded my head and tried to ignore the beads of sweat forming by my hairline. I'd had enough experiences growing up to know that needles always made me vomit and Lyle had never even seen me sick before. There was only so much humiliation I could take for one day.

Just breathe.

Elissa moved out of his way as the doctor started grabbing everything he needed and pulled out a bottle of lidocaine from a drawer.

The doctor then put on a set of gloves and started lightly cleaning the injured area with a variety of liquids and a few cotton balls. That was the easy part, and I was more than happy to have all the excess blood cleaned up. But then, he pulled out a syringe with a *very* big needle attached to it and inserted it into the vial of lidocaine.

"Alright Miss Reddick, if you're ready I'm going to go ahead and numb you, okay?"

Deep breaths, deep breaths!

"Aspen, it's going to be okay, I promise. Just look at me," Lyle soothed lovingly.

He clenched onto my hand, and I squeezed it tightly, anxiously waiting for the lidocaine to go in. I closed my eyes as the doctor's hand came closer and closer to my face.

The syringe needle was then inserted near the deepest laceration, and I nearly passed out after he pulled it back out of my face.

"Okay, we'll just let that sink in for a few minutes and then we can put the stitches in. Sorry for the pain!"

The doctor closed the curtain behind him, leaving the room and I was sure at this point I was as white as a ghost.

"Aspen, are you going to be sick?" Elissa asked concerned.

"Uh, I don't know. I'm hot, really hot. Are you guys hot?"

The whole room started to spin, and everything was fading in and out of focus. I was going down, *right that second.*

"Fuck, fuck Elissa get her head!"

She cradled my head as I fainted. Sweet relief from all the nausea and pain at last.

Amongst the murmuring voices, I slowly woke up to the bright hospital lights and squinted my eyes at how harsh the fluorescents were.

"Oh, Pen, you're awake! Wait, don't sit up too quickly. How are you feeling?" Elissa asked, putting a hand on my shoulder to slow me down.

I looked over at Lyle and tried to sit up more slowly without any dizziness. "I'm okay, I think. How long was I out for?"

My words were partially slurred by the lidocaine that had now taken effect and made the entire bottom half of my face numb. I immediately tried to touch my chin and was surprised at just how numb it was.

"Not that long, about ten minutes. You scared the shit out of me though. I was seriously freaking out. Let me call the doctor back in so he can give you your stitches now," Elissa said.

I nodded instead of speaking and Lyle stroked my back to soothe me.

"Aspen, are you sure you're okay?" Lyle's brow furrowed. "You went down really fast."

"For the most part. The worst of it's over." I grasped his hand and took a long, deep breath.

The doctor returned. "Hello again, Miss Reddick. I'll make this process as quick as possible, and it should be painless now that you're completely numbed."

"Okay, sounds good. I just want it to be over with."

"No worries, I understand. But you two might not want to watch this. It can be a bit much for most people to handle," the doctor said as he grabbed his medical tools to start stitching me up.

As soon as Elissa saw the needle and thread he was going to use, she threw her hands up to say she was going to leave.

"I'll go talk to Clara and let her know where we're at on things. Good luck, Aspen!"

As she left, the doctor had things ready to go and was about to insert the threaded needle to do the first suture.

"Lyle, you don't have to watch. Why don't you go with Elissa?" I tried to reason with him, looking down.

"No, I want to be here with you. I can handle it. Just relax, Pen."

The doctor gave him a sideways glance but continued on and started suturing.

Lyle winced in some places as the doctor skillfully wove the needle and thread through my chin. I didn't feel a thing, but I was sure the sight of it was a much more disturbing picture.

I could feel some tugging here and there, but not enough to actually feel pain. It was a very weird sensation, having your skin pulled and yanked on but not completely feeling it. It was not a feeling I liked very much. Hopefully it would be the last time I ever had to get stitches on my face.

"Alright, I'm just going to tie this off and then you should be good to go. The first layer of stitches was to close the deepest part of the cut and will dissolve, but the second layer will have to be removed in about a week by a nurse or a doctor. In my professional opinion, I don't think it'll scar too badly but it was quite deep so there's always a chance," he said as he finished up.

A scar?

"Have a good evening and be careful next time running out there. Goodnight to you both."

We checked at the desk before leaving to make sure I didn't have anything else to fill out. And lucky me, I'd be getting a bill at some point.

Without medical insurance.

But my face was all fixed up at least, so I guess that counted for something. Except the chance that it could scar and permanently alter my face which I was not expecting.

We finally left the hospital around three in the morning, and I was absolutely exhausted. I hoped those onboard had been able to get some sleep while they waited for us, otherwise we were going to have a team full of cranky people in the morning.

As I came back on to the bus, the driver let out a sigh of relief. "Nice to see you feeling better, Aspen. I'm glad to see you turned out okay."

I peeked into Harlow's bottom bunk to let her know I was okay as Lyle went to our room to get ready for bed.

"Hey, I just wanted to let you know I'm back," I whispered to her as she woke up half asleep.

"I'm so glad you're okay, Pen. Even though it never should've happened in the first place, trust that we will be discussing this tomorrow." She rubbed my arm affectionately. "Now get some rest, you deserve it."

I let her fall back asleep and found Elissa holed up in the bathroom still, getting ready for bed herself.

"Aspen, I really don't know how you just made it through that. You are stronger than I am, that's for sure," she laughed as she changed into her pajamas.

"I guess, I was just really embarrassed honestly. I know how late we're running now, and I just wanted to apologize."

"Aspen, you do not need to apologize to me! You were *not* responsible for what happened, do you understand me?"

"I don't know Elissa, it's just become a whole mess now. I feel guilty!" I grabbed the pack of makeup wipes and started taking off my makeup.

"Look, we're all going to sit down and talk about this in the morning. This was a serious safety incident, and we are responsible for what happens to you on this tour. We're going to make some changes to ensure this never happens again, okay? Now please get changed and go to bed, you need some sleep after all that."

At nearly four in the morning, I finally laid down in bed and curled up to Lyle and together we drifted off to sleep.

Chapter Four

RAYS OF SOFT YELLOW SUNLIGHT PEEKED THROUGH the tiny window in the back bedroom and slowly woke me from my delightful sleep.

I couldn't remember the last time I'd slept that well since coming on tour. It was like I had completely skipped the lucid state and went straight into a deep sleep. Which was much, *much* needed after that night from hell.

The sheets were cold beside me. Lyle was gone, probably prepping for the show that night. It was rougher than normal when we had back-to-back shows.

A light knock on the bedroom door woke me all the way up as I yawned and stretched.

"Aspen! We made breakfast, and your favorite! Bacon!" Harlow yelled from outside the door.

"I'll be there in a second!" I shouted back as I slowly pulled myself out of bed and grabbed my shower caddy from the nook by the side of the bed. I had to look somewhat presentable to go out there after being awake until four in the morning.

I squeezed myself into the bathroom and tore off the big t-shirt I'd worn to bed, turning the shower water on. My hair needed to be washed honestly but the scarlet color would fade even more than it had already, and I couldn't spend any more time in the shower.

I instead threw my hair into a bun and quickly washed my

body off, avoiding my stitches. Time was ticking away so I jumped out soon after getting in and hurriedly toweled myself off. I opted for a cropped tour tee, courtesy of Harlow and a pair of scissors, and cutoff jean shorts to wear for the day.

I finally looked decent enough to see everyone and stepped out of the bathroom feeling much refreshed. All the bunks were empty as I passed by them and into the front lounge area where I found everyone sat talking loudly.

"Hey guys, sorry for sleeping in. Rough night," I laughed.

"Of course, we understand," Elissa smiled as she shoveled some egg whites onto her plate.

"I'll get you a plate started, Pen. Go ahead and sit down, babe," Lyle said, offering up his seat on the couch.

I gladly accepted and sat down next to Christian who had been stuffing his face full of food with his plate sloppily sitting on his lap.

"Wow, man, look at those stitches! Those are kinda gnarly," Chris laughed, getting a look at my face for the first time since I came back from the hospital.

"Christian! Stop being rude!" Harlow said, defending me.

Chris had practically no filter and blurted things out without fully thinking about if what he was saying was offensive. I was used to it and was sure my face looked rough, so I just brushed it off.

"I know it'll be a hassle to stop between shows, but the doctor did say they would be able to be removed in about a week. I won't be like this for long at least."

Lyle handed me a full plate loaded with eggs, bacon, and toast. It was just what I needed after not eating for so long, I was practically starving. I thanked Bryson, the bassist, for making so much food. We were very used to fast food and packaged foods and whatever we could get our hands basically, so having a cooked meal was always really nice.

Lyle squished himself onto the couch beside me and wrapped his arm around my shoulders. I was finally able to scarf down my food as some conversation continued and the bus driver continued wordlessly on the way to the next show.

Clara and Elissa, who had been privately talking in the kitchen, came and sat on the couch opposite to mine.

"Hey, Aspen. Is now a good time to talk?" Clara asked as I tossed my paper plate after eating.

"Uh, yeah, I guess so. Is something going on?" I replied, wiping my mouth off. I hated how stiff and professional they looked, with their legs crossed and lips pursed. Like I was another client of theirs.

"Well, I suppose so. We have something very important to discuss that we went over with the record label and Lyle's other manager yesterday. Clara was a busy lady while we were in the hospital," Elissa explained.

I looked over at Lyle who had no reaction and I realized he was already aware of whatever it was they were talking about.

"Okay. What exactly were you guys discussing?"

Clara and Elissa exchanged a look, and Clara cleared her throat before replying.

"Well, I explained the incident that had occurred and how dangerous it was becoming to you and Lyle to not have more private security at the shows. While we didn't think it was too big a deal at the beginning of the tour and were able to use each venue's security, Lyle has skyrocketed in popularity since then. We can't let a premeditated incident happen again."

"What? That girl didn't mean to trip me. I seriously doubt that she had some personal vendetta against me or something."

"Yeah," Elissa laughed awkwardly. "Neither did we. But we did our weekly check-in on social media and Aspen… it's everywhere. People are talking about it on all different apps and we found out much more about what happened."

I looked over at Lyle again and he put his head down shamefully, completely avoiding eye contact with me.

"Well? What did you find out?"

They glanced at each other again and Clara shook her head before answering.

"Look, I don't like being the one to tell you this, I really don't. But it was apparently something that had been planned by a particularly vicious and dedicated group of girls online. It seems like they had been trying to just find the right time to do it, mapping out approximate times Lyle left the shows and when he went backstage," she explained. "But Aspen, they *intentionally* wanted to hurt you."

My mouth went dry, and time stood still. I morphed into a scared fourteen-year-old girl again who was so hurt, she anxiously sought any type of feeling to distract from the pain she felt inside.

"I-I don't understand. Why would they want to hurt me?" The words rushed out like a waterfall as I tried to fight the urge to cry, thinking about people actually plotting to *hurt me*. I began picking frantically at my nails, destroying the skin around my fingers.

"They seem to think you're a threat to them in some way. I guess in their heads, they think they have a shot with Lyle, or they think he could… do better."

I could see how painful it was for them to tell me, but it was something I wish I never knew. I could have lived peacefully with the knowledge that what happened to me was an accident and we were just caught at the wrong time.

The truth was much darker. And I didn't know how to handle it.

"I just can't believe this. I mean, I'm not a threat to anybody! I've been with Lyle since I was eighteen when he was still singing at random gigs. They didn't even know who he was back then! Why would they have a problem with me? This is insane!"

I jumped off the couch and paced pacing back and forth as the others on board disappeared to their bunks to stay out of the conversation.

"I know, Aspen. It's a lot to take in. We are the ones who dropped the ball truthfully, and we should have taken it more seriously. We never realized they were a genuine danger to you. That's why we're going to fix it. We're going to have a full security team," Elissa said, grabbing my arm to stop my pacing.

"Private security? Really, that's supposed to fix everything?" I asked incredulously.

"Look, Aspen, we've thought it all out and the label agreed to pay for four security guards while on tour, one being your own personal bodyguard!" Clara boasted, as if it was some great new add-on to the tour.

"And Lyle, what about you? How do you feel about this? People following you around every day, watching your every move?" I shouted at him.

He shifted in his seat uncomfortably and could hardly look me in the eye. "Pen, I know it's not ideal, okay? But things have gotten out of control here. I can't let anything happen to you again."

"Fuck," I sighed as I sat back down and wiped away the stray tears that had made their way out. "I don't want private security and I especially don't want my own bodyguard. I can't have someone watching me when I eat, when I sleep, having to let them know when I need to use the bathroom. It's too much!"

"I know, Aspen, I'm sorry. But we can create rules and set boundaries, so it doesn't have to feel so suffocating. The label is willing to work with us and provide the best security that money can buy. These are guys that worked for presidents, movie stars, the most famous people you can think of. They know and understand the need for privacy very well," Clara comforted me.

Deep breaths, deep breaths.

"It's for the best, so nothing ever happens again like last night. The label is very much in favor of this so there's really no way out of it. They'll be with us through the rest of the tour and possibly longer if they're a good fit for our team."

"And what if they're not a good fit for the team? If I hate them then can you have them pulled off the tour?" I asked, full of hope.

Elissa stifled a laugh. "Not exactly. There is pretty much no debate to be had for the tour itself. They're staying."

"And you're really just fine with this, Lyle?"

He picked his head back up and held firm this time.

"Yes. I know it'll take some getting used to at first, but the last girl put her hands on me, and you split your chin open. If they keep us safe, then that's all I care about."

I scoffed. How could he seem to care so much now when he ran away when it actually happened?

"I see I have no choice in this then. I guess we can all enjoy an even more packed tour bus whenever these bodyguards show up. They could sleep… on the floor perhaps. When is your flight leaving Clara?"

"In about three hours. The arena is an hour away from the airport but it's just as well. The new security team will be arriving at the same airport around the time I'm set to depart. Kills two birds with one stone by going there first."

"*What?* They're coming here today? You must be joking, Clara!"

"Nope. The label worked fast when they found out Lyle was in danger. Be grateful, please. This is for the best."

Grateful my ass.

Chapter Five

ASPEN

I WAS ALREADY ANNOYED AT THE IDEA OF HAVING A security team, but to have them come so soon? I wasn't even given a full day to get used to the knowledge that someone would be following me around every waking moment.

That's not the kind of thing you can just spring on someone and expect them to be okay with.

I pulled out my phone and scrolled through social media to distract myself, so I didn't lash out at anyone. I had to keep reminding myself that they had good intentions, and it was the label who made the decision.

Safety or not though, I was dreading having them join us.

Lyle disappeared into the back to start getting himself together for the next show. He always misplaced his in-ears, so finding them before the show was a must-do, amongst a hundred other important things.

Harlow came and talked with me for a bit, while I rehashed the whole nightmare of what happened. She was one of the only people to really validate what I was feeling, which meant a lot to me.

The tour bus stopped to fill up on gas before we made it to the airport. We all got out and stretched for a minute as we looked around the middle-of-nowhere Virginia. We were on our way to Richmond, but I'd underestimated the amount of dirt roads we'd take to get there.

I took a nap for an hour to pass the time after my chin started to throb, having not taken any pain medication for a while.

I caved eventually and put a nude-colored bandage over the top of my stitches after Christian's comments. I had really tried to not let everyone's stares get to me, but I couldn't take it anymore. I felt slightly better with them covered, although I knew it was still obvious when you looked at me that something was there. Better than nothing.

Eventually, we dropped Clara off at a small airport.

"I'll miss you. You always keep me sane on this bus, so please call me when you can. Have a safe flight," I told her before hugging her neck.

I really would miss the hell out of her.

She wasn't one for long, drawn-out goodbyes though, strutting to the private jet without so much as a glance backward.

The security team was to arrive an hour and a half later, ready for the show that night.

The wait ticked by slowly, the delay making us all antsy. Elissa's stupid precise timing had an effect on all of us, as it was all I could think about while waiting.

Harlow had at least taken the liberty of getting started on Lyle's hair back on the bus so it wouldn't take him nearly as long to get ready. Not that bleaching his hair took all that long compared to coloring my waist-length hair, but it was a frequent necessity to maintain his label-mandated look.

"How much longer?" I whined, resting my head in my hands.

"Should be any minute now. Why don't you go check the board again to see when they're landing?" Elissa suggested.

I tiredly got up and checked the big board that showed the economy flights for what felt like the hundredth time.

"Should be here in about twenty minutes. Why can't we just go wait for them on the bus? They can figure it out," I groaned as I plopped down into the hard plastic seat next to her.

"I'd prefer it if I didn't have four tall, muscled dudes just walking around outside not knowing where to go. You think they've ever been to this airport before?"

"Doubt it. But if they're all so tough, I'm sure they could handle it. Just a big waste of time on our part."

"Maybe so but this is a part of my job. Why don't you try to perk up too? I know they'll be more pleased with the welcoming committee if you try to smile some more."

I rolled my eyes at her and refreshed my social media feeds to find something to eat up the rest of the time.

"Flight 2776 from LAX to RIC has landed," a lady's voice boomed over the intercom system.

Thank God.

"Alright, Aspen it's showtime. Please put on a smile and act polite so they don't run back to L.A. screaming."

"Yes, your majesty, you got it," I said.

We made our way down to baggage claim where the four men would be to pick up their bags.

Although given how tight airline security was for us normal folk, I didn't know how they'd do much protecting with no guns or knives in their carry-ons. Seemed kind of pointless to me but I was sure they'd get their hands on some in no time.

Otherwise, how could they protect us?

"Clara sent me their profiles from the security company. I have pictures of all of them, so I'll let you know when I spot them," Elissa said, glancing around.

"You're telling me you've had pictures of them all this time and didn't show me? Ugh, that would've made this so much more enjoyable!"

"Quiet, Aspen, they're right there," she grumbled.

Straightening her blazer and running her hand through her sleek black hair, she made her way over to a group of men who were dressed very casually to be bodyguards.

"Good afternoon. I'm Elissa Kwon, and I'm the tour manager for Lyle Hawthorne. I hope your flight was pleasant."

Two of the men were absolute beefcakes, arms bulging through their white t-shirts that accentuated how built they were. I estimated they were in their mid to late thirties, but you couldn't tell it from a distance.

One of the other men was slightly shorter, and less brawny but had a face of cold steel. The plum-colored shirt he wore complemented the deep umber of his skin tone, and I could see from across the airport his eyes constantly roaming, scanning the faces of everyone around us. Oh, he was good.

And then there was *him*.

Sharp icy gaze, olive skin, and gorgeous obsidian curls.

I think my jaw hit the floor.

"And this here is Aspen Reddick. She's Lyle's girlfriend, but also helps keep everything moving! I don't know what we'd do without her." She gave a forceful laugh, gently touching my shoulder.

Whatever flatteries Elissa was giving me disappeared from my head as the mysterious man looked me right in the eye. I swallowed roughly, captivated by the man who held a room's attention without speaking a word.

It was the kind of stare that made you grow small, unavoidably averting your gaze somewhere else to relieve the tension.

But I wasn't looking away. And neither was he.

"The tour bus is right outside so we'll go ahead and get

going. It will be a tight fit onboard, but we'll do the best to make everyone comfortable. Aspen, would you lead us please?"

"O-of course," I stuttered.

I finally dropped my gaze to the floor when Elissa babbled about the tour and Lyle's success which I was sure they all wanted to hear.

But I could feel the man staring at me from behind, sending chills up my spine. I resisted the urge to turn around but could actively feel his eyes boring into my back. Maybe he was just staring because of my ugly chin?

I was suddenly very conscious of the way I was walking, straightening my shoulders to fix my posture, and questioning what my hair looked like from behind, things I'd never contemplated before.

As we approached the bus, I took a long deep breath and knocked on the door.

I finally had the courage to turn around and give a half smile to Elissa as I subtly shifted my eyes to the man in the back.

He was already looking at me.

I cleared my throat and tried not to sound as nervous as I was feeling. "Go ahead and climb aboard. I'll be the last one on."

I smiled at all the men and tried to be upbeat, so I seemed more outgoing.

Elissa boarded first and the men followed suit behind her.

As the last man went to board, I found myself naturally wanting to say something. But he was so intimidating, I was stopped in my tracks.

"You go ahead. Ladies first," he said in a deep voice, motioning for me to go in front of him.

"Thank you," I squeaked out as I walked up the stairs and he filed in behind me.

I sat down on the couch with Elissa and tucked my hair behind my ears, extremely aware now that I was being watched.

"So, we currently have five of the bunks taken, and one bunk that the driver sleeps in during the day that can be alternated with whoever sleeps there at night. The couch does turn into a queen that the band members sleep on sometimes, but someone can sleep there, I think. And the last option is either on the floor, or on this couch that doesn't fold out," Elissa explained.

"I'll alternate with the bus driver. No big deal for me," the shorter man said. His voice was gravelly, and his stiff exterior gave me the feeling that he was ex-military.

"I'll just sleep on the couch. What about you, Daniels?" the older, muscled man asked the other one.

"I don't really care. Kostas?"

Kostas, the man who hadn't peeled his gaze off me, finally spoke. "I want the couch that folds out into a bed. It'll be… nice."

I didn't like the way he hesitated to answer that. Especially not while looking at me.

"Okay, seems like that's sorted then. Now onto assignments."

Lyle and Harlow came out of the bathroom while Elissa took out her iPad.

"Hey guys, I'm Lyle. Nice to meet you," he said, holding his hand out.

They all gave him a manly handshake, with my new stalker finally taking his eyes off me to shake his hand properly.

"Glad it went okay," Lyle smiled before squeezing in next to me.

"Alright, Carson Holcomb, you and Tyler Daniels will be assigned to the overall team. So, you might float a bit, being with the band members or myself or something like that," she said as the two men fist-bumped each other.

"And then Koen Gray will be assigned to Lyle Hawthorne himself."

The military man, who was the very definition of if looks could kill, simply gave a slight head nod.

"Which leaves Dominik Kostas. You will be assigned to Aspen Reddick."

The man who finally had a name. He smirked and leaned back in his seat.

"Excellent."

Chapter Six

ASPEN

THANKFULLY, THE NEW ADDITIONS TO THE TEAM HAD packed light, making their presence onboard slightly less jarring.

But four new bodies were hard to ignore with one bathroom, one hangout space, and less than a couple hundred square feet between us all.

The only positive was that the airport was relatively close to the venue, and we'd be off the bus to go to the show soon enough.

That made me feel a lot better about the man who wouldn't put his eyes back in his skull.

I eventually hid in my bedroom to get away from him and his longing stares. And while I understood there wasn't much else to do on the bus until we got to the venue, I had not planned on being anyone's visual entertainment.

I was surprised that Lyle hadn't noticed it, but he was in his own world before show time of course.

I breathed a sigh of relief when we finally got to the arena and were able to be away from each other for a little bit while Lyle did his rehearsals.

Elissa had some important business to take care of at the show with it being the halfway point on the tour, so I'd be spending showtime with Harlow. She usually wasn't one to stick around for the backstage craziness, especially in the really big venues and their abundant chaos. But she'd agreed to hang out that night just so I'd have someone to stick with while being guarded for the first time.

Guarded. I didn't like how that sounded.

All the men had changed into full black attire while back on the bus, trying to blend in while still showing that they were part of our crew. Each had been given a handgun that they carried at all times, as well as a set of earpieces that connected to each other so they could communicate with each of them stationed throughout the venue.

As much as I had been able to relax while watching the crew set up and hearing Lyle rehearse, it was a monotonous routine of the same day on repeat. Just in a different city.

However, my alone time was cut short when I saw Dominik coming straight for me.

"Miss Reddick, is it?" he asked, although I was sure he already knew the answer.

"Yes?" I replied annoyed, shifting my weight from foot to foot.

"I'll be accompanying you throughout the show tonight. Daniels and Holcomb will be stationed with the band as well as Miss Kwon, and as you know Gray is with Mr. Hawthorne. I'll be with you and Harlow."

"Okay? Thanks for letting me know?"

"You're welcome. I'll be here if you ladies need me at any point," he said with a handsome grin, completely ignoring my sarcasm.

"You got it, buddy," Harlow replied with a thumbs up. She didn't like it any more than I did.

As rehearsals ended and showtime got closer, the air had become thick and sticky with rain hovering nearby. That was not ideal for an outdoor show.

Lyle could handle a little rain, and so could the equipment for the most part.

But if there was too much lightning or a full-on thunderstorm, they couldn't perform in the conditions. It which would mean possible refunds, missed revenue, and just a nightmare for everyone.

And if that was the case, I'd hoped I wouldn't be by Elissa when she found out. She would raise hell about it.

I had no idea what kind of storms Virginia had late in summer and if they were even big enough to be a real concern. Regardless, there was a noticeable enough difference in the shade of gray sky that I started to become concerned.

"Harlow, look at the sky. It's getting really dark," I told her, watching the clouds move in.

"That's pretty nasty looking. I wouldn't be shocked if we had a total torrential rainstorm."

"That's just great. We're already here and everyone's ready to go and yet the show will likely be delayed, or god forbid, canceled."

"Don't take it so seriously, Aspen. Only people really losing money is the record label, so who cares," she sighed. "Rain is rain, Mother Nature is always going to win. Let's just enjoy it."

Dominik had been lingering a few feet behind us but hadn't said much. I preferred him at this distance.

"Ladies, just got word we're expecting a storm in about thirty minutes. We're figuring out the best safety route right now," Dominik informed us as he lightly touched my back.

Shaking him off, I turned to face him directly. "Wouldn't the best safety measure be to head backstage? Where else would we even go?"

"You'd be surprised how safe the bus is. It would certainly be much safer to have everyone already on the bus than to try and run everyone out in the pouring rain. Do you object, Miss Reddick?"

"God, stop calling me that. Please just call me Aspen, or Pen if you're feeling less annoying."

"Pen?"

"Short for Aspen. And no, that does *not* mean you can call me Penny."

"Well, you're in luck that I don't prefer any of those. They don't suit you very well. I'll call you Aspen out of the kindness of my heart," he smirked. "Or Red. Considering your hair and your last name, it's rather fitting."

"While I appreciate the gesture, that's not part of your job description. Just let us know if we're moving to the bus or not, okay?" I jeered at him.

"Rather snappy, Pen. Dude is just trying to help out," Harlow said quietly, trying to calm me down.

I didn't even realize how quickly I'd lost my patience with him. He was just so damn good at being so damn aggravating.

Dominik suddenly held his hand over his earpiece as he got new information from one of the other men.

"Looks like the venue has officially announced a delay. We're going to move everyone back on the tour bus until a decision is made about whether the show is happening tonight."

I rolled my eyes and let out a deep sigh. "Well, that's just perfect. Only time we're able to be off that stupid bus and now we have to get right back on."

Before Dominik could even reply, I grabbed Harlow's wrist and started marching back to the tour bus. I didn't want him to think he had the power to decide when and where I moved. He inevitably followed behind us.

"Terrance, I'm sorry but the show is delayed. Doesn't look like we'll have to get on the road yet, but it will disrupt your sleep some with everyone back here. Sorry again," I told the bus driver who had finally tried to lay down and sleep for a little bit.

"Not your fault, Miss Reddick. Hopefully, the show will go on as planned," the older man said with a soft smile.

It had distracted me long enough to forget about the annoyingly tall, gorgeously tan man who was still stalking me.

"Would you back up some? I can feel you breathing on me," I grumbled as I walked away without even looking at him.

"You're a tough one, aren't you? All pissy because you got stuck with me somehow?"

Apparently with fewer people onboard, he'd decided to drop the professionalism.

Two could play at that game.

"Yes, I am. I didn't want this. I didn't want you here and I certainly didn't want to be the object of all the girls' hatred that started this whole charade. That's the whole reason you're even here!"

"Does that explain your chin?"

I instinctively put my hand over the bandage and knew my cheeks were bright red with how embarrassed I was.

"I assumed someone would've told you before you came," I mumbled, completely humiliated.

"Nope. We get an assignment, and we go on it. I didn't even know who Lyle was when I got the call at five this morning."

For some reason, I doubted that.

"So, why don't you tell me what happened, so you'll calm down and get over your little 'the world hates me' act?"

"It's not an act! I was attacked, *intentionally*, by fans at the last show who had been planning to hurt me. I split my chin open when I hit the pavement and had to get stitches. It was a horrific experience, actually!"

He seemed entirely unfazed by my shouting which bothered me more than if he would've reacted to it.

I softened my approach. "Look, I don't know what kind of famous people you usually work with, but I'm not one of them. Nothing about me is fake or an act, or some new version I'm testing out. I'm just a regular person who got caught up in all this."

"Hm, that's interesting," he noted to himself. "And just for the record, I didn't say anything about your chin looking bad. You don't need to be embarrassed about it."

"That's easy for you to say. Have you ever been attacked by a group of crazed girls and possibly permanently scarred from it?"

He shifted his jaw but didn't respond.

"Exactly. Now I would appreciate it if you could ease up on the whole 'breathing down my neck, staring a hole through me' thing. It freaks me out."

"No, it doesn't."

"And how would you know that Einstein?"

"Because every time I'm looking at you, you're looking back at me."

Speechless, the door suddenly opened, halting our conversation in its tracks. Loudly, everyone else started shuffling in with the rest of the team talking and laughing to one another. I cleared my throat, trying to regain my composure.

"Then don't look at me so much."

Chapter Seven

ASPEN

AFTER ABOUT AN HOUR OF HEAVY RAIN AND LIGHTNING, there would have to be a final decision about the show going on.

Everyone was bummed out, and the mood was pretty poor. I still had hope that the show might be able to happen regardless. The rain had significantly slowed down, but the stage was likely drenched.

"I don't know, Elissa, do you think this will still work?" Lyle asked her, knowing it was just about time to make a decision with the venue.

"It'll be a big pain to make it work, and honestly, we don't know the condition everything is in. You can't be running up and down a stage that wet, you'd bust your ass."

"That's exactly what I need right now," he laughed dryly. "Just tell them to cancel then. I know there's tons of people already here, but I don't see another way for this to work."

Elissa sighed and pinched her temples. "Well Lyle, that's a big decision and comes with repercussions. Refunds will have to be sent out; we'll have to reschedule the show."

"We have to reschedule it? Really?" he whined.

I hit his arm and gave him a look with how insensitive he was acting.

Obviously, it was a huge hassle to try and reschedule the

show and extend the tour to make it happen, but there were only so many options available. Keeping the fans happy should've been a priority, but apparently it wasn't to him.

"Yes, I'll call the label tonight and let them know what's going on. They'll have to get back to me with a new tour date but it's most likely going to have to be added on to the end of the tour," Elissa explained.

Lyle groaned loudly and we all cringed, me personally just annoyed that this meant even longer until we could go home.

"Are you sure they can't try and switch it to tomorrow night while we're still in the city? Same venue, same show time, and everything? Our next show isn't for three days anyhow," I suggested.

"Yes, but those three days were supposed to be our break. If we make a new show happen tomorrow, we're looking at back-to-back shows again for a while."

Of course, being sent into that chaotic, nightly show schedule again wasn't ideal, but it was the best solution to try and keep the tour on track.

"Yes, I know it will really suck, but wouldn't you rather deal with it now then be at the end of the tour and have a new date to deal with? This would work for everyone," I proposed.

Elissa leaned back and thought about it for a minute, probably running through all the possible solutions and if there was something else they could do instead.

"Well, Aspen, that's not a bad idea. I'll call the label now and get their opinion, but as long as the venue works with us then I don't see why not. It'll keep fans from having to get as many refunds too since it'll be the next day, which helps us."

Not that we ever saw that kind of money but whatever.

"What do you think Lyle?" I asked him gently, resting my hand on his thigh.

"I think I'd rather just get it over with and do it tomorrow.

We do have the daytime tomorrow for a small break, and tonight too, although it's still raining."

"Alright it's settled then. I'll start calling around and letting everyone know. You guys are free to do whatever tonight, as long as you're not dead in a ditch somewhere," Elissa said with a wave of her hand as she pulled out her iPhone.

I was so happy, I could scream.

This was the first night off where we could actually do something not tour-related in a very long time.

"So, what do you want to do Lyle?" I asked him excitedly.

He awkwardly shifted his leg out of the way and away from me. "I want to go and get some sleep, honestly. It's been a long day and I'm not really in a mood to go out tonight. Sorry, Pen."

I swallowed my disappointment and tried to understand where he was coming from. It had been a rough couple of days, so I didn't blame him.

"Of course. I'll see if Harlow and Christian want to go out instead."

"That's fine, just take Dominik so you're safe out there."

"No way. He's for shows only," I insisted.

"Yes, you will take him. You're in a city you don't know, and you could use all the protection you could get. He's here anyhow so might as well use him."

I turned around and shot a death glare at Dominik who was entirely amused by the situation on the other side of the bus.

"It'll be fun anyway Pen! Come on, let's go!" Harlow smiled, grabbing my hand.

I let the situation go to not cause any problems, but I was very irritated. Restraining myself, I wordlessly got up with Harlow as the group of us left the bus and headed for the city.

With Dominik following us of course.

The rain had subsided, with only a few stray raindrops falling every now and then. It was cooler out too, which was nice considering how hot it had been the previous few days.

I tried to pretend like Dominik wasn't ten feet behind me and continued to walk side by side with my friends in blissful ignorance.

But it was hard to do that when I could feel his eyes practically boring into the back of me.

As much as I hated to admit it, Lyle was right that we had no idea where we were. We had been going up and down the same street not really able to figure out what was what. There were a lot of fans still out on the streets near the venue too, who all looked very disappointed.

I felt bad for them honestly. But that's Mother Nature for you.

Further down, restaurants and bars hummed with activity in what appeared to be the downtown area.

"Oh guys, look, there's a pizza place! We should definitely get some," Chris said, staring into the lit-up 'Pizza Kings' sign.

I was starving and we never got to do fun stuff like this.

"Alright, alright, let's go get something to eat," I agreed.

The pizza place was moderately crowded, but still quiet enough that it could be enjoyed.

The hostess sat the four of us at a booth back in the corner of the restaurant and I, perhaps a bit too eagerly, took the empty seat by Harlow.

Which just so happened to be directly across from Dominik.

"Alright, guys what can I get you?" a young waiter asked the table.

"We'd like the eighteen-inch pepperoni pizza for the table, please. Waters all around as well," Christian told the waiter, not bothering to ask us first.

"You got it."

"All water? No beers?" Dominik asked inquisitively.

"Well yeah? Don't you know the rules?" Harlow asked knowingly.

"Apparently not," Dominik replied, slightly annoyed.

"Sober tour, rules set by the label since almost all Lyle's fans are like 13. Squeaky clean image and all that," Harlow said in air quotes. "It includes everyone so that also means you and your buddies can't drink either. Lyle and Chris got their asses kicked already for smoking weed so I suggest you follow the rules."

Dominik blew out a breath that turned into a dry laugh. "I was not informed of that. Good to know though."

"It sucks but you get used to it eventually. They just aren't very lenient. Which is really annoying since Aspen's birthday is coming up," Harlow unfortunately mentioned.

I shot her a glare and shook my head because I did *not* want him knowing about my upcoming birthday plans.

"Oh, is that so?" he asked me, suddenly showing interest in me for the first time that night.

"Yes. So what?"

"Sounds like you planned on drinking so it must be a big one," he tried to suggest casually although it was clear to me, he had an ulterior motive in asking.

Smart ass.

"21 actually."

He looked almost dumbfounded by that.

"Wait, you're turning 21? You're saying right now you're 20 years old, Aspen?"

"Yes. Stop acting weird about it," I grumbled.

Dominik very quickly regained his composure and put his facade back on in front of everyone.

"Right. Well, that's fucked that they won't let you drink on your 21st. You should say something to someone higher up."

Harlow and Christian looked at each other and almost burst out laughing hearing him curse like that.

It seems like I had been the only one so far to get a taste of what he's really like behind the 'professional asshole' farce.

"Elissa might be able to do something but it's a big might. She already covered for this dumbass and Lyle for being high the other night, so I doubt she'll want to cover for me too," I explained. The waiter brought our waters out, but we continued our conversation.

"And how exactly is the label able to figure all this out if they're not onboard the bus? Who's going to tell them?" Dominik questioned once the waiter had walked away.

I laughed at his lack of knowledge about how the business works.

"People always find out. I think it's one of the band members who keeps blabbing about it, but who knows. Secrets are hard to keep unless you have someone to be your alibi here so don't make any enemies," I cautioned him.

He bit back a laugh at that.

"No enemies. Sure, I can do that."

The pizza arrived, hot, greasy, and delicious. I couldn't remember the last time I'd been able to go out so casually, eating in a restaurant like a normal person and just sitting around with a group of friends.

It made me sad in a way to see how much I'd been missing out on since being on tour with Lyle. How much everything had changed since he signed the record deal.

We ate every last slice and talked about all sorts of things, largely leaving Dominik out of the conversation, much to his dismay.

But as I'd told him about being on the bus, it was rare you got to speak freely like we were doing without any fear of someone eavesdropping on you. We all were enjoying it to the fullest and had much to discuss.

"Man, that was good! I didn't know Virginia had some bomb-ass pizza like that. It's a shame Lyle didn't come out with us," Chris said as we walked out of the restaurant.

"Definitely. It would've been nice to be able to go out with him normally for once."

"Normalcy flew out the window a long time ago, Pen, but at least you got to hang with us for a while! You know we're always here for you," Harlow laughed.

"Of course. Being on that bus just makes you so stir-crazy. It's like a whole new wave of freedom just being able to walk around downtown like this!"

I looked at the busy streets, all the people passing by who didn't know who we were and didn't care. And I felt peace. Peace at being unacknowledged, and not being linked to Lyle.

"The tour will be over soon enough. But then it'll be back to making a new album and promoting it and then a new tour that'll probably be international. The cycle will never end," Harlow joked.

I laughed at what she said but that very notion was one that haunted me all the time: the fear that this is where I'd be for years to come.

It was enough to dampen my mood.

I slowed down and walked behind them as I fell into pace with Dominik.

"So, is this how it'll be now? You, always here somewhere, just lurking in the background?"

"Maybe I like to lurk. It gives me time to figure out people better."

"Well, excuse me, then," I scoffed.

"You're easy to read, Aspen. I didn't need to walk behind

you all night to be able to see it. I just can't figure out why no one else has."

I grabbed his arm and made him stop walking. That was the final straw, him walking around acting like he knew everything when he didn't have a clue. I had to talk myself down from the mouthful I was about to give him, so angry I could spit.

"Dominik, you don't know anything. Stop with your insistent need to understand me or read me or any other kind of shit like that. I much prefer the front I put on so please just leave it like that."

"A front is a front. You can't keep it up forever, Aspen."

I let go of his arm and straightened myself back out.

"Oh yeah? Watch me."

I sped up to catch up with the others, determined to prove him wrong. I could continue to put on whatever happy face I had to, and it would be believable damn it.

"So, guys, want to do something else tonight?" I asked them, coming around to Harlow's side. She wrapped her arm around my shoulder, squeezing me tight against her.

"Ah, the world's our oyster! We can do anything you want, Pen."

"Snacks! We've got to load the bus up with some more junk food. All of Elissa's healthy shit and green juices are nasty." Christian shuddered, launching a discussion of Elissa's gross food.

"Alright, sure that sounds good. Let's see where we can find some food."

Leaving Dominik behind us, we started walking further downtown to see if we could find some kind of small convenience store of sorts. Just enough to get us by for the night. We were so preoccupied that we hadn't even noticed the alleyway we were passing by.

Until all of a sudden, flashes of blinding light flooded my vision, sending me stumbling back.

"Yo Aspen!"

"Lyle's girlfriend, tell us what his new song will be!"

"Smile, Aspen!"

Paparazzi cameras were being shoved in my face from every angle, and the flashes were so disorienting I couldn't even see in front of me. Apparently, they'd been hiding in the alleyway, waiting to catch us.

"I've got you," a voice said in my ear, as strong hands met my waist.

Dominik put himself between me and the hordes of paps as they grew more aggressive, still trying to get their shots while I covered my eyes with my hands to try and see through the flashes of light.

"Dude, back off." Dominik didn't change his position, creating a barrier as the paps lunged at me.

"Miss Aspen, pose for us! Come on!"

One pap's arm reached out for me, and I instinctively dodged him, but Dominik's hand flew in front of me and pushed the man back before I even realized it.

"What the fuck did I just tell you? Move back!"

The pap stepped backward in surrender, as Dominik was becoming more aggressive. He was alone, and we were vastly outnumbered by the number of men crowding us.

We hauled ass, trying to get out of their line of sight before they got a shot they could attach to some bogus headline. The last thing I needed was to have to explain to Lyle and the team why there was an article about me, and my face plastered online everywhere.

Finally getting out of the way, we all paused and tried to take a breather, having basically run through the streets to safety.

"Holy shit. I can't breathe," Harlow panted.

We all echoed her, with Christian doubled over as he tried to suck in some deep breaths himself.

Dominik was further away from us, angrily raking his hands through his raven-colored hair.

As confused and shaken up as I was, I didn't understand what he was so upset about.

"Dominik?"

At the sound of my voice, he turned around and shook his head at me.

"Not right now, Aspen."

"Why are you so frustrated? Everyone's okay, we made it out fine. The bastards didn't get anything usable I don't think."

He laughed dryly, rubbing his hand over his jaw in one fluid motion. "You just don't get it."

"Then help me understand!"

"You almost got hurt, Aspen!"

His pupils were wide and staring into mine, as I realized then what he was getting at. I'd been so unnecessarily angry with him over what happened to me, even though it wasn't fair to him. Angry and stubborn enough that I completely ignored my surroundings and almost got hurt again.

"Oh," I said quietly, taking a step back from him. "I'm sorry, I know I didn't help any by not paying attention to what's around me. I honestly just didn't see them. I was so busy talking to Harlow and Christian and I—"

"I don't care about them. I care about the fact that *you* were almost taken advantage of again. And that shit doesn't happen when I'm here."

The vein in his neck pulsed and I had to avert my gaze to control a sudden pang of lust.

This is his job.

"I'll be more careful next time. I'm sorry again."

"You really are something, you know that? You undermine

your status, and this is where you keep ending up. Their prey, yet again. Let's just get you back safely and call it for the night," he sighed.

I understood he was upset over how easily the situation could've gotten out of hand, and I knew my stubbornness had only made it worse.

So, I agreed with him for once and didn't reply with any snarky comment as we started our journey back to the tour bus.

Keeping my distance from Dominik was difficult, but necessary after that unexpected flare of desire after he protected me.

This was wrong.

I couldn't let it happen again. The walls I'd built around myself were there for a reason, and his protective nature wouldn't suddenly break through them. It was just him doing his job.

Right?

Chapter Eight

ASPEN

EITHER MY MIND PLAYED TRICKS ON ME WHEN I WAS half asleep, or there was someone in my room that night. I'd never questioned before how delusional I was in the middle of the night since I had usually been out cold for quite a few hours and could make mere shadows into beasts. But I had since come to wonder if I was actually that crazy after all.

We had come back to the bus quite late, all of us slightly rattled by the whole paparazzi experience. But everyone tried to act cool, and that nothing was the matter when asked.

The band members were playing some video games, and Elissa had finally been able to relax for once, with a face mask on. Even Lyle was kicked back in the bedroom, although he did oddly seem a bit spooked when we came back earlier than expected. The band members were surprised too but didn't say anything.

As weird as that was, everyone was in good spirits, and I didn't want to ruin that.

But Dominik refused to leave me alone, his eyes trailing me no matter where I moved to on the bus. It was overbearing, and I was doing my best to make sure Lyle wouldn't notice. He wouldn't understand and I didn't want to explain the whole paparazzi incident, which seemed to be at the root of Dominik's gazes.

It was irritating me, especially after I'd just told myself again to put my walls back up. I had to get away from him.

Annoyingly squeezing past everyone, as the extra bodies now aboard had made things very tight, I eventually made it to the bedroom. Thankfully most of the other bodyguards just kept to themselves. I appreciated that considering I could only take one stalker at a time.

Lyle was asleep, so I had sunk into the covers with nice, warm body heat already there. The small electric fan we had by the bed blew a steady breeze and I was able to drift into a peaceful sleep.

Normally, I was used to tossing and turning in bed while we were constantly moving since any small jolt would wake me up during the night while on the road. But that wasn't what woke me up this time.

It was just one of those gut feelings. Like when you have a nightmare, and you wake up with chills and your heart racing because your body thinks you're still in it.

I woke up with that kind of instinctual feeling that I couldn't shake off but thought that I had hallucinated it.

I convinced myself so much that it was nothing that I fully did not expect to see a silhouette in the doorway in the middle of the night. Not only did it ignite my fight or flight, but I was so scared that I could hardly breathe.

And to make matters worse, I still wasn't sure it was even real once I was awake that morning. I might have just convinced myself that it was, and I was starting something over nothing. It could've been my imagination, or one of the many people aboard stopping in for a second. Which was what I hoped had *not* happened, since there was only one person to consider who would've actually done that.

I chose to say nothing, because it would have given Dominik

too much satisfaction for me to make such an accusation when he'd just deny it.

I instead went into the kitchen that morning like a normal adult, fixing a hot cup of coffee in my father's beloved Raiders mug with a splash of half and half. It was a miracle that the mug hadn't broken yet with how much we traveled, but I was always really careful about where I stored it. We'd had enough broken cups in the past that had taught me that lesson.

"Hey, Pen! You sleep okay?" Harlow asked. She didn't know what had happened that night, of course-she was just making small talk.

"Of course, yeah. I'm good to go," I smiled at her.

I picked through the cabinets and found the box of breakfast protein bars I loved. I took one out and went to pick up my coffee when my attention was suddenly pulled to Dominik entering the kitchen area shirtless. In gray sweatpants. *Only sweatpants.*

"Morning ladies," he grinned.

I quickly attempted to remove myself from his path and focused as hard as I could on anything but his bare chest.

He ended up sliding behind me to grab some food out of a nearby cabinet.

"Sorry, just have to reach around you," he whispered, touching my hip lightly as he squeezed by me.

Fucker. Why was he toying with me?

I cleared my throat and started talking to Harlow again to get my head out of the gutter.

"So, Harlow, do you think you'll have time today to dye my hair? I know you just dyed Lyle's yesterday, but the red is starting to fade," I said, picking up a lock of hair that had lost its beautiful color.

"I can probably fit it in. It looks kind of nice with the muted red tones though!" she said, eating a protein bar herself. Red hair was notorious for fading quickly but I wasn't personally a fan of the dull look.

Dominik sat on the couch across from Harlow, and I remained at my spot in the kitchen to stay completely focused on my conversation with her.

"Thanks, but my roots are coming in and they look awful. I'd much rather the royal treatment from you," I laughed, hoping she just might agree if I complimented her enough.

"That can be arranged. Just make sure there's nothing else you need to help Elissa with before the show since it'll take a while."

I nodded at her and finished my lame breakfast, sneaking looks at Dominik's half-clothed body.

He was rather hard to ignore. The biceps, the defined chest and large shoulders. I would have been kidding myself to try and say he was anything less than gorgeous.

"What about you Dominik? You doing anything else until the show?" Harlow asked, trying make small talk with him.

"No, nothing. You can do something to my hair if you want to help pass the time. I'm kind of tired though. I didn't sleep much last night. What about you, Aspen? You get much sleep?"

He was admitting it. He was sitting right there in front of me, admitting he was in my room in the middle of the night, and purposefully doing so in a way that didn't resonate with anyone but me.

A very calculated approach. Disturbingly calculated in fact.

But I would be the last person to give him the kind of satisfaction he so desperately wanted from me.

"No, I actually slept great. I had dreams of rainbows and butterflies. Doesn't get much better than that," I said with a fake smile.

He didn't seem surprised by my rebuttal and just shook his head and laughed.

"Sounds fun, I wish I had those kinds of dreams. Maybe you could help with that sometime."

Don't lose it, not because of him. Relax and take a deep breath, Aspen.

"Maybe you should take some sleeping pills then, Dominik. Or try and find some joy in your life. I'm sure that would help your dreams."

Harlow chuckled at my attitude, our argument amusing her.

"Who knows, after Harlow fixes my hair up all nice, I might find myself a new source of joy. Plenty of die-hard fans out there. Isn't that what tour life is all about?"

If he had been trying to make me speechless, that was a good way to do it.

"Dominik! Please tell me you are not reducing us down to the kind of tour management who lets groupies run rampant. Clearly not the vibe here if you couldn't tell," Harlow gasped, only slightly offended.

"Then I won't bring them here. There's a lot of places you can have fun."

"Ew! God, Dominik please get a grip! Take a note from your colleagues who are minding their business quietly right now. I don't need your testosterone levels ruining the image we've kept up this whole time for the label. Get it out of your system another way please," Harlow scoffed in disgust, rising and leaving Dominik and me alone.

"So. Any thoughts?" he asked, trying to dig at me again.

"I think your constant need to taunt me to lose my shit is ridiculous and immature. You can screw whoever you'd like as long as you keep it out of here. Some of us actually care about our morals and our dignity and would rather not see whatever trash you pick up. But if you don't have any morals then sure, go ahead."

"You really think *my* dignity is the one in question here?" he retorted.

I walked up to where he was sitting and leaned down to his level.

"Stop this game you're playing. It's pissing me off and only making me want to ruin you and your stupid cocky image. I suggest you don't let it get to that point."

He simply looked me in the eye with an air of smug superiority.

"I think I will, actually. Perhaps I want you to ruin me."

I'd never met someone who knew just how to rile me up and get away with it. No one had gotten under my skin like that in a very long time, and I refused to be sent down that road again.

"Come on, Pen! Let's start on your hair!"

Not wanting to entertain the conversation any longer, I gladly walked away from him and to Harlow who was gathering her supplies from the tiny drawers of the sink's vanity.

"You two fight like cats and dogs, I swear. Apparently, it seems that's what he needs though, given his attitude. If you don't check him on it, then I will and that will not be pretty," Harlow laughed as she grabbed a chair for me to sit in.

"It seems like that's all I ever do nowadays. Keep everyone in check," I sighed.

"Not a bad gig to have, Pen. You're the only one to keep us sane here."

I didn't respond to what she said but felt a pit in my stomach at who I'd become on the tour. I didn't want to keep anyone in line or be seen as Lyle's babysitter.

And I certainly was not about to start that again with Dominik.

Chapter Nine

DOMINIK

Pissing Aspen off first thing in the morning wasn't what I'd had in mind, but damn was it fun.

She made it too easy with the way she reacted to everything I said. I could have said the sky was pink, knowing she'd take the bait and argue with me.

Letting her think she was in control was the most enjoyable aspect for me though. It was clear to me that she lacked control in every other aspect of her life. If she needed to take it out on me, I was fine with that.

But I'd never let her see just how much I was pulling the strings.

The paparazzi incident, however, was not something I prepared for. Whatever bullshit she'd spewed to me about not being famous was a complete lie. And I was kicking myself for taking a job where I had to deal with assholes like that. The past gigs never had people that aggressive. And she had completely undermined the entire thing, which really got to me.

That girl was going to be the death of me.

"Hey Daniels, what's up? Are you ready for the show tonight?"

He had stepped outside for a minute to smoke, ready for a break from that hellscape of a bus.

"For sure. Just hope it's not rained out again tonight. I'm

ready to move on from this shitty city," he groaned. "And that short one doesn't help matters any. She acts like we're below her and orders us here and there like we're fucking dogs, man."

By the short one, he meant the manager Elissa, who he wasn't fond of in the slightest. While she was the closest thing to our boss while on tour, she had an unfavorable disposition and a lack of people skills.

It also didn't help that she didn't quite understand our jobs and acted like we were always servants to her, which wasn't the case.

"I know it, it's ridiculous. Can't blame her though. This shit sucks. Being stuck in there all day with all those people."

"Better than what you got. You've got your hands full with that redhead no doubt. She is pure fire, Dom. You better watch out or else you'll get burned."

Little did he know, that's exactly what I wanted.

"Ah come on, you know she's no match for me. Fun to mess with though," I said.

"You better be careful, playing games with her like that. I see the way you look at her, and she's been with Lyle for two years, Dom. Can't figure out their dynamic yet but I wouldn't get in the middle of that. And please don't stir the pot either for our sake."

Their 'dynamic' could have been spotted from a mile away. Daniels was just an idiot.

"I enjoy a good game. Plus, she'll be a rather... interesting distraction while we're stuck here."

"Whatever you say, man. Just don't come crawling back to me when you get burned." He took one last drag and looked me in the eye. "If I were you, I would keep my distance from that one."

He snubbed his cigarette out on the ground, and I only paused for a millisecond to think about what he had said. Back on the bus, I plopped down on the faux leather couch to unwind.

Those that did have their own bunks spent a lot of time there, as all six of them were occupied.

But they were like being in a coffin, so I couldn't fathom how they did it. Each bunk was smaller than a twin bed, and Daniels' feet had to be scrunched up for him to even fit with how tall he was. Having a completely personal space was nice, but the pull-out couch was sufficient enough for me.

And while we all slept like shit every night, because he was the star of the show, Lyle of course got a whole bed. Which I envied with my neck all screwed up from the poor cushioning of the pull-out. But I reminded myself that it was all temporary and I'd have a nice king bed again after the job was over.

After only sitting down for a few minutes, a melody of delightful giggles filtered from the bathroom. My feet were taking me over there before my brain even registered what I was doing.

"I look ridiculous, Harlow! It's everywhere!" Aspen laughed, looking in the mirror at herself.

Red hair dye had gotten smeared all over her forehead and some on her cheeks even, which they both found hilarious.

I'd yet to see Aspen act so… herself before. Her cheeks rose, the corners of her lips turning into a wonderfully radiant smile. She looked so lively, and carefree.

I had never seen a woman laugh as beautifully as her.

"What's so funny, girls?"

The laughter died as soon as I said something, and Aspen's spirits instantly dropped when she saw me standing in the bathroom doorway.

"Just Harlow and I messing around," she said quietly, not meeting my eyes.

"Well, Debbie downer Aspen needs to lighten up every once in a while! If I had known it was this easy, I'd always make a mess when I dyed her hair," Harlow joked, hands coated in red dye. "So, are you still going to hold up to your offer from earlier, Dominik? Because I think I could give you a great haircut."

With our earlier discussion being brought up, I studied Aspen's face and how her smile fell when thinking about our conversation from that morning. It was an intentional topic brought up to test how Aspen felt about me with other women. I hadn't been able to tell before then if she was attracted to me, and I *needed* to know how she really felt. It worked perfectly.

And while my hair was longer than I liked, the haircut wasn't to attract some groupie girl.

It was for her.

Sure, I did find some additional joy in bringing up the idea of looking nice for other women and getting a rise out of her, but it was a very purposeful discussion. Seeing just how much she tried to hide that it upset her to think about, was the real answer to my question.

The groupies were never something I planned on actually pursuing though. Just part of the game.

"Sure, have at it. Just let me know when Aspen's finished."

"Perfect! Your curls are amazing, I know just what to do to make them pop!"

Curls were curls. I had learned when I was a teenager how to style them better with water or gel, but I didn't know what exactly she could do with my hair beyond the cut. If she had a vision that Aspen would like however, I could go along with it.

Although if I looked at Lyle as any example of Harlow's abilities, maybe I should've lowered my expectations.

While the 'beach boy' blonde hair might have looked nice on some people, it was hideous on Lyle. It didn't help that it washed out his already pale skin, and made him look younger than he actually was, which didn't work in his favor with his occasional patchy beard. Pair that with his whiny voice and shit attitude, and Lyle was absolutely pathetic.

The fact that Aspen couldn't see how much of a self-centered, asinine human being he was astounded me.

She was a smart girl. Very clever in fact yet acted as if she couldn't speak for herself when around him. She didn't say more than a peep, beyond trying to settle things between parties. I really didn't like the way she seemed to shrink around him.

It bothered me. A lot.

Yet I wasn't even surprised. Me and my guys had figured out pretty immediately that the client would be awful when we got the call. It really took a girl going to the hospital for the label to realize they needed better security?

The whole way it went down sent a very obvious message that they thought they were above our 'lowly' security. The arrangements were made so quickly, sending us on some shitty economy flight at an ungodly hour. That label made it very clear what their priorities were.

We'd had some difficult clients in the past, but none were ever rushed like this one was. It was almost a guarantee that it was going to be a shit job for a shit person, but it was *good* money.

Koen and I almost didn't go through with it. We'd done most jobs together for the past few years and everyone had that line they drew in the sand as to what their limits were. This contract was dangerously close to ours.

We didn't do pop stars for one. They were known in the business as all being self-centered crybabies. Movie stars were a hell of a lot easier to deal with than these people were. We liked the movie stars because they were usually too strung out or drunk to even know what was going on which made it an easy job.

Second, we knew there would be a lot more people involved than just the primary client while in a transient setting.

And wouldn't you know it, everyone on the team was insufferable. Know-it-all, demanding, you name it. I regretted agreeing to it as soon as I stepped off the plane.

But then there was Aspen.

Charming, aggravating, and drop-dead fucking gorgeous all in one.

Her sarcastic, bold nature was absolutely alluring. When she wasn't busy being mouthy, she secretly had an enormously big heart. It was amazing how much she cared for those around her, even Lyle.

Younger than I'd first thought, considering she was only 20 to my 27 years, but it made no impact on our connection.

I might not have started the job with the intention of finding someone like her, but I'd be damned if I didn't do everything in my power to keep her now that I had. And while the paparazzi incident was a complete mess, it really scared the shit out of me, so much so that I couldn't sleep without checking on her to make sure she was okay.

I didn't mean for her to catch me doing it, but it didn't faze her a bit.

My usual tricks meant nothing to her. She treated me as if I was a bug flying by her ear and she was constantly swatting to get me out of the way. If she wanted me to chase her, then I would happily do so until she was mine.

But she would be lying if she claimed she didn't feel the tension the way I did. The chemistry between us. It was absolutely fucking addicting.

I'd left the girls alone after I killed the mood, only slightly annoyed that Aspen clammed up around me. But I met up with the boys in the front lounge area who'd pulled out the gaming console.

The band members were pretty chill and were some of the only tolerable people around. They were much more for watching movies, playing video games, or just really keeping to themselves.

"Sup' guys, can I play in a minute?" Lyle asked, coming up

to where we all sat. The guys looked around at each other, testing the waters to see if anyone was going to speak up first.

Someone say no, please.

"Sure, you can play the next game with Dom," Holcomb replied, like the dick he was.

Fuck me.

"Cool bro," he said casually, grabbing a soda from the fridge.

He came and slid in next to me on the couch and I was hoping that he wouldn't actually try to start a conversation with me. I was trying to avoid him as it was.

"So, was that you I heard arguing with Aspen this morning?"

Great.

"Yeah, we were just talking," I replied nonchalantly.

He shifted his jaw but didn't dispute it.

"She doesn't get upset often so if she is for some reason, you should tell me. I'd hate for something to be going on that I don't know about."

Bold of him. Not that I'd ever tell him what Aspen and I had going on.

"Nah, it's all good. She just didn't like me bringing up groupies," I said, trying to throw him off my trail.

"And why would the two of you be discussing groupies? I can't imagine Aspen bringing that topic up," he said.

I appreciated the masculine approach he was trying to take but he'd never win.

"We were just going over what's allowed here. I figured there must be a good amount of ass that goes around so I was hoping to get a piece of it myself. Seems like that isn't the kind of ship your leader has running here though, so it's all good."

He smirked, and it seemed I'd convinced him of my intentions. But then he came in real close to me and whispered, "You'd be right. I actually had a chick over last night, so I was a bit freaked when you guys came back so soon. Just let me know at a show when you're wanting some and I'll hook you up."

He winked at me and gave me a brotherly slap on the shoulder. I gave him an all-too-convincing smile back at him. "Thanks, you're a real one."

Fuck.

That could only mean one thing. Something I'd selfishly hoped was going on under wraps to give me a way in with Aspen, but something I didn't want to be true for her sake.

Lyle was cheating on her. And she had no idea.

Chapter Ten

ASPEN

IT WAS AMAZING WHAT SOME FRESH HAIR DYE COULD DO. My confidence had been through the roof since Harlow had been able to do my hair a few weeks ago. It was bright and definitely made a statement, but that's exactly what I wanted. And Lyle had even told me it looked nice, which I appreciated since he rarely ever complimented me.

Everything was smooth sailing, with the shows having gone well too. We had a system, and it honestly wasn't as bad as I thought it was going to be with the new security. Pretty much everyone minded their business and stuck to their job of making sure we were in and out safely and moving at appropriate times.

All except for Dominik.

For some reason, I'd drawn the lucky straw when I got stuck with him because he wouldn't leave me alone. No other bodyguard hovered the way he did, and I couldn't stand it.

Every show he was breathing down my neck, always right where I was and if I even tried to move an inch, he clocked it. But it wasn't just at shows, it was *everywhere*. If I wasn't in his line of sight, all hell would break loose according to him apparently.

I considered just running off to see if he'd chase me, but I had a feeling he would.

And on top of that, my snarky replies meant nothing to him.

Every time he would respond with something equally sarcastic or annoyingly witty and it was driving me up a wall.

Because I actually liked it.

I liked having someone to banter back and forth with. Someone that actually seemed to care what I had to say and would respond with more than a basic one-word reply.

There was a shred of guilt over what my increasingly positive feelings about Dominik. But it was easily forgotten when I found myself smiling more and significantly happier than I'd been in a long time. I didn't want to feel guilty for that.

Not that I'd ever admit it to Dominik.

He would get way too much satisfaction in knowing how much I enjoyed his company.

Things were just better the way they were.

Thankfully, we were going to get a slight break from the tour schedule starting that week. We had been on the road for just over five months, with the security crew being with us for two months. And trust me, no one needed to be stuck on a bus for that long.

We were all just about at our wits' end.

Elissa was crankier than normal, Christian had gotten snappy a few times, and two of the other bodyguards were a little annoying.

But Dominik did a good job at keeping them cool. While he was getting along well with virtually everyone onboard, he and I always argued about something.

He was meticulous onboard, so much so that if you didn't know any better, you'd assume he didn't even live there.

I however was quite the opposite. Clothes on the floor and leaving dishes out, which sent him spiraling. Yet another point of contention between the two of us. It was like that on practically everything.

Except for one incident.

I had my stitches removed at a random hospital along our route. And despite everyone's ridiculous pleading, I just went in by myself and had them removed. It was quick and easy, and I didn't have to hear any more comments about it.

While it had left a small indent in my chin, the doctor had convinced me that the scar would be gone in a year or two. *Lucky me.*

But Dominik had gone a little soft on me, showing me his scar in comparison to mine that day.

"You'll be good as new," he told me. "Don't worry about it. Mine was deep enough that it never fully healed but yours is not nearly as bad."

He rolled his sleeve up and showed me a scar that grazed his forearm and followed down to his hand where it became much deeper and almost pitted.

"That looks like it was really bad. Did you get that from bodyguarding?"

He quickly looked away and rolled his sleeve back down.

"Uh, no I didn't. It was a long time ago and it's all healed now so it's fine. Bodyguarding isn't a word anyways."

"Shut up, yes it is."

We'd gone back to our usual dynamic quickly enough, but I hadn't forgotten his vulnerability that day. I questioned how I'd even missed his scar given how deep it went into his hand, though it seemed to me that he tried to keep it hidden for the most part.

I never said anything about it, but the comparison he shared between the two of us that day actually warmed my heart. Maybe we weren't complete opposites, which I secretly kind of liked.

"We've arrived, Miss Kwon," the bus driver announced as we stopped at our destination, yanking me from my memories.

"Alright guys, last show!" Elissa said. "Hotel life soon awaits. For most of us at least."

"I don't even care that it's a hotel. It'll be a queen size bed at last!" Harlow laughed.

"Yes, well we still have the show tonight so look alive people! We'll all be out of here before we know it. With the exception of you of course," Elissa said pointing at Lyle.

"Why is that?" one of the band members asked.

"Lyle will have to fly back to L.A. to record the new single the label sent over. He gets to stop off at home before joining us again, but we won't be able to do the same. We have a show directly after the break in Missouri, so we'll have to stay close."

"That blows," one of them complained, and I was right there with him.

"It would take time and money to fly all of you to your respective homes and back within the week. Unless each of you can afford yourself to fly home and then to Missouri before the next show, I suggest you quit your whining. Paid hotel life is better than none."

As much as I wished I could go home for the week, Elissa was right. None of us could afford ourselves to fly back and forth in such a short period of time. Well, maybe the security team could afford it. I heard through the grapevine they were getting paid handsomely by the label.

"Think we'll get to share a room?" I asked Harlow excitedly. It would be like the sleepover I always wanted from when I was a kid.

"Definitely. We should see who's making the arrangements and make sure we get the same room," she said, putting on her eyeliner.

"Aren't you forgetting something?"

Ugh. Dominik.

"What would I be forgetting, Mr. Kostas?" I turned around to his large stature towering over me.

"Unless you plan on Harlow sleeping in the same bed as you, *I'll* be the one taking the other bed in the hotel room."

"You're joking," I laughed dryly. But the look on his face told me he was not. "You can't seriously expect to stay in my room with me! That would be, that would be…"

"That would be my *job*, is what you mean. Don't bother trying to change it. The room assignments have already been sent over."

I wanted to stomp my foot like a child. I hated his power over me, always feeling like I had no say in anything. I'd already lost all control of anything on the godforsaken bus, and yet again I had no say?

I swear I could've screamed.

I didn't trust myself to share a room with him, probably unable to sleep knowing it was just us two in the room together. Separate beds or not, I'd never slept in the same room with a man that wasn't Lyle.

"You really couldn't stay with Koen? He's your buddy, isn't he?"

"No, I can't. Koen is flying back with Lyle, but it wouldn't matter anyways. My duty is to you and that means being there to actually protect you. I can't do that from a separate room, now can I?"

I narrowed my eyes at him, ready to explode. There was the part of my brain that knew this was professionally what would be expected of him, but God did it drive me absolutely fucking crazy. I didn't know how to feel about it and the lack of control over my own feelings was scaring me.

"Fine. Try not to gloat so much about it, will you?" I said.

"Gloat? I don't gloat."

"Then you should wipe that smile off your face because trust me when I say if I could find any way possible to get you off my back, I would. I didn't 'let you win' this, I backed down out re-spect for your job."

Dominik furrowed his eyebrows sharply, and he wasn't the only one surprised. My tone was much icier than I intended. I just didn't appreciate the way he gave me those cocky looks when my brain was still on overdrive trying to decipher what the hell I was feeling.

"Yes, of course, Aspen. My apologies," he murmured.

Did he seriously just apologize to me? I'll take things I never expected to happen for 200 please.

"It doesn't even matter. Let's just get this show over with so we can finally have a break. I'm on the verge of ripping my hair out as it is," I admitted. It was my own way of trying to explain and apologize for me lashing out.

"That would be a shame. Better off not letting that happen."

I couldn't hide the small smile it brought to my face that he didn't have to acknowledge my form of an apology to understand it was the best I could do.

"Well, I think if I'm trapped here any longer it'll happen soon enough. I've been here even longer than you, remember?"

"Certainly. It's a miracle that your hair hasn't fallen out any-how from how much you dye it."

I openly laughed at that.

"That's a valid statement. Although Lyle's is much more at risk considering his is bleached every few weeks, thanks to the label. Did you know he's originally brunette?"

Dominik's smile fell just a hair, but not without me noticing.

"I didn't actually, but that's not surprising. These labels al-ways have a perfect vision in their heads. The blonde seems to be his… signature look now."

The way he hesitated told me all I needed to know about how he really felt. I found it slightly amusing.

"He'd go back brunette if he had the choice but all the label cares about is selling the image."

"And what about you? You don't care to go back to your natural color? Whatever it may be?"

I cringed. Although it was a simple and valid question, I didn't want him to bring it up.

"No, I don't. I have no interest in that and won't be going back to my natural color again for a very long time."

"Oh, come on, you can't tease me like that. Now I have to know why you won't go back to your natural color."

I sighed and started picking at my fingernails nervously.

"It's complicated, just leave it be."

"Aspen, you know I won't say anything."

I looked up at him and tried to ignore the flutter of my heart at how intently he was staring back at me.

"It's brown. My natural hair color is light sandy brown," I admitted finally. "The same color as my mother's."

I could almost see the gears turning in his head as he figured out what this meant.

"So, you dye your hair red to not look like your mother anymore?"

"Precisely."

He leaned back into his seat and thought it over for a minute.

"Interesting. See, I clocked you as a rich girl from the suburbs who's on her rebellious kick right now with the hair dye and being on tour. I was sure your mommy and daddy were in their big white house just waiting for you to come back home and settle down into a normal life."

My mouth dropped. I thought he was the only one who saw me for who I was. How could he have been so wrong about me?

The reality of my past was much more depressing, and I hated even having to think about it myself. The fact that he somehow thought I was a rich princess, was truly crazy to me.

"Well, I haven't talked to my mom in over two years actually, and my dad is dead. We never had more than a few hundred dollars to our name most of the time so you should keep your assumptions to yourself," I said coldly.

"Ah fuck Aspen, I'm sorry. I didn't realize —"

"No, don't. Don't backtrack now out of pity. Clearly you don't know as much as you think you do."

"I don't, you're right."

My head snapped up at his admittance. He *never* admitted when he was wrong.

"I never should've assumed that about you. I really am sorry, that was completely out of line."

I didn't reply and turned away from him, wanting to keep him outside my walls.

"Is it because you think I'm judging you? Because I don't judge you for your upbringing. Mine is more similar than you'd think."

"And how is that?" I chided.

"My parents are immigrants from Greece. They moved here with hardly anything and we grew up in an awful neighborhood, but it was all we had. My parents did the best they could and worked odd jobs to keep a roof over our heads."

The puzzle pieces started to all connect, and perhaps I was slightly touched that he was sharing his backstory with me. But I couldn't. When someone hurt me, all I wanted to do was hurt them more.

"Well, mine weren't nearly as devoted to those endeavors. My mom was a drunk who couldn't hold a job after my father died and I single handedly raised my younger brother until I finally got out at 18. So not so similar, really."

I turned away from him again and he didn't try bothering me after that.

For some reason, I wished he did.

Chapter Eleven

ASPEN

S IF THINGS COULDN'T GET ANY WORSE, THE LAST show before break was a nightmare.

The venue had almost no security, letting people stomp all over each other as they fled toward the stage for the best spots. Inevitably people were upset, and complaints were starting to file in rapidly.

The lack of security wasn't only an issue for fans, but for us too.

Elissa was over it. She was a firm woman on normal days, but on days she was pushed too far? She would rain hellfire on anyone in her way. We all knew to stay clear of her as much as possible when she was on a warpath.

She demanded to know what outside security group the venue had hired, likely to send them out of business.

Lyle of course, barely noticed the chaos ensuing and all the upset fans crowding the stage. He'd gotten into this monotonous routine during shows while on tour, and it's like any kind of personal touch for his fans wasn't important anymore.

He didn't sing any special songs, say anything different in his lousy speeches that attempted to make each show feel special. Although we all knew it was the same rehearsed lines he'd said at the last fifteen shows.

But that was the least of my worries during showtime.

It had truly been just a miserable day and Dominik still on my heels didn't help matters any. We had hardly said a few words to each other throughout the day after I blew up at him.

In hindsight, I felt guilty for being so harsh with him and couldn't stop beating myself up for how I ignored him sharing his whole life story with me. I was being a stubborn asshole, and I regretted it fully. I just didn't know how to apologize to him.

Even though we weren't on the best of terms, he still refused to let up at the show. I was already exhausted and half-asleep backstage, just trying to make it through the night and his hovering was unneeded. But apparently the lack of venue security bothered him immensely.

I understood that it increased the odds of someone or something slipping through the cracks, leaving our team's security on high alert. It was *him* that was driving me crazy.

"Please move to the side of me at least."

I'd asked him twice already, since having his tall self in front of me meant I could hardly see anything.

"No. What good will it do if I'm at your side? I'm doing my job."

I rolled my eyes, just about ready to head back to the bus and call it a night. I didn't feel like putting up with him nor his attitude.

"Just wanted a break Dominik, that's all," I sighed.

As I turned around to head back to the tour bus, he caught my arm.

"If you leave, then I am too. I'm not letting you walk back to the bus by yourself. Stop pretending like you don't need any help."

He looked at me in that way that could've single-handedly tore all my walls down. When he showed how much he cared about me without using words.

Shaking myself out of it, I ripped my arm away from him,

and he didn't fight me. "If I need your help, I'll ask for it. Either let me go alone, or back off while we're at the show."

He took a deep breath and our eyes locked on each other. It was as if I could physically see his confliction. Alas, he shook his head and turned his back to me. "Fine. Go."

Two words. That's all I got from him.

I could feel the hurt in his tone, the palpable ache as if the last thing he wanted to do was turn me away. But this was for the best.

Though temporary, the week-long break would be exactly what we all needed after the day in, day out chaos. And for me to try and get my act together. I was acting like a teenager again with a stupid crush.

It was ridiculous.

Instead, I was going to focus on much more important things. Like lying in bed all day, watching ridiculous reality TV shows, and enjoying a nice full-size shower for the first time in five months. Since it was on the label's dime, we could all relax without thinking about the costs and I hadn't been able to do that in a long time.

Everyone eventually piled onto the bus one last time, exhausted from the show. On the verge of falling asleep again, I was startled awake when a certain issue finally reached a boiling point.

Christian and Lyle had not seen eye to eye on things in over a month. Christian was focusing less on his duties of being an assistant to Lyle, and more on wanting to party. There was already some disdain for his behavior following the smoking incident a few months back, but he was determined to get Lyle into trouble again.

Elissa and Lyle had already had enough arguments about it, with Lyle always somehow convincing her to keep him around. But eventually, enough was enough. Christian's attitude was awful, and his constant pleas for someone to go out and 'have fun with him' were getting on everyone's nerves.

Elissa finally stepped in and tried to have a stern talk with him before the show that night, but it all fell on deaf ears.

He attempted again to bring drugs on the tour and Elissa put her foot down for good this time. She cornered him on the bus, forcing him to admit to her that he was bringing them for Lyle. And with her already upset from the show, she was not backing down.

But neither was he. It went back and forth for a minute, her telling him that he was, "sloppy, useless, and completely un-needed," and him saying she was a crazy bitch. Eventually, the fighting got worse and Christian absolutely lost it. Screaming about all sorts of things, and how she was going to regret this.

It was quite unsettling to watch.

But people who don't like to be very disciplined certainly don't change their tune when under such intense conditions. I personally would've let go of him much earlier on the tour to save us all the headache, but I didn't run things.

Once Harlow intervened to calm things, Elissa told him he was fired and that was the end of it. He was subsequently dropped off in some random small city and told to get the hell out of there. Tough blow but it needed to happen.

One less person onboard though meant a little more space and it really did make a difference. Holcomb, one of the other bodyguards, was now able to take the free bunk, although I had offered it to Dominik first out of the kindness of my heart.

He'd just insisted that he wanted to stay in the pullout bed.

Dominik may have been the world's greatest pain in the ass, but he was always polite and cordial to everyone. That grew on me a little.

Finally making our way across state lines about two hours away, we were almost at our destination. It was late at night, and

I was having a hard time staying awake on the couch as we drove through the winding back roads.

Dominik sat across from me, and my chest clenched at how defeated he looked. He and I had both quietly watched the arguing and I had a hunch that he was feeling the same way I was at the moment.

That our fighting was ridiculous by comparison.

When we crossed into the next state, Lyle was dropped off at the airport for a private flight to head back to L.A. for the week and all I got was an awkward kiss goodbye. He didn't even acknowledge that it was my birthday that week.

I imagined if it was someone else in my position, that his coldness would've been quite upsetting. Yet I wasn't all that fazed by it.

We were growing more distant every day and his lifestyle wasn't made for couples to thrive in. There were only so many hours in a day and with Lyle's career occupying almost all of them, it was clear that I'd become the afterthought.

Watching your relationship disintegrate was a really shitty feeling. But what was even worse, was that neither Lyle nor I would bring it up to one another. I wondered sometimes if he was hoping I'd be the one to initiate the "talk" or if I'd ride it out until the tour officially ended.

Neither option was one I wanted to pursue.

Maybe there was a piece of me that wanted to make things work still. But when only one party cared to put in the effort, there were only so many options before it came down to the ultimate ending.

I figured the week apart from each other would give us both time to reflect and think about things. We hadn't been apart for this long in a while. Everyone needs some healthy distance from their partner every once in a while, even if it's just going out separately once a week. I didn't have that option while trapped on the bus from hell.

So, the week at the hotel needed to be perfect. Even if he wouldn't be there for my birthday, I was determined to make the most of it.

I wanted to enjoy it with no strings attached or worrying about anything but relaxing.

That sounds easy enough, right?

Chapter Twelve

ASPEN

"**T**HESE ARE YOUR ROOM CARDS."

The man handed Dominik and I two room cards at around one in the morning and I was already heading to the elevator before he could even turn around. I needed to sleep desperately, and the quicker I could get to the room, the better.

I had decided that my birthday week would still be perfect, even with Dominik lingering around. But that didn't mean I was going to change all my plans to accommodate him. I hit the elevator button of the floor I needed, and figured Dominik would catch up at some point.

"Could you slow down, Aspen? Jesus," he muttered, slamming his hand in the elevator doors before they shut.

"Oops."

He pursed his lips, and I could tell he wanted to say something sarcastic right back at me. Instead, he simply swung his bag over his shoulder and entered the elevator.

"Is it going to be like this the whole time?" he asked as the elevator began moving.

I'd rather watch the floor numbers change on the digital display than answer him.

Because the truth was that I didn't know. If I acted any other way, I was worried that my real feelings would come through. I had to keep up this show for as long as possible.

"Maybe."

"Aspen, I'm serious. After all the fighting and chaos, I want to enjoy the week here. Don't make this harder than it has to be."

He looked me in the eyes, and my breath hitched in my throat.

I couldn't think when he looked at me like that. All that clouded my mind was him, and it made me want to do some really terrible things.

"I-I won't. I'll be good," I stuttered.

Dominik looked down at my lips, then back to my eyes. My heart was about to rip through my chest. His full lips, framed by his dark facial hair he'd grown out, were coming closer and closer and I knew I was going to let him kiss me.

The elevator suddenly dinged as the doors opened to our correct floor with a few people waiting to board.

If the noise hadn't disrupted us, I would have made a very big mistake. One that would've completely affected this week.

I cleared my throat, and awkwardly rolled my suitcase out into the maroon carpeted hallway. Looking at the sign on the wall, I followed the line of doors until I found the one that matched our room cards.

Sliding the card in, the door clicked open, and I almost shit myself.

One. Fucking. Bed.

"You've got to be fucking kidding me."

Dominik leaned over my shoulder and saw the dilemma. And he laughed. Fucking laughed at the sick joke that was my life.

"I'm going to go back downstairs and see if we can get the room switched to two queens," I muttered, turning my suitcase around.

"Oh, come on, you big baby. It's a king bed, just put some

pillows in between if you don't want to touch me. Which is kind of offensive, you know."

"Excuse me but I don't feel like having to try and share a bed with a sasquatch like you. I'm 5'9" as it is and guess what? These long legs, and your tree trunks don't mix."

"You worry too much. It'll fit us both just fine. You need to get some rest anyhow, so why don't you just deal with it for the night?"

I rolled my eyes, knowing I was sounding like a total asshole, but it was not at all what I had pictured. Sure, I was being too extreme, but my tiredness wasn't helping any and I was frustrated. I looked again, and realized it was technically large enough for us both.

"Fine. But you're in charge of stacking the pillows."

"I can handle that. I'll make sure there's no chance of interaction, since you seem to care so much about that," he scoffed.

I thought I heard a hint of edge in his tone, and I couldn't put my finger on why exactly it would irritate him so much. It was for the best interest of both parties for us to stay far, *far* away from each other after the incident in the elevator.

Dragging my suitcase to the corner of the room, I grabbed my toiletry bag and made my way over to the bathroom. I had to take off my makeup, wash my face, and go through my whole nightly process before I could go to bed.

But holy shit was it so much better when you had a wide bathroom counter and full-size sink to spread everything out on. I could've filled the entire counter with makeup and skin products and still had some room left over.

The shower, however, looked like it was sent straight from heaven.

Large glass doors, floor-to-ceiling white subway tile, and a gigantic rain showerhead were calling my name.

There was so much space, so many…*things* that could be done with that much room.

Get your head out of the gutter.

"Dominik!" I yelled out to him.

"What?"

I opened the bathroom door to find him neatly stacking a line of pillows between both sides of the bed.

"I'm going to take a quick shower, okay? If you need to shower, then you can just go after me. I'll be done soon."

"Wow, thanks for the courtesy."

"Whatever. I'll be in here if you need me," I said, grabbing a stack of clothes from my luggage to change into. I grabbed my underwear with superhuman speed before he saw anything.

He waved me off and I took everything into the bathroom with me. If he wanted to be all snappy with me, then so be it because I was *not* going to rush this shower.

I had waited for a shower like this the whole time we'd been on tour, and I certainly wasn't going to rush through it just because Dominik was with me now. He could wait his turn.

Slipping out of my clothes and into the warm water, I almost melted at how amazing it felt. The steady water pressure, the perfect temperature that didn't turn cold after a few minutes.

It was absolutely like being in heaven.

Until a loud knock banged on the bathroom door.

"Aspen!"

"What do you need Dominik?"

"I need to take a piss. Can you hurry up?"

"For fuck's sake Dominik! No, no I cannot. Go aim your dick off the balcony for all I care!"

"You can be a real ass sometimes, you know that?"

Most certainly. And I didn't feel a damn bit of shame about it.

"Just hold on for ten damn minutes and I'll be out!"

I huffed at my lovely shower time being interrupted and tried to hurry my shower routine along. I could've been even more of an ass and shaved my legs or applied a hair mask, but I decided to be nice for once.

Shutting the water off, I grabbed one of the white fluffy towels hanging off the bathroom wall and wrapped myself tightly in it. I huffily grabbed my clothes and took them with me to change into.

My wet feet slapped against the tile floor as I unlocked the door and swung it open.

"I'm done now. Have fun."

Dominik took one look at me, and I could've sworn I saw his cheeks flush considerably.

He didn't say anything. There was no need for words with the gaze he held me in, undressing me with my eyes. Wordlessly, he stared and then stared some more before I felt inclined to finally say something.

"Go now please, so I can finish getting ready," I said motioning to the open door.

He got up eventually from his position on the bed, but not before I caught the noticeable bulge in his pants.

I held back a grin but found myself quite happy to have had that kind of effect on him.

Leaning over into my suitcase to grab some socks for the night, the door opened unexpectedly, and I shot up, my back going ramrod stiff.

My ass had to have been fully visible with me leaning over. Maybe even more than that.

"If you're done with the shower, I'm going to rinse off while I'm in here," he said casually.

Okay, maybe he didn't see me semi-naked then.

"Yeah, that's fine. I'll just finish up when you're done," I choked out as he started to close the door.

"Oh, and you might want to make sure I'm actually gone *before* you reach into your suitcase next time. Just as a friendly reminder," he winked, finally closing and locking the door behind him.

Heat rose up my throat and seeped into my cheeks, my heart flying through my chest yet again.

Of course, he had seen my entire bare ass. That's just perfect.

I quickly dried off the rest of the way and tried to catch my breath. The fact that he had seen my somewhat naked body was… exhilarating.

But I absolutely could not be thinking so egregiously.

I changed into my pajamas while he was in the shower and braided my hair into one long plait so it wouldn't tangle while I slept.

Finally feeling somewhat back in control of myself, I waited for Dominik to be done so I could finish my night routine.

After a few minutes, he emerged from the steamy bathroom already dressed for the night.

His hair was sopping wet still, dripping onto his white shirt and I couldn't fathom him sleeping on that wet of hair without doing anything to it.

"I'm done if you want to go and finish your weird nightly rituals."

I laughed out loud and went and grabbed one of the extra towels still hanging on the silver rod in the bathroom.

"You're going to catch a cold if you leave your hair this wet."

I stood on my tip toes and ran the towel through his dark curls, trying to soak up some of the excess water.

He was incredibly still, not moving a muscle as I dried his hair. He was so much taller than me that it was a bit more intensive than I thought it'd be, but he didn't have any complaints. He willingly let me do it.

"That's better," I said quietly.

He looked at me with lustful eyes, tracing my every move. I couldn't let things go any further and put the towel down before trying to go back to the bedroom.

"Why didn't you say anything when I cut my hair?" his voice graveled, layered with desire and a yearning for transparency.

I stopped in my tracks and turned around in the doorway.

"Probably because you wanted it to look nice for groupies."

His gaze darkened, and he slowly walked over to where I stood.

"That wasn't the truth. You know that."

"I…" My words trailed off, his eyes pinning me in my place. "I think it suits you," I finally said weakly.

"Is that so?"

It wasn't a question. He was taunting me.

"Because I did it for you," he admitted. "So, I would appreciate you saying something next time."

He did it for me?

"Why on Earth would you do that? I like your hair either way."

"Because Lyle's hair is short. Figured long hair wasn't your thing."

The last thing I wanted was to be thinking about Lyle.

"Don't mention him again," I pleaded. "Not when we're talking about you."

His hand moved to my hip and fit into the curve of my waist like it was made for me.

"For the record, I like long hair. What I don't like is you making decisions like that based on me. We can't…"

"Who says?" he whispered.

I gulped, desperately trying to find a way to reason what we were doing in my head. I *wanted* things to progress, I wanted Dominik. More than I ever thought was humanly possible.

I wanted to give into my urges more than anything. The way

he ignited me was unlike anything I'd ever experienced before. But it was wrong, for more than one reason. I couldn't jeopardize either of us.

"I told you I'd be good. For the sake of both of our positions, you need me to be good right now," I breathed, my face mere inches from his.

"Yes, I do. Be a good girl and tell me no. Find a way to shake me out of this."

"*We can't,* Dominik. We are better off just remaining client and bodyguard." The words didn't even sound believable to me coming out of my mouth.

"Not good enough. Find another way or I swear I'll bend you over right here," he said darkly, his hand moving up my waist and toward my breasts.

I wanted that. I *really* wanted that.

Don't give in. Find a way to distract him, Aspen.

"I'm sorry," I blurted out. "For earlier. Pushing you away when you were just trying to do your job. And I never should've been so cold to you after you opened up to me about your life. I got defensive because of how shitty my own childhood was and I lashed out at you."

The hunger in his eyes waned slightly, and I knew I found a way in.

"I don't trust myself around you… you're changing everything for me. I acknowledge every time you open up to me, even when you think I don't. I remember all of it because it makes me feel less alone, and I'm sorry I never wanted to admit it to you. You're the only reason I don't break down and cry about the scar on my face. You're the only reason I'm making it through this."

My hands instinctively went to his as I found his scar and traced it with my thumb. He blinked a few times, seemingly coming out of the haze we'd both been in.

"I don't know what to say."

"Don't say anything. I just wanted you to know how sorry I was, and that I pay more attention than you realize. You know I won't ever be this transparent again."

He nodded his head, accepting this new knowledge, but didn't say anything else. He wrapped me in a tight hug instead that single handedly broke down my walls and showed he understood me in every way possible.

It was what we both needed. It doused the flames between us to a sizzle, a necessary splash of water to bring us both back down to Earth.

Going to bed that night with a line of pillows between us, my heart physically hurt. I secretly wished I'd never asked him to build the pillow wall and that I could cuddle up close to him. Because I didn't want distance anymore. I wanted him to know every piece of me, and I wanted to know everything that made him Dominik.

But the wall of pillows was all too symbolic of the real wall that our worlds had put between us.

We couldn't be together.

And I couldn't change that.

Chapter Thirteen

ASPEN

THE HARSH MORNING SUN BLED THROUGH THE SLIDING glass doors of the hotel room and slowly woke me.

Rolling over to look at the clock next to the bed, I could hardly believe my eyes. It was ten in the morning, which was much later than we ever slept in while on tour. I guess when my body was given the opportunity, it finally decided to catch up on all the missed sleep.

I searched the other side of the bed for Dominik, but it was completely empty.

I figured he had woken up earlier and already got his day started, which left me with a big, empty hotel room. And even though that was what I wanted at first, I almost couldn't picture being there without Dominik after what happened between us.

Despite how much I had urged my body to sleep, my brain couldn't stop replaying the night before. It was so heated, so passionate, and yet I couldn't act on any of it without there being serious repercussions.

It was getting increasingly difficult to spend each day with him acting like my feelings weren't growing. And being alone together seemed to be making it even worse.

I couldn't be left alone with him again all day. To prevent myself from doing anything rash, I decided to find something to do on my own for a while.

Harlow was conveniently in the same hall and had some-how gotten an entire room to herself. I thought we could go down to the pool and hang out for a while without Dominik shitting a brick.

I'd have to run it by him though when he got back so he wouldn't get all upset if he found me not in the hotel room.

Until then, I flipped on the TV and went through the pro-grammed channels until I found some ridiculous trashy reality show I could play in the background while I got ready for the day.

I stretched my body out and eventually pulled myself out of bed to wash my face and brush my teeth. I then picked out a bright pink swimsuit from my luggage and a skimpy crocheted cover up dress to go over it. I was almost done changing when a light knock was at the door.

"Yes?" I yelled out.

"It's me," Dominik's deep voice sounded.

I went over to the door and opened it up to Dominik car-rying two cups of hot coffee.

"I uh, went downstairs and grabbed these while you were still sleeping. It's a vanilla latte, just the way you like."

Speechless, I grabbed the warm cup of coffee from his hand. I couldn't believe he knew my coffee order, let alone that he'd picked it up for me unasked.

"Oh, wow. Thanks… how'd you sleep?" I asked kindly, try-ing not to freak out as I took the cup from him.

Our fingers brushed and I ignored the surge of electricity that flooded my body.

"Pretty good, actually. It was pretty nice to sleep in a real bed."

I took a sip of the coffee, and it *was* just the way I liked.

"Definitely agree with you there. I have no idea how I'm going to be able to sleep back on tour after being treated to this," I laughed.

"Well, at least it's almost at an end. Then you'll be free to go home."

Home.

The Calabasas ultra-modern mansion Lyle had purchased before the tour started wasn't home to me. We'd only been there for two months before we left for the tour. I didn't even have time to move things in fully. But where else was there for me to go? Back to Tennessee with my trainwreck of a mother? Definitely not.

"Right…" I sighed, trying not to make it a big deal. "Won't you be going home too then?"

Dominik visibly winced and sat down on the bed.

"Look Aspen, I know you haven't been the fondest of the idea, but it seems like the label is interested in extending Koen and I's contracts."

"What?"

"Elissa let us know about a week ago. It's up to us now if we want to go through with it but it seems like Koen wants to. It's good money, and he tolerates Lyle pretty well."

"Okay, but what about you? What do you want to do?"

He scratched his head awkwardly and had trouble maintaining eye contact.

"I don't know. It would be a really different gig than we're used to, and we'd be signing on for a year. Essentially, we'd be with you everywhere you went. It would be a lot to handle, Aspen."

I had barely been able to handle them on the tour as it was, how the hell was I supposed to handle them going with me everywhere back home? To the grocery store, to the pharmacy? And I'd be saddled with them for an entire *year*? Where would this end!

"Yes, it would be," I said quietly. "I don't want to sway your decision, so I'll just say that I'll support whatever you want to do. I understand this is your livelihood and I don't want to get in the way of that."

"There'll be other contracts I'm sure—"

"No, it's okay. I want you to make the decision yourself. I know I'm not the easiest to deal with and everything so if you turned it down, I would understand that."

"But then I wouldn't be able to see you anymore." He grabbed my hand and threaded his large fingers between mine. I melted at his touch, unable to hide how much I enjoyed his vulnerability.

"I know, and I can't say I'd like that very much. But you would be free from the contract at least. You could find a client you like better."

"And what about your freedom? You don't want to be followed everywhere. I know you, Aspen."

"Well, I don't exactly have many choices. I do what I have to do."

Dominik's face fell and I didn't want to go into further detail about how much I was used to doing what I had to in order to survive growing up. When my father was still alive, things weren't all that bad. I tried to hold onto those memories.

"I've always loved music you know," I said on a lighter note. "Before my dad died, we had an old record player that he always played Pink Floyd records on," I laughed lightly, recalling the memory. "It doesn't shock me sometimes that I ended up here. Sure, Lyle's music is… perhaps a bit more pop than what I'm used to but it's still good I guess."

"You guess?"

"The world likes it well enough. It's all created by the label anyway; Lyle just performs it. They already want him to produce a new album once the tour ends."

"Interesting."

There was a beat of silence, and I awkwardly tried to fill it.

"So, I'm going to see if Harlow wants to go to the pool with me for a little bit. I'll be right downstairs, and you can look out the window to make sure I haven't disappeared. Don't go down there with me please."

"Where's the fun in that? Why don't you just let me hang out with you guys?"

I contemplated it, thinking about him all sad and alone in the hotel room. Then I started to feel guilty.

"Alright, fine. But you stay at least twenty feet away from me. I don't want people assuming anything, okay?"

"Yes, your highness. Although anyone with eyes could figure it out," he taunted.

"Considering that anyone here could be the one spilling the secrets to the label, it's for the best if no one finds out about… this. Yes?"

He rolled his eyes at me, and I tried to hide the smile on my face as I finished getting ready.

I texted Harlow to ask if she was interested and she was absolutely down for it. We'd tried to see if the other bodyguards were interested but it looked like they were more inclined to continue relaxing in their hotel rooms.

So, the trio of us went down to the pool area and found some empty lounge chairs to set our bags and phones down.

"Twenty feet, Dominik," I reminded him in a hushed whisper as he sat down in one of the chairs.

"Yeah, I got it."

Of course, he did.

I pulled off my cover up, ignoring the way Dominik's eyes roamed my body, and chucked off my flip flops. Harlow sprayed my back and chest with sunscreen we bought in the lobby to make sure my fair skin didn't burn.

I adjusted the straps to my bikini top to make sure my boobs weren't hanging out and felt a sharp kick to my shin.

"Ow! What the hell?"

Dominik yanked me down to his level and whispered in my ear.

"It's hard enough watching you like this. Don't make it any harder."

Just to spite him, I purposefully let the top strings of my bikini go and *almost* let the strings slip before pulling them back up and retying the top around my neck. Having nearly flashed everyone at the pool, Dominik was left fuming.

Excellent.

"Okay, let's get in!" I told Harlow excitedly, completely ignoring the absolute tease I just was in front of Dominik.

We went down the pool ladder and the water temperature was spot on. I melted into the crystal-clear water and could've happily stayed there all day.

"This is so nice! It's practically like bath water," Harlow commented as she floated on her back. Her bikini showcased her many tattoos, and I loved getting to see them all out on display. She had some really fun designs and a huge tiger piece on her back that I hadn't seen yet.

I waded in the water, submerged up to my neck as I enjoyed the nice summer breeze.

"Hi ladies, how're you doing?" A bald middle-aged man approached us.

"Fine, thanks," I said with a weak smile.

"Where are you guys from? Anywhere around here?"

Fuck. He was going to keep asking questions.

"No, just visiting," I replied politely. I was trying to keep my answers short without setting off any alarms.

"Oh really? Well, you girls should have a night out on the town. I could show you all the best spots," he suggested flirtily.

I nervously turned around to look for Dominik and found him already watching the interaction intently, waiting to see if he needed to jump in.

"We won't be here for long unfortunately but thank you for the offer!" I said a bit more confidently as I tried to move on.

The older man was getting agitated at my answers, and I was growing more uncomfortable as he followed me around the pool.

"Oh, come on, I'm sure you could spend one night out," the man pleaded once more, moving closer to me.

I tried to give Dominik a pleading glance, but he was already coming over before I even had the chance to.

He ripped his shirt off and didn't even bother climbing down the pool ladder, jumping straight in instead.

The splash made the man turn around and eye Dominik up and down.

"Something going on?" Dominik asked, wiping the water out of his face.

Dominik had moved in front of me, covering me with his much larger body.

The man, now seeing there was someone else in the picture, held his hands up in a surrender motion and got out of the pool.

"That's what I thought. Fucking asshole," Dominik muttered under his breath.

I tried not to ogle at his insanely toned upper body as he turned around toward me.

"Thanks for that. People are weird," I said as I tried to laugh it off.

"You need to be more observant. He'd been fucking watching you since you tried to take your top off."

Okay Aspen, maybe not the smartest thing to do in a public place.

"Well, that's unfortunate. Guess it's a good thing you were here, just like you wanted."

"You're driving me insane, Aspen. Absolutely fucking insane," he gritted out.

"Hey Dom! I missed you coming in. Wanna swim with us?"

Harlow asked, completely oblivious to what was going on between us.

She'd drifted away during the incident with the older man, which had left me to deal with it alone. Of course, she came back just to find us in a more precarious position.

"No, he's not swimming with us. He was just helping me with a situation," I said glaring at him. I did not need any more incidents between us that would give people the wrong idea.

"Ah, Aspen, give the guy a break! He deserves a day off work too."

"Trust me, there are no days off with Aspen," he retorted.

"Well, I think we should give you the night off for Aspen's birthday this week. She'll get to let loose and have fun, and I'll be there to watch her. You can relax and take a break!" Harlow suggested.

"Your birthday is *this week*, Aspen?" he asked me genuinely.

"Yes. It's on Thursday."

"And you didn't say anything to me because…?"

"I don't know, it's not a big deal to me."

"Can you believe her? Aspen, you are too modest. It's your 21st birthday! That's like the one birthday that is supposed to be a big deal," Harlow joked.

I just shrugged my shoulders.

"I don't think that's a good idea, Harlow. If you guys are drinking, I should definitely be there," Dominik insisted, crossing his arms across his chest.

"Oh, of course we're going to drink! I know the label has their rules but technically we're on a break right now. This is your rite of passage, Pen!"

I groaned at the whole idea of it. "I hate drinking, Harlow. I don't think it'll be very fun."

"Oh, come on, girl! It'll be so much fun! We can go out together and get drunk as hell and just have a blast!"

"Harlow again, it really is best if I'm there," Dominik demanded.

"Dominik, it's only one night. I think I'll be okay. I don't need to be treated like a child at my own 21st birthday," I butted in, annoyed at his insistence on coming with us just to bodyguard.

Dominik shifted his jaw and scoffed at my response, unsurprised. He didn't say anything though, and angrily got out of the pool.

"Wow, what's his problem? The other guys won't say anything about him having a break for the night. He must really take his job seriously."

I rubbed my hands over my temples and tried not to say anything insulting about how ignorant she was being. She either couldn't read our body language at all or was choosing to be blind to it.

"Something like that. Why don't you look around online and see if there's any bars or clubs nearby? I won't agree to a whole big celebration, but a few hours will suffice," I suggested to her.

"Yay! It's going to be so much fun, especially with a baby drinker! I'll make sure I get you the best stuff."

As Harlow continued blabbing about her favorite drinks and the best way to order them, I couldn't help but tune her out and think about Dominik.

I hated the way he stormed off, and hated even worse that I was so worried about him that I couldn't focus on anything else.

"So, Aspen? What do you think?"

I didn't know what she had last said, but it didn't matter. All that mattered to me was going and finding Dominik.

"Yeah, that sounds great. Just text me the details and we can get ready together."

"Perfect! Can't wait," she said excitedly.

Chapter Fourteen

ASPEN

BOUNDING UP THE STAIRS TO THE HOTEL ROOM TO avoid the wait for the elevator, I was anxiously trying to get back so I could talk to Dominik.

Sliding my room card in, I found Dominik sitting on the bed with his head in his hands.

"Hey."

He lifted his head up and scoffed at me being there. "Don't you have somewhere else you need to be?"

"No. I wanted to see if everything was okay."

"Okay? Aspen, you just acted like me being there at your birthday was the worst thing you'd ever heard. I'm not exactly interested in seeing you right now."

"That wasn't what I meant when I said that. I was annoyed because it seemed to me that you only wanted to come so you could protect me. I have to have some line drawn in the sand here. There is a separation for me between you doing your job, and you outside of your job," I argued to him.

He glared at me from across the room still, and I crouched down to where he was sitting on the bed.

"Look, I don't want 'Dominik the bodyguard' on my birthday, but that doesn't mean I don't want *you* there. I just want to be treated like any other person you know." I laid my hand over top of his, and he shook me off.

"That isn't something I can just separate, Aspen. They're both me, and we're in this situation regardless. You're not just any other person to me."

And cue the butterflies in my stomach.

"You're not to me either. I just want you to see me as someone else for once, with nothing related to the contract. Please, this is all so complicated."

"It's not really. It just seems to me that you don't know what you want. I can't change who I am on and off the clock just to please you!"

"Dominik, no it's not like that!"

"I think it is. You need to figure out what the hell you want, Aspen. I'm not just going to sit here forever and wait for you to make up your mind based on if I'm your bodyguard for the day or not," he said loud and clear. "I have shown you exactly what I want. Now you need to decide."

Dominik got up abruptly, and stormed past me, slamming the hotel door shut behind him. I didn't even have time to register the argument we just had, and then he was gone.

It felt like the world was crumbling around me. I couldn't hold my emotions back anymore and let myself succumb to it all as I crawled into bed and bawled.

I felt like a truly horrible person, and I had never felt that way before. But it was hard to deny the facts. I did wish the contract didn't exist and we'd met outside of this as two normal people. Because the truth was that I was pursuing something with Dominik, while still attached to Lyle and yet struggled to find remorse in it.

Who does that?

The question Dominik asked was an important one, but one that I had yet to figure out in the slightest. I didn't know what I wanted, or who I wanted, or who I even was. I didn't ask to be an extension of the pop star life or to meet Dominik while I was with Lyle.

My world was hardly my own and I didn't know how to get out of this hole I had dug.

But Dominik was right, I couldn't just leave him without an answer and make him wait around for someone he'd never have. That would be entirely unfair of me, and I did recognize that.

And yet, I didn't want to lose him either. Selfishly, I wanted him to stay there with me and I knew that I was really far gone to be wishing such a thing because I was never known for being a selfish person. But I still wanted him all to myself.

Crying while tucked in the safeness of my bed was the only way I could cope. I hadn't been able to cry at all while on the bus, surrounded by people I didn't know all that well and didn't want to embarrass myself in front of.

The emotional release was needed more than anything.

Day turned to night and before I knew it, I had spent hours cooped up in the hotel room. I felt a numbness that I hadn't felt in a very long time, and I'd be lying if I said it didn't scare me. It was all too reminiscent of the days of my youth when I longed for anyone to care and appreciate me.

I felt utterly alone, and that was never a good thing.

The worst decisions I made when I was younger were fueled by my feelings of loneliness and not having anyone to tell me right from wrong. It sent me down a path that almost left me even emptier than I was before.

I couldn't let myself go down that road again.

If I had to make a decision to get myself out of this mess, then that's what I would do.

Rolling over to grab my phone off the nightstand, I dialed Lyle's number and hoped it wouldn't go to voicemail.

"Pen?"

"Hey, Lyle. I just wanted to check in on things and see what's going on," I said clumsily.

"It's good to hear your voice. Things are going great. I was in the studio all day working on the single and I think it's going to be a huge hit."

I could tell how excited he was through the phone.

"Wow, that's great news! I'm so glad it's going well. How has it been being back at home?"

"You know…different without you here. This house is just too big for only one person. Trust me, I'll be glad when we're off the road and back home again."

"So will I. This hotel they shacked us up in for the week is nice, don't get me wrong, but it's just like we're in limbo waiting to get back on the bus again."

"I'm sorry, I wish I had more control over that kind of stuff. We're so close to the end though, Pen. I know it hasn't been what we were expecting but it's been such a huge help in my music journey. I've finally made it."

It pained me to hear how happy he was when I felt the complete opposite.

"Of course, I know. And honestly, at the end of the day, I'm happy if it's helped that much," I said with the most amount of sincerity I could muster. "I have a question for you though."

"Sure, go ahead."

I twirled the comforter of the hotel bed around my fingers, almost too nervous to ask. "So, my birthday is in two days which I'm sure you know, but I just wanted to see if there was any possibility that you could come back early to help celebrate?"

The line went silent for a second, and I thought I might have lost the connection.

"I don't know, Aspen. The team was really hoping to use me for every last second before I left. I don't think I can swing that."

I swallowed my disappointment the best I could and tried to be understanding.

"No worries. Poor timing and all but I know that wasn't your fault. We can celebrate when you get back."

"Totally, and I'll still call you of course to tell you happy birthday. I've got to go but I'll talk to you again soon, okay?"

"Yeah, no problem. I'll see you soon," I said, falsely cheerful. "See you."

I wanted to slam my phone on the ground but resisted knowing that I couldn't afford another.

If I was worried about us pulling apart before, the phone call proved that we were worse off than I thought. His career had taken precedence once again, and I was on the back burner. I knew what I had asked was far-fetched, but the old Lyle would've made it happen.

It seemed like it really would just be Harlow and I for my birthday. It wasn't her fault, but I didn't think I'd be all that peppy or fun to be with considering how shitty I felt.

With that phone call being an absolute bust, I started to let my mind wander to where Dominik had gone.

I had assumed he was just with the other bodyguards blowing off some steam, but I couldn't be so certain. He was unpredictable at times, and I didn't know the lengths he would go to get away from me.

All I knew was that I did not want him with another girl.

If he was with the boys, then I could sleep peacefully and accept that he just wanted some time apart. But I needed to confirm it. Selfish or not, I didn't care.

I texted Harlow quickly, asking if she knew the room number of where the other bodyguards were.

They were in the same hall, making it all too convenient for Dominik to have been down there.

Changing into some other clothes that didn't make me look

so unkept, I grabbed my phone and room card and went to find their hotel room.

It didn't take me long until I reached the end of the hall and found the room that matched the number Harlow gave me.

Hesitantly bringing my fist up to the door, I thought about what I could be walking into. Did I truly want to see him if he was in some kind of precarious position with someone else?

But I just wanted to know for sure. I couldn't take the what ifs anymore.

I knocked on the door and waited for someone to answer.

Carson, mostly just referred to by his last name, answered the door.

"Hey, Aspen! What's up?" he asked nicely.

"Nothing really. I was just wondering if Dominik happened to be here?"

"Yep, he sure is. Come on in."

I walked into the room and found Dominik sitting in a chair talking to one of the other bodyguards.

He didn't look pleased to see me.

Thankfully though it was just the guys hanging out in the room I realized after doing a quick scan, so I instantly felt better.

"What're you doing here Aspen?"

Dominik sounded defeated and I didn't blame him.

"Just trying to see if you're staying here for the night. Didn't want to lock up if you're coming back."

Excuse.

One thing about Dominik was that he was rarely embarrassed in front of other people. I didn't doubt he would answer me as candidly as he would any other time when not surrounded by his friends.

"I'll be back later," he said sternly.

No other explanation, no other words. Just that.

"No problem. Hope you guys have a good night," I said with

a small smile. The other guys waved to me as I awkwardly turned around and headed out the door.

But I had a feeling his friends would be asking questions.

I pressed my ear up against the door once it shut behind me and heard muffled voices going back and forth.

"What's going on dude?"

"You sure you know what you're doing?"

"You've got to be careful, man."

All I wanted was to hear Dominik's voice reassuring them that he knew what he was doing, and that he was sure of this.

"I don't know."

The voice was clearly Dominik's and while I couldn't blame him for his lack of faith in me, it hurt to hear. Whatever I was feeling only continued to grow stronger and it was hard to accept that he was unsure of things. But with Lyle still around, I had my own skeletons to handle. And until I truly dealt with that, I knew it wasn't right for me to expect so much out of Dominik.

How could I expect him to be so sure of this when I wasn't myself?

Confronting my own feelings happened to be something I was not very good at. I had mastered the art of concealing my true opinions and beliefs in order to please others, so much so that I suppressed virtually everything. I was so used to shoving it all down, I feared what would happen if I continued to do so given how intense my feelings were growing.

It was becoming clear to me that I needed to talk to Lyle when he came back from L.A. We needed to sit down and have a serious conversation about what was happening to us and if we could survive this.

It was a last resort, and I felt sick to my stomach even thinking about it. But I couldn't continue what I was doing.

I sulked back to my room, tempted to just stay awake until

Dominik eventually came back but there was no telling how long he'd actually be gone for.

I went through the motions of getting ready for the night and made my way into bed just shy of midnight. The deflated wall of pillows glared at me, and I decided to just leave them.

Turning out the light, I hoped to wake up with a clearer mind on what to do.

But all I really wanted was Dominik.

Chapter Fifteen

ASPEN

I SLEPT SOUNDLY ALL NIGHT, UNAWARE OF DOMINIK'S return in the middle of the night.

I assumed he was purposefully quiet so he wouldn't wake me, but I wished he had to some degree.

It was clear that there were things left unsaid. A certain decision he was hoping to get from me, whenever that might be.

I however had nothing of the sort figured out by the next morning. I was still a mess, exhausted by the sheer number of thoughts whizzing through my brain. When I woke, Dominik was asleep beside me.

He'd slept as though he couldn't get far enough away from me however, practically about to fall off the edge of the bed.

That didn't feel so great.

I hauled myself to the bathroom to shower off and get my day started.

I had to do something to get my spirits up because my birthday celebration was the following day. And while I could have just moped around the hotel again, I figured that wouldn't help my case very much.

I texted Harlow instead and recruited her to go explore the city with me.

We were in some small town up north, and I didn't know

anything about the area but figured there had to be something to do to pass the time.

After quietly getting ready while Dominik still slept, Harlow knocked on the door to come get me.

"Hey! Ready to go?"

"Yep, just about. Come on in," I whispered, holding the door open.

Dominik shifted in his sleep with the commotion but didn't appear to be awake otherwise.

"So did you find any cool places around here?" I asked her while applying a few more touches to my makeup. We'd considered inviting Elissa to see if she wanted to relax for a bit, but she was likely still swamped with work. She never really got a day off while on tour.

"Sure did! There's a coffee spot a few blocks from the hotel and a great brunch place a little further away. Does that sound good?"

"Sounds great! We can walk to the coffee shop and maybe take an Uber to the restaurant after?"

"No."

I whipped my head around to Dominik who, in a half-asleep state, refuted my suggestion of our plans.

"And why is that?" I asked as he rolled over in bed.

"Two girls out alone. Bad idea," he mumbled almost incoherently.

He wasn't really in a state to be making demands. And there was no way in hell I was going to walk that far. I wanted to take an Uber damn it!

"Sorry, but you don't have a choice in it. I'll be back later, okay?"

I figured he'd say something else about me going somewhere without him like he usually did.

"I don't like this."

"I understand, but it's time for us to go. See you later," I said, cutting him off.

Harlow of course didn't intervene but watched our argument play out per usual.

We headed out the door and started to make our way downstairs, when footsteps echoed behind us.

I didn't need to turn around to know who it was.

Of course, Dominik had to come. How hopeful of me to assume he might just get off my ass for one day.

"Don't try and pull that shit again." He maintained a composed tone, but I could sense the bitterness in his voice as he pulled a clean t-shirt on.

I was back to wanting to rip my hair again, slowly suffocating under the incessant need for control.

Knowing that there was no way I could just send him back to the hotel room, I ignored him and kept walking to the lobby.

I stopped at the hotel concierge desk to make sure we knew where we were going and then we continued out to the street.

The little town did have a lot of charm to it, with old brick buildings that reminded me of where I grew up. It was so quaint, most people just living their daily lives as they walked to work or the stores nearby.

It did strike a bit of jealousy in me that they got to live every day like that. So calm and peaceful, never any chaos.

I felt just like a regular girl again, noticing the small things for once like the carefully maintained tree-lined streets or the slight breeze in the air that twirled my scarlet locks. I hadn't felt like that since before Lyle signed his contract.

Eventually we reached the coffee shop, and I got my same latte as usual, with Dominik getting a nasty black coffee that I made a face at. But we kept moving right along, Dominik only offering his helpful commentary when need be.

His eyes roamed everywhere while we walked though, his

head almost pivoting like an owl to try and catch everyone's movements. He was wildly more observant than I ever was, and picked up on any slight action that could appear to be a little off.

He was a lot of things, but I could never say he was bad at his job.

Dominik sat at a separate table during lunch, indicating to me that he was still upset after the argument we had previously. While he was technically on the clock, he'd eaten with us before with no problem. I had hoped he would still feel comfortable enough to eat with me without having to lose sight of his duty.

But it appeared that wasn't what he wanted.

It was hard for me to focus on the conversation with Harlow when I could feel Dominik's stare penetrating through me from across the room. I had to force myself to pay attention when I noticed the conversation only being one-sided.

My attempt to try and lift my spirits before the big day did not work.

I was somehow left feeling even more empty than before. Dominik was there yet acted like I meant nothing to him.

Lyle was halfway across the country, not a bit concerned with me or what I was doing.

And at times, although I adored her, Harlow felt like a friend by circumstance and not by choice.

These thoughts clouded my mind all throughout lunch and after we left too. We wandered the streets for a little while, considering that we weren't allowed to Uber, taking in the atmosphere and all there was to see.

We conveniently happened to pass by a nightclub with a big, flashing neon sign that said 'BAR' to light the way.

"No way! Look at this, Pen!" Harlow squealed.

"Looks like a dingy nightclub to me?"

"No silly! This will be perfect to celebrate your birthday tomorrow! It's got a full bar, dancing, music, the whole works!"

I cringed internally at just the thought.

"I don't know, Harlow, it looks a little sketchy."

"I agree," Dominik said sternly behind me. His tone was detached, yet I could feel the ice in his words.

"Please, Dominik! Just let us have fun for the night. We'll be home by two and everything, sir," Harlow joked, barely suppressing her laughter.

"I really appreciate it Harlow but maybe we can do something else for my birthday?"

"Please guys, it'll be so fun! I haven't drank in ages, and this is our only free pass!" she whined.

"Harlow," Dominik said sternly. "No. Neither of you belong in a place like this. I will not allow you to go."

I glared at him and his overbearing need for control over me. I didn't enjoy the use of the word 'allow.'

"Dominik, please! Just let us have a girl's night!" Harlow pleaded with pretend puppy dog eyes.

"Really Dominik? It's just for the night. We're not even that far from the hotel."

"Aspen, no is no. You will not be spending your birthday in a trashy bar with men waiting to get their hands on you when you're finally drunk enough." He spoke calmly, but his words were like daggers, piercing through me.

It was like everything was about to reach a fever pitch again.

I was not going to argue with him about what I was doing on my own birthday, despite knowing he was being more realistic than I was. Trashy bar or not, I refused to be treated like a child anymore.

"You know what Dominik? If you hate the idea so much, then you should really just stay at the hotel. I'm smart enough to not just go home with any random man who shows interest, and the fact that you don't see that is mind blowing to me."

He waited for a second, trying to analyze his best plan of

attack. I was on my toes, fully revved up to go at it with him again, and then he simmered down unexpectedly.

"Fine, Aspen. If you want to go at this alone then be my guest. You can rely on Harlow for your protection."

His demeanor was calm on the outside, but laced with a coldness only I could see. He didn't want to fight. He didn't have the strength.

"Sounds like we're good then! Yay! This will be so fun, Aspen! And I promise I won't do anything dangerous or get us into any kind of potentially bad situation."

She started to go on about how I should dress and do my hair for my birthday, but I tuned all of it out. I still didn't even want to go, but now had to out of spite and a need to prove Dominik wrong.

He walked a few paces behind us, completely silent and I yet again was cursing his existence. I was just about at my wits end with him and I didn't know what would happen the next time he pushed me.

Chapter Sixteen

ASPEN

HARLOW HAD DEFINITELY FOUND THE NASTIEST CLUB possible to make the experience authentic. The floors were sticky and covered in who knows what, and there was an undetectable stench that permeated the air. There was a collection of girls standing in the back as we walked in, and a few men seated at the bar, but it was otherwise quite empty.

"Why is there hardly anyone here? It's ten o'clock?" I asked her as we walked up to the bar counter.

"Oh, Pen you have much to learn. Give it a few hours and we will be basically on top of people," she said with a laugh.

She walked up to the bartender with such confidence, I couldn't help but feel even more out of place.

"What will it be ladies?" the stout bartender asked while cleaning some glasses.

"How about we start with a Cape Cod and two Long Island iced teas?" Harlow said flirtily as she leaned across the counter.

"You got it, sweetheart. ID's?"

I proudly took mine out of my wallet as the bartender glanced at me and then back down at the picture on my ID from when my hair was still a natural brown. I could see him squinting at the birthdate and I wondered if I really looked that young.

"Happy birthday," he said gruffly as he took one look at Harlow's and waved her off as being good.

I smiled to myself at finally getting my first legal drink and was now *almost* excited to see the place start to fill up. It had been way too long since I let loose. As Harlow slid her ID into her back pocket, she turned around and very quickly realized the attention she was getting from other patrons.

She was hard to ignore, with her bright hair, and sleeves of colored tattoos that mirrored her natural vibrancy. I understood the allure of someone like her, and being in a small town, I was sure she was not the kind of girl you could find just anywhere.

I'd be lying though if I said it didn't make me feel inferior.

The bartender delivered the drinks and Harlow took a sip of her iced tea before moaning at how good it was. "That is incredible! Go on, take a sip Aspen."

"Okay," I chuckled warily as I took a very tiny sip of the drink.

I coughed on instinct, trying my best not to spit it out. It was extremely strong. I could hardly taste anything else in it but pure alcohol.

"Pen!" she laughed as I nearly coughed a lung out. "Come on, you can do it. It's really not that bad, you just have to keep drinking!"

"I don't know if I can drink this, Harlow. It's really strong," I admitted while pushing the glass away from me when I finally stopped coughing.

"Okay, why don't we do a shot first then? It'll loosen you up some!"

I instinctively scrunched my face up at the idea and shook my head no.

"Look, I'll show you a trick I used to use when I was in college, okay?"

Hesitantly, I agreed, and she ordered us two lemon drops.

"Okay ready to try?"

I contemplated it again and had to think about how willing

I actually was to drink the pale-yellow colored liquid in front of me. But I really did want to have a memorable 21st birthday, despite how much I was dreading drinking.

"Alright, fine. Show me."

"Okay, I want you to pinch your nose and gulp down as much as possible in one go. Most new drinkers try to take more than one sip, but you should *not* do that," she said in a way that lingered on sounding demeaning. "You need to do it fast or else you'll feel some burning and might want to puke. You wanna try?"

I somehow just knew I was going to regret this.

"As long as you don't laugh when I vomit all over you, I'll try I guess."

'You'll be fine!" she said, grabbing her own shot glass. "On your mark, get set…go!"

She took hers in one seamless gulp, so I pinched my nose with my fingers and tried to just take one big gulp like her.

It went down like pure acid, and I definitely still felt some burning as I swallowed it one go. The pinched nose did help some, but it was absolutely foul.

I sat the shot glass down and coughed some more but was feeling much more encouraged now to try another.

"That was good! Only took you five seconds. I bet you can handle this now like a champ." She clinked her glass to mine, and I just started guzzling as much of the iced tea drink as humanly possible. My ears popped with the first gulp, but I just kept going.

"Aspen, you can slow down!" she laughed.

Harlow's voice faded off into the background as I tried not to stop with how much my throat was burning. I just wanted to get as much down as possible while I still had the nerve to do it.

As I reached the bottom of the cup, I was on the verge of losing it, but I was finally finished.

I pulled the empty glass away and sputtered out some coughs before reaching for a lemon on the table to get rid of some of the lingering alcohol that made me want to gag all over again. No vomiting though, which counted as a win.

"Oh my god, Aspen, you did it! Ahh, I'm so proud of you!" she squealed, wrapping her arms around me.

I laughed with her and actually felt proud of myself too. It may have seemed rather pathetic, but I finished my first real drink. And I was finally getting the chance to have the college experience I always wanted.

Now it was time to keep going.

"You definitely will be able to make it through tonight if you were able to get all that down so quickly. Cape Cod is next! This one is cranberry and vodka, so I think you'll like it."

I shrugged my shoulders and confidently picked up the glass, taking a long sip.

I couldn't help but still sputter at the first gulp as the liquid scorched my throat. It was at least a little better than the Long Island iced tea. I'd be hard-pressed to ever get that again.

"This one is really not that bad. I think… I'm going to have fun tonight!"

"Woooo!" Harlow yelled as we both started crushing our drinks and ordering more rounds.

If this was just the beginning of the night, I couldn't wait for later.

"Pennn, why don't you go out and dance?" Harlow whined in a drunken stupor over the incredibly loud music.

Sweat glistened down her face and chest as she came back up to the bar where I was still sitting. She was drunk off her ass and had enough drinks that I had stopped counting after a certain point.

I had just about four drinks myself and was going in and

out of being on top of the world and having the most fun I'd ever had, to sitting down and feeling like I was about to go to sleep any minute.

I was feeling like the latter at that moment.

"You know why, Harlow. Lyle isn't here and I don't want anyone getting the wrong i-idea," I groaned with a nasty burp in between.

"Well, I'm going to have fun all by myself then! Your loss, Penny!"

I paused for a second, my drunken brain registering what she just called me.

"*Don't* call me that again Harlow. I'll go if you'll only say my real name," I said only half-joking. I didn't play when it came to that nickname.

"Yay! Come on, Aspen!"

She excitedly grabbed my hand and pulled me into the sweaty tangle of men and scantily dressed women who were far better looking than myself. I put the thought out of mind and started casually swaying with her to the upbeat music. It seemed to be all Harlow could manage after spending so much energy dancing around before that.

The song switched and ironically, one of Lyle's more popular songs came on. Great.

"No way! What are the odds!" Harlow gasped as she began pulling out some very unique dance moves.

I could tell she was just feeling the beat and going for it, and I honestly admired her. I was too shy, even with so many drinks in me, to dance so freely in front of other people.

I did secretly try to gauge people's reaction to the song however as I looked around at the dance floor. Some people started to leave once it came on, which I found quite interesting. It made me question how much of his core audience was made up of young girls if adults were so disinterested in it. It was supposed to be one of the most popular ones.

"Pen, you've got to loosen up some more! How about we get you one more drink? Then we can close out the tab and put it all on the business credit card!"

While one more drink sounded tempting, I didn't want to overdo it for the night. Lyle still hadn't called to wish me a happy birthday and I didn't want to be a hot mess talking to him. It was clear as day that I was going to be hungover enough the next morning as it was. And while I wanted to have a good time, I didn't want it at the expense of becoming a sloppy drunk.

Like my mother was.

"You know what, I'm going to get it for you anyway! Just stay here, I'll be back in a sec!" she shouted as a new song came on.

People flocked back to the dance floor as the song had a much slower and sexier R&B vibe to it. The new song was much more my speed, and I felt my worries slowly slip away as I began moving to each beat.

Lost in my own world, I started dancing more and just feeling the rhythm of the song. I didn't even notice how many people were crowding around me.

"Ugh, everyone is so rude! Sorry it took me forever to get back over here. Drink this!" Harlow complained after squeezing through people. She then shoved an unknown fruity-looking drink at me as she took long swigs of her own.

The cocktail was red in color and looked kind of unappetizing, but I had already drank so much that I figured I might as well finish out my birthday strong.

Remembering what Harlow had told me earlier, I tried to drink it as quickly as possible to avoid so much burning. Whatever was in that one though was instantly vomit inducing and I had to hold back a gag as I finished it.

"Jesus, Harlow what was that?" I yelled at her.

"Oh uh, good question. Maybe something with vodka? I don't know, the bartender just recommended it. Now come on, let's dance!"

She grabbed my hands and started jumping all around as she moved in time with the music and forced me to move with her.

I felt like I was flailing around like a fish and getting in everyone's way around me as they all practically humped each other.

After a little while though, that last drink started to kick in and I had an entirely new wave of energy. Harlow miraculously never stopped dancing and seemed to have gotten an energy kick as well from her last drink.

"This has been the best night ever! I love you so much, Pen!" Harlow smiled as she wrapped me in a very sweaty, but sweet hug.

I eventually forgot there was anyone else there but me as I finally let go and just let myself be free. Dancing how I wanted, singing to the songs, not caring how I looked.

I couldn't remember the last time I'd felt like that, if I'd *ever* felt like that.

As time stretched on, I didn't question anymore why Lyle hadn't called me or what he was possibly doing. All I knew was that as drunk as I was, I was so happy, and that feeling was one I wanted to last forever.

"This has been a really great birthday, Harlow. I can't tell you how much I appreciate it. I could stay here all night!" I happily yelled to her over the music.

"You sure about that?"

I jumped back, startled half to death to see Dominik in a white button-down, the top buttons half undone, and his signature smirk plastered on his face.

"What are you doing here? I asked for one night without you on my ass, just one night! God, can't I ever get a break?"

I immediately turned on my heel and tried to get the hell

away from him, when he grabbed my wrist and swung me back to face him.

"Relax, Aspen. I wanted to tell you happy birthday."

His face was inches from mine, and it was then I realized how strikingly blue his eyes were. They were like the color of the sea, layered with hues of cerulean. My heart rate spiked with him so close, his stare held on me and me alone.

I was too drunk for the kind of emotions I was feeling.

I twisted my wrist out of his grip and stomped off anyways, making my way out of the crowd.

"Wait, Pen! Come back!" Harlow called after me as I headed out of the club.

I repeatedly told myself that I just needed some fresh air and some of the alcohol to wear off because whatever the hell I had felt so intensely could *only* be explained by my drunkenness.

I needed my clarity to come back immediately.

The breeze was comforting, and the world seemed to move just a bit slower outside. The streetlights illuminated the sidewalk enough that I could thankfully see my feet in front of me as I stumbled along the entrance of the club and tried to sober up.

The door squeaked open, and Dominik appeared.

"Aspen, can we just talk for a minute?"

I crossed my arms and only gave him a side glance as I continued to walk around aimlessly, hoping at some point my mind would return to a clear state.

"Please, Aspen. I know you didn't want to see me tonight and that I'm directly going against what you asked but I had to make sure you're okay."

I glared at him and still refused to respond. He knew I didn't want him there and yet he came anyway. I turned my back to him and walked faster to get away from him.

"Aspen, fucking respond to me. Stop doing this silent game," he demanded, stopping me in my tracks.

"I don't want to! You ruined my night, and I was having fun. I was the person I've always wanted to be. I just wanted to enjoy it while it lasted," I cried.

I sat down on the curb of the sidewalk and wiped away the stray tears attempting to escape. I was drunk crying, for Christ's sake.

"I know, Aspen. I saw you. Was mesmerized by you more like," he tried to joke although all it did was make my stomach flip flop.

"It did look like you were having fun for once," he said more gently as he sat down next to me. "You seemed so free."

"I don't look like I have fun normally?" I asked sadly, my brain choosing to skip over the mesmerizing part for a half second.

"No, Aspen. You don't," he replied honestly. "Although I can't really blame you. It hasn't been the easiest situation and I know you're doing your best. Plus, whatever you have going on with Lyle isn't helping, I'm sure."

"You know about that too?" I said shamefully as the tears continuously fell.

"Yes. It slipped out from someone that he hasn't been the most concerned with calling you while he's been gone. Which I'm sorry for," he apologized genuinely. "It's my job to keep secrets though so don't worry about it. And I'm sorry I ruined your night too. That's not what I meant to do."

His tone was so gentle, and calm. There wasn't even any condescension in the way he spoke.

I sniffled and looked up at him as he had a softness in his eyes I'd never seen before. Like I was the only thing that mattered to him at that moment.

Snap out of it!

"That's okay. I'll be suffering enough tomorrow as it is. Harlow gave me about five drinks and some shots so I think the hangover will be pretty bad," I said, turning away from him so I could ignore whatever drunken urges were emerging.

"Five?" he shouted. "You had five drinks tonight Aspen? And shots?"

"At least I think so. I have no idea, they were all really strong. I just drank whatever Harlow gave me," I mumbled through a yawn.

"That Harlow, I swear," he mumbled. "I could kill her for this. Fuck, Aspen, you're going to be really sick. Come on, let's get going then. You need to lay down," he said, offering his hand to help me up.

I put my palm in his and melted at his touch. His hand was soft and warm, and I felt a shot of electricity go up my spine as he helped me up.

"I like your hands," I giggled.

He glanced at me funny as I stood up with him. "What?"

I nearly tumbled over after standing back up again but he was quick to catch me from falling.

"Whoa, I feel dizzy," I said, rubbing my temple with my free hand.

"Aspen?"

It was cut off by me leaning over the curb and hurling my guts up in the most unpleasant, unladylike manner I ever thought possible.

Dominik was quick however, and pulled my hair out of my face before it could get caught in anything as I emptied my stomach out completely.

"Wow, I feel better," I sighed after finishing.

"God, Aspen, did you drink on an empty stomach?"

"Um… yes? I mean I ate lunch but that was a very long time ago. Actually, I'm hungry," I laughed.

Dominik clenched and unclenched his fists as he tried to restrain his anger in front of me.

"Listen, I'm going to go find Harlow inside and get you some napkins to wipe off with. You stay right here and do not move, okay?"

I nodded at whatever nonsense he said but heard maybe a third of it.

Feeling much refreshed with all of that out of my system, I wiped my mouth off with the back of my hand and onto my jeans. I started swinging around the streetlamps and singing to one of Lyle's songs that had been stuck in my head.

"Hey sweet face! Come on over here!" a man yelled from across the street.

The man's figure was hidden by shadows and with only his silhouette shown, he looked rather ominous.

"Come into the light," I yelled back to him.

He obeyed, and willingly stepped closer to the streetlamp that illuminated him completely.

"You like what you see, princess? Why don't you come on over and we can have some fun!"

I may have been drunk, but never drunk enough to be that stupid.

"No thanks, I think I'm going to stay over here," I said politely declining him.

"Ah, that's no fun. I won't hurt you baby, come on," he insisted, walking over to where I stood.

I started backing up, slowly trying to get closer to the door of the club where I could duck in quickly.

"Now, little girl, where you going?" he spat angrily as he started walking over at full force.

I screamed a very high pitched, horror movie level scream as I started running back inside and toward the bar counter.

I ran straight into Dominik.

"Aspen? Look at me, are you okay? What's going on?" he asked concerned as he held my shoulders.

"The man outside, he tried to get me to come with him, he was going to come grab me!" I sobbed as I held onto Dominik as tightly as I could.

"You're okay, Aspen, you're with me," he said consoling me. "Look, stay here, I'm going to go check things out."

His hand reached into his waistband to pull out his gun, and I couldn't bare the thought of him going out there alone.

"No, please! *Please* don't leave me!" I begged him, clutching onto his shirt.

He looked at the door and then at me and there was no questioning the pure fear in my eyes.

"I won't, Aspen. It's okay," he said calmly as he put his gun back and held me in his arms.

I felt myself slowly start to calm down as I felt completely safe and sound in Dominik's grasp. He let me rest my face in the crook of his neck as my heart rate climbed down from the insane peak it had reached.

"Oh my god, Aspen, are you okay?" Harlow asked after she finally found us.

"Look who's here, Pen," Dominik whispered, using my nickname for the first time, as I lifted my head up to see Harlow. I'd never been so grateful to see her again.

"I'm okay," I wept as I hugged her neck. She looked at Dominik questionably.

"Harlow, please stay here with Aspen while I scope everything out outside. We are leaving right now," he demanded. She quickly nodded her head.

Dominik stepped outside first, keep a hand on his gun just in case. He surveyed the entire area, looking behind walls to make sure we couldn't be ambushed or attacked unexpectedly.

"Okay, I think it's safe. You two stay behind me, and do not do anything that'll draw attention. Stay silent, walk with your eyes ahead, and do not look around at anything."

We both nodded our heads and stayed right behind him as we walked back to the hotel.

Dominik's eyes were circulating the entire time we were walking, not quite convinced we were safe. He still checked multiple times once we got to the hotel to ensure no one was following us and then allowed us to go in.

Before we went back up to our rooms, we stopped at the concierge desk and Dominik discreetly talked to the man working and warned him about the creepy man I'd encountered earlier.

The hotel staff agreed with whatever Dominik had said and Dominik then gave us the go ahead to go up to our rooms.

Holding onto my arm, he guided me into the elevator, and I accidentally stepped on his foot as I swayed slightly, not having my full balance yet. I tried to apologize but I was so sleepy that it came out more like incoherent mumbling.

Once to our floor, Dominik saw Harlow off to her room and then brought me back over to ours.

I sat down in the room's sole fabric chair, still feeling like the world was moving too fast and I was processing everything too slow.

"Aspen, are you sure you're okay? I can go back and try and find him you know if that'll make you feel safer," Dominik offered.

"No, no it's okay. I think I want to sleep. I've drank enough to last me for at least a year," I mumbled through a yawn as I threw my shoes off.

"Aspen, why don't you go get in bed to try and sleep it off? I can sleep on the floor tonight," he offered.

I looped my arms out of my bra straps and pulled it off under my shirt to keep a small shred of my dignity. I thought about taking my jeans off but that seemed like a lot of work.

"No, that's okay. I think I'll sleep right here."

I clumsily tried to curl up in the chair but didn't get very far before Dominik pulled me out of my drunken state.

"We're going to bed now. Come on, lay down," he soothed as I tiredly climbed into the bed.

"Fine but you sleep here too," I mumbled as I patted the bed beside me. "No pillows."

He sighed but gave in for my sake. "Okay, then. I'll be right here all night so if you need me just call my name, okay?"

"Mhm," I yawned again as I pulled the covers over me and all the layers of sheets.

Dominik then pulled a thick blanket over top of me and slid into the remaining bed space, being very careful not to touch me without a wall of pillows to separate us.

"Goodnight. Thanks for saving me," I said sleepily.

"Anytime, Pen. Anytime."

Chapter Seventeen

ASPEN

AN INTENSE WAVE OF NAUSEA STARTLED ME AWAKE from my desperately needed sleep.

I looked at the digital clock on the nightstand: five in the morning.

Rolling over on my side, Dominik was still asleep, but had done little to stay separate from me.

At some point during the night, he had migrated from the edge of the bed, to practically smothering me. His arm was secured tightly around my waist, his head by my shoulder as he was undisturbed by my rustling around.

He was delightfully warm, and a very soft pillow to be curled up against. I almost wanted to just continue laying there and staring at him, enjoying his body so close to mine.

But I was truthfully going to vomit all over the bed if I tried to stay there for one more second.

I carefully untangled our limbs from each other, moving slowly and carefully to not wake him. He looked rather beautiful like this, his eyelids closed and relaxed.

As much as I tried to go back to sleep and ignore the nausea, I couldn't hold it off anymore.

Throwing the blankets off me, I made a run for it to the bathroom, flipping the light switch on.

Just as predicted, I once again puked but there wasn't so

much to throw up that time with practically nothing in my system. Great.

I felt like actual hell, wondering why I didn't just take off my damn jeans with how uncomfortable they were as I sat down on the cold bathroom tile. I had never been hungover before. Everything felt like it was vibrating.

I sat on the ground for a while longer, hoping the intense throbbing of my head would calm down more.

After some time had passed, I felt well enough to stand, pulling myself up by the bathroom sink.

Finally more coherent, I decided to get out of my uncomfortable clothes. I rifled through my suitcase and found a pair of pajama pants and a t-shirt. I turned around to see if Dominik was awake, but he still seemed fast asleep. My head was starting to pound worse though, and all I was focused on was getting changed and going back to sleep again. So, I quietly shimmied out of my jeans and tank top and just slid things on as fast as possible.

I climbed back into bed and slid in close to Dominik. Cautiously moving closer to him until I was by his chest. Willingly snaking my body around his, thoughtfully moving every piece of me to interlock with him, I sighed contently.

He stirred slightly, turning over and pulling my waist closer to him. His hand laid across my torso, and I was situated just perfectly into the curve of his body.

Comfortable once more, I drifted back off to sleep on cloud nine.

Waking up was even more brutal than I'd expected. The nausea had subsided, but I felt like I'd just been hit by a truck.

I sluggishly opened my eyes and shielded them from the bright sunlight coming through the bedroom's sliding doors. I groaned aloud as I covered my face with my hands and tried to make everything dark again.

Every time I opened my eyes, it felt like the world was spinning and intensifying every feeling.

But my head really hurt the worst.

The pain bloomed across my temples and into my skull, a migraine forming more rapidly once awakening. It wasn't a dull pain I could ignore. It was harsh, stabbing, and unrelenting.

"You should look on the nightstand," a voice said just above a whisper.

I moved my hands away from my face and found Dominik standing in the doorway, arms crossed over his chest, nodding to the table beside me.

Looking over to my right, I found a glass of water and some ibuprofen already set out. It was exactly what I needed.

"How long have you been up?" I whispered quietly.

"A while. It's about nine now and we have to get back on the road today, so I started to pack up our stuff early," he said, like it was nothing.

Our?

Sure enough, my suitcase was zipped up and waiting by the door.

"Thank you." I was still in a daze but took the pills off the nightstand. "When do we have to be out?"

"We have about forty-five minutes. Lyle has already flown in so he's taking a private car over here, but he has some virtual interview for a news site he must do first, so it'll be a minute before we actually get on the road."

I had totally forgotten. Lyle had that big interview scheduled for the afternoon and then a show that evening. Which meant a jam-packed schedule courtesy of Elissa.

Kill me.

"Thanks for the reminder. I'll try not to be the one who

slows us down. That's the last thing I need today," I mumbled while taking another sip of water.

"Well, I'm sure you're going to feel like hell the rest of the day. Harlow never should have had you drinking that much last night. That was a lot for a regular drinker, let alone someone who never drinks."

I rolled my eyes at him.

"I'm serious Aspen. And who knows what would have happened if I didn't show up. One of these days you're going to have to get off your high horse and accept me being here."

"Oh, trust me, you're pretty hard to ignore by now. I just would rather not have a stalker all the time."

He cracked a smile at that.

"Well, I'm going to go and take our stuff out to the bus. Terrance pulled into the parking lot already, so time is ticking. Go ahead and get ready and I'll be back."

I rubbed my tired eyes and nodded, craving a little more sleep.

I had forgotten what it felt like to be a normal person until I stayed at the hotel, and it was a very welcome change of pace. It had been a real breath of fresh air, and I was finally able to relax and feel like myself again.

But alas, it was only temporary.

My movements were slow and lethargic as I got ready, like I was stuck in a mental fog. It was a very odd feeling with my body and mind both feeling heavy, as if I were moving through quicksand. It seemed I wasn't getting over my hangover as quickly as I thought.

Just as I finished getting ready, Dominik came back. I went through my normal morning routine and took a quick shower, my actions still feeling mechanical and disconnected, but enough to get me by.

Just about at the time I finished and grabbed my remaining toiletry bag, Dominik came back.

"Hey, are you ready to go?"

"Yeah, I'm good. Just hoping that the bus movements won't make me any sicker. I still feel like shit," I groaned, double checking that I had everything from the room.

"Well, you're not alone in that. I just checked on Harlow, and she is also moving slow this morning. Both of you aren't doing so hot."

"Alright, well let's go grab her so she doesn't miss the bus."

We left the room together and went further down the hall to where Harlow's room was.

I knocked on her door a few times.

"Harlow? You ready?"

It sounded like there were hushed voices going back and forth through the door.

"Yeah, be down in a second!" she yelled back.

Dominik and I looked over at each other, wondering who else was in there with her.

After a few minutes the door swung open and out came Elissa with Harlow following behind her.

"Good morning. Let's get a move on, shall we?" Elissa instructed, pretending like the whole situation wasn't weird.

Elissa and Harlow rarely ever spoke about anything, let alone something that required that kind of privacy.

We wordlessly followed them down to the lobby and out to the tour bus that was parked outside.

The other bodyguards were already there, waiting for us to board.

One after another, we all piled in, and I thanked Terrance for coming back to drive for us. I always tried to give him my appreciation when it usually was a thankless job.

Once everyone was settled in, I started asking if anyone

knew when Lyle would be done with the interview. It had become vividly clear to me that we needed to talk, and he had a lot of explaining to do as to why he didn't call or text me once for my birthday.

I had not been drunk enough to forget that.

Elissa had let me know that he was just finishing up and would be on his way soon.

I tried to keep my nerves at bay, scrolling on my phone to distract me from checking the time every five minutes.

Eventually, after a little while the bus driver pulled up to the office where Lyle had been recording the interview and I finally felt my anxiety slow a little.

He boarded the bus, and I was eager to greet him at the door.

Wrapping my arms around his neck, I tried to shake some of my nerves off.

"Hey, Pen. I missed you," he grinned as he released the hug.

I gave him a half smile back. "You too. How was L.A.?"

He threw his duffle bag off his shoulder and sat down on the couch next to me. "Crazy, you won't even believe how much has changed since we were last home."

"Well, we weren't there for long before we left anyhow," I laughed halfheartedly. "How is Clara doing?"

"Fantastic. She was a huge help while I was recording. She has such a great ear for this industry."

Realizing that we were still surrounded by people, I figured it might not be the best place to air out our dirty laundry. We could handle this privately.

"That's great. We should talk later. You know after the show."

"Sure, yeah, we definitely can."

I mustered out the best smile I could manage and tried to ignore that he hadn't brought up my birthday. *Once.*

Dominik came out from the back of the bus and saw that Lyle was now back.

"Hey man what's up?" Lyle said, giving him a head nod.

I watched Dominik carefully as he sat down on the couch across from us and stared at him.

I awkwardly shifted in my seat, hoping he wouldn't say anything about us.

"Not much. Just trying to make sure everyone's good after last night," Dominik said casually.

Lyle's eyebrows furrowed with confusion. "Last night?"

"Aspen's 21st birthday? Her and Harlow went out last night to celebrate."

Lyle's face immediately fell, and my cheeks turned bright red.

"Aspen…" Lyle trailed off turning to look at me. "I'm so sorry I didn't call. Happy birthday."

I froze, feeling like everyone was staring at me and just waiting for me to validate his mistake.

"Thanks," I whispered.

Dominik wasn't so happy with that answer.

"About a day late dude."

Dominik tried to appear light-hearted, but the tension in his voice and stiff body movements gave him away. He was seething.

Lyle turned around, shocked that he would be called out for once.

"Simmer down, bro, it's all good."

Dominik's jaw tightened, and he breathed heavily, trying to restrain his anger.

"Not really *bro*. You should try and figure out what you missed out on before saying it's all good."

"Aspen?" Lyle asked me incredulously.

I felt more uncomfortable with the pressure shifted on me and didn't know what to say. Dominik trying to punish Lyle was inadvertently punishing me too.

"It's nothing. The night was just a little hectic, is all."

"What does that mean?"

Dominik laughed under his breath.

"Dom, get out of this conversation. Seriously," Lyle scoffed.

Dominik narrowed his eyes, not too fond of being dismissed by Lyle. But I pleaded with him silently, and eventually he put his hands up and walked away. Although he had thoroughly started a rift between Lyle and I only minutes after he got back.

Lyle, no longer wanting the attention of everyone, brought me into the back bedroom where we had some more privacy.

"Aspen what happened?" he asked quietly.

"It's not like you'd know. You never even called me last night. On my *birthday*," I hissed.

"Pen, I'm so sorry. Time got away from me after recording the song so many times and I was struggling to even stay awake. I promise I'll make it up to you," he proclaimed.

"You really think I believe that? No way, it's a bunch of bullshit! Should I call Clara?"

"Clara? You're threatening me now, Aspen? Why are you getting so upset?"

"You missed my goddamn birthday, Lyle! And you don't even care about it! Or what even happened last night."

"Fine, then tell me!"

"I was almost attacked, okay? Dominik was there to help us back to the hotel, but it was really scary. I wasn't in the right state of mind to be able to handle that."

"The hell does that mean? I'm sorry you got attacked again, I truly am," he sighed, pinching his temples. "Were you okay to sleep last night?"

"Yeah, I was fine, I was with-" I paused realizing what I was about to confess to. "I was with people, so I felt safe."

"People? Who were you with?"

I didn't want to confess to him where I ended up sleeping

so I opted instead to silently start unpacking some of my clothes and ignore him once more.

"Why won't you answer me, Aspen? Who did you sleep in bed with? Was it Harlow?"

As he rattled off more questions, I continued to pull out clothes and wipe my hair out of my face as I gathered my remaining clothes up and threw them in the corner of the room.

"I slept on the floor, okay? You can relax," I finally responded slightly louder than planned.

"You better have. I don't know what would possess you to do that when there was a bed, but if you slept alone then that's all I care about. You did sleep alone, right?"

I rolled my eyes at whatever bullshit he was spewing and went back toward the front of the bus.

"Stop, Aspen! Answer me!"

That was loud enough to start getting people's attention. I slowly turned around and gave him a death glare. If he wanted to hash it all out in front of everyone then so be it.

"If you were there last night, you would've seen that I was drunk off my ass and could hardly walk straight. I went to sleep the first place I saw comfortable enough, and that was the end of it. You need to calm the fuck down," I snapped.

"Harlow really got you that drunk last night? You're supposed to drink in *moderation*, Pen. You never should have had that much."

His tone was so condescending that I was practically speechless at the way he was talking to me. I took a long deep breath to control my temper.

"I had fun. It was a great experience and I loved getting to act like a normal 21-year-old. If you have a problem with that, I do not care. Now please leave me alone so I can go back to sleep with this god-awful hangover of mine."

He gritted his teeth and seemed to be holding back from saying what he really wanted to.

"Fine. But, please come sleep in the bedroom. You don't need to go back on the couch for Christ's sake."

It hadn't occurred to me until then that I had subconsciously just resorted back to where Dominik had last been, my body trying to find him again before it even registered in my brain.

I couldn't set off any more alarms though. Lyle was mad enough as it was, so I took the path of less resistance.

"That would be nice," I whispered with my head down.

Back to that agreeable girl who did anything Lyle asked of her.

He kissed my forehead tenderly as we went back to the bedroom, and I slipped underneath the covers.

Lyle got himself comfortable and moved close to me. He started caressing my arm, and across my collarbone. I tried to discreetly move away from his touch and nestle into the pillows, but his hands went wandering again.

Up my shirt.

My head felt like there was a tsunami knocking on the gates, waiting to drown everything out and crush my skull. I felt like shit again, was in an awful mood, and had thrown up multiple times in the previous twenty-four hours. It was most definitely not the time for that.

"It's been so long, Pen. Why don't we enjoy this time to ourselves?" he whispered seductively by my ear, laying kisses down my neck. His hands continued to grope and pinch my naked flesh and I felt absolutely nothing in response.

Everything in me wanted to say no. To say that all I wanted was to sleep away my headache and eat something when I woke up, feeling more refreshed for the show that night.

But I didn't say anything. I didn't move a muscle or respond to his touch. I pretended like it wasn't happening and that I was somewhere else entirely, letting my mind float away into any reality that wasn't the real one.

Lyle, like the genius he was, picked up on how disinterested I was after a few minutes of me not responding and sighed deeply. I thought he might've assumed I was asleep, which I was thankful for.

He didn't say anything, just rolled over and tucked himself away from me as I finally went back to sleep at last.

Lyle started moving around next to me and I got out of bed to not disturb him. Since he needed his beauty rest and all.

I rubbed my tired eyes and checked the clock to see it was midafternoon. We were going to arrive at the show venue any minute.

My stomach suddenly lurched, and I thought I was going to puke again. I high tailed it to the bathroom and leaned over the toilet just in case, but nothing ended up coming out. I heard footsteps but couldn't look up to see who it was.

"You okay, Aspen?" Dominik asked, crouching by me on the floor.

"Fine, thanks. Just living the dream."

"You know I was going to take a shower before the show since *someone* was in the bathroom all morning. But whatever, you go ahead and take up all my precious time," he said sarcastically.

I couldn't help but laugh at that.

"Unless you can fit in this bathroom with me, you'll just have to wait until I don't feel like I'm going to puke everywhere. Make yourself useful and go fix your hair or something," I suggested half-heartedly.

"I would if I could, Red. It is a shame this bathroom is so tight," he smirked. "And are you saying my hair looks bad?"

No. It didn't look bad. His curls still looked remarkably good and didn't even need much done to refresh them anymore since Harlow cut them short a while back. But I certainly wasn't going to admit that to him. Or acknowledge his suggestive comment.

"I don't know, does it?"

He rolled his eyes at my sarcasm, and I knew I was being even snappier than normal. But my head was throbbing, and I couldn't take being so close to him in the same room and not doing anything about it.

"You know you snore some when you sleep," he joked, still trying to raise my mood.

"Excuse me, I do not!"

"You do. And you're grabby."

He was really going to sit there and accuse me of the position we ended up in when sleeping together that last night? That wasn't going to fly.

"Your arms were around *me* when I woke up, okay? And I told Lyle I slept on the floor so lower your damn voice."

He laughed sardonically at that.

"Really? Lyle got upset that you might've slept in a bed with someone else? That's the pot calling the kettle black if I've ever heard one," he said as he reached around me and turned the shower on.

The stream of water continuously beat on the tile as I registered what the actual hell he just said.

"What are you saying, Dominik?"

"I think you need to talk with Lyle is what I'm saying. Probably Koen as well who was with Lyle the whole time in L.A. And maybe the bus driver too, considering he's seen every person who comes on and off the bus," he said nonchalantly.

Did Lyle have another girl on the bus? Did he fuck someone when he was in L.A.?

Dominik would only be saying that to hurt me, right? There's no way Lyle would ever do such a thing…

"Just my two cents. Sorry for having to be the one to tell you though," he said.

"Get out!" I yelled at Dominik, shutting the door in his face.

Chapter Eighteen

ASPEN

IGRIPPED THE SINK EDGE SO TIGHTLY; MY KNUCKLES WERE pure white. Whatever Dominik was insinuating couldn't have any truth to it. Lyle and I had been together for *two years*. I'd supported him through everything.

And yet despite that, I really couldn't put it past him anymore to have done such a thing.

I selfishly took over Dominik's shower, needing something to wake me up from the dream.

I shed my clothes and let the warm water beat down my shoulders and back as my mind continuously tried to betray me and enter the most pessimistic thoughts.

Maybe that's why he wasn't at my birthday. Maybe that was the perfect opportunity to have me out of his hair and away for long enough to cheat on me. But what if he'd been cheating on me even on the bus?

My chest tightened at the thought, and I found it harder and harder to move through the motions of washing myself or my hair. I just wanted to sit and drown in my own self-pity.

While what Dominik said might not have even been true, I didn't think he was the kind of man to just make up shit for his own enjoyment. Koen or someone had to have seen it firsthand, and I was not going to let Lyle get away with it.

They would have to tell me the truth.

I shut the water off and wrapped a towel around myself, as I debated putting back on the clothes I'd just taken off. I didn't have any other clothes in the bathroom with me and the last thing I wanted was to see Lyle's face if I went back to the bedroom.

I had to find the perfect opportunity to talk to them each individually before confronting Lyle. I wanted all perspectives and the facts before I took this seriously.

Because if I walked up to him and asked him directly without any other proof, I'd shatter any trust left in the relationship and he'd demand to know where I heard anything from. In which, I'd have to give up Dominik and that was something I simply wouldn't do.

I slid my comb through my wet hair in steady motions that I pulled from the sink cabinet, as I looked down at my fading red strands.

As much as the news came as an initial shock, I found myself struggling to be completely heartbroken as I imagined I would be. And there was only one person responsible for me feeling like that.

I subsequently left the bathroom and went to the front of the bus, avoiding Lyle at all costs.

A few band members and Elissa were sitting down talking, her iPad at her side for once instead of being glued to it so early in the day.

"Hey Aspen! Sorry we haven't had a chance to really talk yet! How was it last night?" Elissa asked curiously as she patted the seat next to her for me to sit down.

I anxiously looked around for Dominik, to no avail.

"Really fun. Harlow definitely knows how to have a good time," I nervously laughed. "And we both got very drunk. It was awesome though."

"Good, I'm glad you had a good time. I heard that Dom ended up showing up. Is that…true?" she asked, the end of the

sentence being much quieter to not evoke questions from anyone else.

"Yes. He wished me a happy birthday and took care of
Harlow and I while we were absurdly drunk. I didn't mind him
showing up after all."

"Well, it's a good thing it worked out. I mean I was worried
after Lyle said he wasn't going to be able to talk to you that you'd
be really upset but it sounds like you guys still had fun. You deserved to have a wild night for once," she said kindly not knowing what she'd just revealed.

Lyle had *not* spent all day in the recording studio and lost
track of time, like he'd told me. He'd let Elissa know *before* that
that he wouldn't talk to me, and yet couldn't have spent that
time sending me a quick text instead? He neglected to inform
me of anything.

"Mhm. I know you guys have a busy schedule today so I'll
do my best to help out where I can. Despite my obvious hangover," I offered with a small laugh, trying to act normal.

Dominik, whose curls did in fact look even better than before, entered the room changed into his bodyguard attire, having
to forgo his shower because of me. He walked over to the coffee
pot in the kitchen.

I glared at him from across the room as he acted like he
didn't turn my life upside down.

"That'd be great! I'd really appreciate it since things are so
tight today."

Elissa launched into the timing in between events but I
tuned her completely out as Dominik sat directly across from me.

All I could look at was him sitting there cockily, pretending
to look at his phone and sipping his black coffee.

But he couldn't pretend around me. I knew damn well he
was enjoying it. Having the upper hand, making me question

everything and treating me like I was a fool when it came to my own boyfriend.

I hated that he knew before me, and that I had no idea how long he knew for.

Aware of my stare, he lifted his eyes from his screen and locked in on mine.

I narrowed my eyes at him and stretched my foot out across the aisle to kick his stupid suited leg.

He silently pulled his leg back and acted like it didn't hurt but I delivered a mean kick. It most certainly hurt, and I was glad it did. He was playing a game with me, and it was not one I wanted to participate in.

"…and so, if you could help get him back over here by five, I think he'll be fine to go right into hair and makeup."

I turned back to Elissa and slapped a smile on my face. "Of course! That'll be no problem. As long as *he's* assigned somewhere else."

I didn't need to say his name for her to know who I was talking about. She looked between us, putting together how things had changed so quickly.

This announcement though made him put his phone down finally and interject.

"That's not happening. Aspen is my duty and that cannot be changed. This arrangement is staying the way it is," he said sternly.

Elissa, not realizing truly how serious he was, laughed at him. "Aye, aye captain!"

I gave him a dry laugh and couldn't help but blurt out, "Are you seriously acting like you own me? Koen could easily switch to my bodyguard and there would be no issue."

His jaw tensed and I knew I'd pissed him off now.

"No. Koen has a specific job and so do I. You can't just interchange us for fun when we're under contract. Stop acting entitled when you know better," he jeered.

"Me? I'm acting entitled, really? You're the one who just said that I'm your duty! Me, *a human being!*"

Our voices continued to rise, and I no longer cared if I was attracting everyone's attention.

"Because you are! Protecting you is my assignment, and I won't change that just because you're being a brat."

"No, your duty is to ensure the safety of all of us so why don't you just take a backseat and let someone else be my bodyguard for now. Koen!" I screamed.

Koen, who was on a bottom bunk, rubbed his eyes before coming into the lounge area where we were now standing.

"Yes, Miss Reddick?"

"You'll now be assigned to me. Dominik can work separately for Mr. Hawthorne since he's so worried about his personal endeavors."

Elissa and the band members who were still surrounding us, all looked around at each other, but no one would intervene.

"Uh, yes Miss Reddick of course," Koen responded dutifully.

Whatever Koen would have responded with didn't actually matter. My gaze was situated on Dominik, and only him. He was breathing heavily, his lip twitching and looking like he was about to explode. But I couldn't take it anymore.

"Okay then, looks like we've got that settled how about—" Elissa started.

"Stop the bus!" Dominik yelled, interrupting Elissa.

"Sir, we're on the highway," the bus driver responded, slightly annoyed.

"Take the next exit."

Dominik's tone was so demanding, I knew no one would try and disobey him. He wasn't fucking around.

At that point everyone onboard was staring at us wide-eyed, but I refused to back down. If he wanted to take this all the way, then so did I.

The bus driver did take the next exit as instructed and pulled into a large gas station.

"I'll just fill up the tank," he said calmly before exiting the bus.

"No one else gets off this bus but us," he said to everyone onboard. "Aspen, get off now."

I bit back a nasty remark and entertained the idea of saying no. But the dark look in his eyes told me that would be a very bad idea. And I did not want to handle anything in front of everyone anymore.

It had become personal.

"Of course, *sir*," I snarked.

Still with damp hair and looking like a wreck, I walked outside cross-armed and went far enough from the bus that no one could see or hear us. He was following behind me at a rapid pace, even pressing a hand on my back to hurry me along, as we went all the way behind the convenience store to be completely out of sight.

"You're driving me fucking insane," he said roughly before guiding my back to the cinderblock wall and leaning into me.

His breath hit my cheek and every thread holding my willpower together dissipated. I couldn't restrain myself anymore, and I didn't want to.

I stared up at him and the frenzied look in his eyes as he pushed my hair away from my face.

"Tell me you don't want this," he whispered as our breaths mingled.

"I want this. I want *you*," I breathed before crashing my lips into his.

It was a clash of tongue and teeth, a war for dominance. But I willingly gave in and let him make his claim on me without resistance.

Shockwaves pulsed through me as his one hand gripped my neck, the other latched tightly onto my hip.

My heart was beating out of my chest as his lips continued to devour mine like the world was ending around us. Knees weak and cheeks ablaze, I couldn't stop the growing desire for more. It was the most electrifying kiss I'd ever had in my life.

And despite how many times I'd imagined it, my fantasies didn't come close to how perfect it was.

"Fuck, fuck," his voice traveled as he finally pulled away from me.

Through deep panting breaths, I furrowed my eyebrows at the lack of contact and grabbed his neck to bring him back to me.

"No, no, Aspen we can't," he said disappointedly, pulling my hands away.

He pushed away from the wall and ran his hands through his hair anxiously.

"This is why I never let myself get attached. I'm such an idiot. Fuck!" he mumbled angrily as he kicked the ground.

I came up to where he'd walked off and put my hands on his chest.

"Stop it, Dominik. *I* kissed *you*. I wanted this and I still do," I confided.

He looked down at me and all the conflict in him seemed to ease for a second. He held my face with both hands as he gently stroked my cheeks.

"I've never met someone like you before. You get me so stirred up, I feel like I might explode if I don't get my hands on you," he confessed. "Do you know how hard it is to live like that and not be able to touch you?"

"Of course, I do. I'm in hell every day that I'm stuck in this mess. I understand you, and believe me, I feel everything you do too. I have since the moment I saw you."

I waited for his reaction with bated breath as I hoped he

would realize why I'd always been so difficult with him. It was the only way to express how great my feelings were without using my words.

"No wonder you were so feisty then too. I should've known you'd bring me to my knees," he said smiling.

"To your knees you say?" I asked him jokingly.

"Yes. I've always been at your will, Aspen."

He took what I said literally and got down on his knees in front of me, in the middle of the backwoods ass gas station alleyway.

Jesus Christ this man.

He looked up at me innocently and I let my hand roam across his jaw as I couldn't help but smile from ear to ear.

"It was rhetorical, but you sure do know how to make a statement. I kind of like you actually submitting to me for once though," I smiled.

"I'll do anything you ask of me, Aspen. I swear it. You have corrupted me beyond belief, and I will always fall to you."

I leaned down and kissed him deeply. I took this as his clear admittance that I was the true winner of our games. There was never a question of it, even though he sure liked to play like there was.

He got up off his knees and clutched onto the bottom of my shirt, his fingertips touching bare skin. Back at his full stature, he gazed down at me.

"The only reason I was so mad at you was because you were trying to pull me away from you. And to make myself clear, you will not be guarded by Koen under any circumstance."

"Lyle isn't an idiot. He'll catch on, Dominik, even if he's been with… other women. There will be enough questions as it is about why we're at each other's throats so often. Having Koen guard me is the best way to protect me."

"I don't like that. I don't like it at all. And I most certainly do not want to be guarding your punk ass boyfriend," he said with such venom in his tone. "If you're still calling him that."

But the way he said 'boyfriend' made my heart start to crumble.

I just cheated on Lyle. My boyfriend. That I was in a relationship with.

And I was finding it hard to feel truly guilty about it.

Because there was the reminder in the back of my head that not only had he potentially fucked someone in L.A., but that he'd brought a girl on the tour bus at some point too. The fact that he could've already fucked things up before I ever gave into Dominik was an actual sigh of relief. It made me feel a whole hell of a lot better about what I did.

"What we want doesn't matter right now. We're almost done with the tour and then we'll be done with this. You will switch with Koen to protect me," I said sternly. "You don't have to be physically with me to be protecting me, Dominik."

We both knew it was the best way to not raise suspicion and keep everyone's questions at bay. While they would still ask around with how nosy they were, it would deter them from figuring out what was really going on.

I hoped after our blowout, it had become obvious that we were just two hot heads, and the topic was too sensitive for anyone to get into without pissing one of us off.

"I'll do it if I know that's where you're safest. But I'd much rather you be with me."

He wrapped his arms around my body as I breathed in his scent of pine and cedarwood and melted into his touch. It was the last time we'd get to be so close for a while.

His hug felt like it was a promise, a contract between us.

That we'd do whatever we had to do to make this work.

Chapter Nineteen

ASPEN

"YOU GUYS OKAY?" ELISSA ASKED NERVOUSLY AS WE walked back onto the bus subtly distanced from each other.

"Of course," I replied with a fake smile, knowing she'd likely pick up on it.

I tried to skirt around Lyle, but he grabbed my arm and leaned into me.

"Aspen, we need to talk," Lyle said sternly, shooting Dominik a fierce look.

I begrudgingly nodded my head and followed him back to the bedroom, trying to look as dejected as possible to not cause attention.

He sat down on the bed with me and laced his fingers between mine.

"You need to be honest with me about what's going on, Aspen. This kind of environment isn't fair for everyone to have to live in."

Don't stutter. Don't lose focus.

"Nothing's going on. Dominik is an asshat and I despise living with him," I said too unconvincingly. "Look, he pushes my buttons on the daily and I never even wanted him here in the first place."

"Really that's all? You two were fighting so bad earlier, Elissa almost had to break it up! Hardly five feet tall *Elissa*."

I scoffed, trying to imagine Elissa ever actually caring enough to get in the middle of us.

"Right, and what exactly would you like me to do about that?"

"I don't know! Attempt to be civil with Dom?" he suggested, dropping my hand. "Is he annoying? Yes, but he's just doing his job. And I know you didn't want this in the first place, but it's not his fault he's here. The tour will be over soon enough, okay?"

"And then what? We'll go back to L.A. while you make an entire new album and I sit around doing…what?"

"Pen, you can do anything you want. If you want to get a job of your own, or if you want to go to school, you're free to do so. I'll support you, always."

I got up abruptly, my nerves like a livewire with how nonchalant he was acting.

"I don't see how this will ever work Lyle! You'll never be home, or able to spend time with me. Every spare minute you have will be spent creating this album."

"I'll make time! Look, this doesn't have to be a death sentence for us. If anything, it'll give us some time apart instead of spending every minute with each other."

Furiously raking my hands through my hair, I felt like I was on the brink of losing it.

"Time apart, right. Because that's just what this relationship needs right now after you being in L.A. and doing God knows what when you were there!"

"It is! Just look at you and Dom, likely fighting so much because you're stuck on this bus day in and day out. I get it, I know it's frustrating and it's obviously taken a toll on us too."

"So, you think it's me, that I'm the problem?"

"We need time apart, Aspen!" he yelled.

I could feel tears welling up as he spoke the truth, but I held them back. Regaining my strength, I could see what was going to happen. If it was going the way I thought it was, we needed to have it out and be done with it.

"Well, you'll get your wish. If you don't want me on the tour anymore then just say it."

He sat there wordlessly, eyes looking anywhere but at mine.

"Right now! Say it, Lyle!"

"I don't know, Aspen! You've made things so miserable around here, no one wants to be near you anymore. Harlow tolerates you, but no one else does."

"I see. That's fine then. After tonight, I'll book a plane ticket back to Tennessee and you'll be free to fuck whoever you want. Happy?"

"What? Aspen wait!" he yelled after me as tears freely streamed down my face.

"Don't try and deny it! You've been bringing girls back here when I'm not around! I'm sure you fucked them in L.A. too while I was left here."

At this point I'd run into the main part of the bus where everyone was still sitting, having no shame in letting everyone hear us.

"Aspen, I don't know where you heard that from but it's not true. Just let me explain," he said defensively.

"No! Everyone here has seen it. They know the truth. Tell me Koen, you'd know best. Just how many girls has he brought back here?"

Koen, taken aback that he was being asked such a question, froze in his response.

"Ma'am, that's not in my job description—"

"I don't care! Just tell me the truth, *please*!" I begged him.

"I escort Mr. Hawthorne many places, women are sometimes there and sometimes not."

"Oh, what kind of bullshit answer is that! You're not the fucking president Koen, just tell me!"

He swallowed roughly, looking down at his shoes.

"Yes."

One word. Only one word was needed to confirm that fear that Dominik put in my head. Lyle swung around and almost decked Koen.

"Stop it! You're a fucking coward. I hope you enjoy your life without me in it," I yelled, pulling Lyle back away from Koen.

"Aspen, please, it's complicated," he begged, holding his hands tightly on my cheeks. "I swear!"

"No! It's not, there's no explanation for this," I sobbed, ripping his hands away from me and grabbing my bag that was slung across the couch.

Dominik was on standby, carefully watching the interaction but not wanting to appear suspicious by standing up for me. I didn't care though. This needed to happen for everyone involved.

"Just get me off this bus, please. I can't—I can't do this," I cried, walking up to Terrance whose eyes were still on the road despite the disturbance.

"Ma'am, we're about a mile from the concert venue. Just give me a few minutes."

I continued to cry, huddled close to the bus driver. I wanted more than anything to have been able to run away right then and there instead of being stuck for another goddamn second on the bus with him.

As soon as the bus rolled to a stop, I was out those doors and running.

Where? I didn't know. We were in a big city, but I was sure there was somewhere I could go where I wouldn't be able to hear his voice that night.

Chapter Twenty

DOMINIK

WELL, THAT WENT POORLY.

It was clear to me that it was just a matter of time until the truth came out, and I didn't want her with him anymore. Although I may have nudged her in that direction, I didn't regret it.

Seeing the hurt she was in however, was enough to send me over the edge.

I wanted to slap that stupid ass look off Lyle's face. How the hell he could possibly be shocked that she finally found out was beyond me.

I couldn't fuck his face up before his big show, as annoying as it was. He certainly deserved it, though.

Before I even realized what I was doing, my feet were following Aspen out of the bus and toward the venue.

She was running, full-on *running* through the backstage of the venue trying to dodge the crew members already setting up. And I was right behind her.

I hadn't yet thought out what I was doing following her, but I wanted her to know I was there. I was sure there was nothing I could say to alleviate what she was feeling, but I could make sure she was safe.

Finally making her way to the front of the arena and onto

the stage, she stood still. Glancing at every bright stage light over-head, every empty seat in front of us.

I caught up to her and was out of breath myself, yet my entrance didn't faze her in the slightest.

"Ma'am? We need you off the stage," a crew lady complained coming up to us.

"Back off," I barked back at her.

She narrowed her eyes at me like she wanted to say something else but then turned on her heel and went backstage.

"Aspen, they have to set up for the show. Why don't we go somewhere else?" I suggested gently to her.

"Look at it. All of this, every single bit of this is only possible because of me," she said spitefully. "I was the only one who supported him when he'd used all his parents' money. I was the one who encouraged him to start posting his music online. I gave up my entire life to support him."

She swiped her tears off her face angrily.

"And yet it all meant nothing to him. Not a single goddamn thing."

She turned away from the bright lights, her arms curling in on themselves to try and comfort her body.

"I'm sorry, Aspen. Let's just get away from here for the night."

Aspen agreed and I wrapped my arm around her back to help guide her out of the maze that was the backstage area.

Calling in on my earpiece, I let the other bodyguards know what was going on and looked around outside to try and find any marking or sign that indicated where we were. Eventually I found someone on the crew to tell me the exact part of the city we were in.

Switching locations so often left me in a blur most of the time. My job wasn't directly hindered by the constant shifting of locations, but it left me in a haze more often than not as we moved from place to place.

Yet in the midst of the chaos, Aspen was my anchor, the only one who kept me grounded.

She was the source of my madness and my savior all at once.

The depth of devotion she elicited from me was both exhilarating and unnerving. She had an inexplicable power over me, making me cave to her every whim as she undid me at the seams.

But knowing she wanted this just as much as I did lit a fire in me I didn't know was still there.

And seeing her in this much pain, made me see absolute fucking red.

I was still calm enough to do what was best for her in the moment, but without my past history, I would've lost it already.

Taking Aspen with me, we walked a couple blocks down to a nearby shopping strip.

Her head remained down the entire time, a testament to how upset she was.

I hadn't imagined how much the news would've affected her and I couldn't say it didn't bother me. Her attachment to him went further than I suppose I realized. But I would let her take as long as she needed to handle these feelings.

She sat down on the curb of the sidewalk and immediately put her head in her hands, trying to block her face from me.

She seemed on the verge of a breakdown, and while I couldn't probe her on it yet, I questioned if she actually planned on leaving the tour and flying home like she said earlier.

Because contract or not, I was following her wherever she was going.

There would always be another client out there, with another manager trying to sink their claws in, so losing this contract meant nothing to me. As long as I was with her, I didn't care what it took.

I just felt guilty trying to bring it up with her still so distraught. I needed to get in contact with Elissa and see what could be done if this was going to be taken care of in a single night. If there was a red-eye flight Aspen could get on by the end of day, I had a feeling she'd be up for it, given how heartbroken she seemed.

I didn't want to pour salt into an open wound, but I had to ask her if this was what she truly wanted.

"Aspen? Are you sure you want to leave the tour?"

She looked up at me with glassy brown eyes, tears still clumped to her lashes.

"I don't know," she cried, her voice cracking with each sob. "I can't believe I even said that."

She turned to me with a tear-streaked face and a nose blanketed with red, yet she still looked absolutely ethereal.

"It's okay, Aspen." I rubbed her back with a soft touch. "Is going back home something you really want to do?"

She sniffled and tried to wipe away the tears sliding down her face.

"No, not really. I haven't been back home in years. *This* has been my life, everything to do with Lyle and his career and I don't know anything different now. Without this tour, without Lyle… I have nothing."

I grabbed her chin lightly and angled it up for her to look at me.

"Yes, you do. You have your dignity. You have your strength. You have a choice," I emphasized to her. "And you have me."

"Don't say that right now," she exclaimed painfully, forcibly moving my hand away from her face.

"Why not? It's the truth."

"Because I don't deserve you!"

I took a step back, shocked that she would ever say that. It was purely incomprehensible that she couldn't see her worth, or thought somehow, she wasn't good enough for me.

I exhaled sharply, lightly touching her forearm as she refused to look me in the eye.

"I don't believe that. I don't think you're deserving of most of what you've dealt with in your life, Aspen. But to say you're not deserving of someone who knows you and is there for you?"

"You don't understand, Dominik! I haven't had someone like that in a long time. I certainly don't deserve it now when I'm crying over another man. Do you know how pathetic that is?"

"Look, Aspen, neither of us was expecting this. I never planned to meet someone like you, but God, am I glad I did. That's the funny thing about fate. It happens when you're least expecting it."

Her honey-colored eyes met mine and she was hanging on the end of every word like it was her lifeline.

"But I know we were meant to meet. I haven't cared one bit about you being with Lyle because I knew you two wouldn't last. You belong with someone who can give you a better life, Aspen. One where you are cared for and cherished, where you're *loved*."

"And I'm just supposed to let you throw away your life for me? I can't, Dominik, everything is in the way! I don't have a job, an education, a car, even a place to live!"

"All of that can change. You haven't had any of that because you've been too busy living in Lyle's shadow to make a life for yourself. I don't care anymore, Aspen. I will support you so you can build a new life. I'll do whatever it takes to get you to a place where you are happy again."

Overwhelmed, she got up suddenly, feeling the need to pace back and forth, an anxious habit of hers.

"I can't ask that of you. I'm a mess right now, literally falling apart at the seams," she stammered. "But I also can't imagine my life without you now. I want you to come with me so badly, but you're under contract, Dominik. I know there's a penalty for breaking it."

"I don't care. Tell me you want to go back to Tennessee right now and I'll break the contract today."

She scoffed at that, pulling at her hair exasperated.

"No, absolutely not. I will not be the cause of you losing your job. That's not fair to you!"

"I'm serious, Aspen. I'll find new work like I always do. Lyle is not my first client and certainly won't be the last. If you want to go back tonight, I'll book the plane tickets with Elissa right now. Just say the words, and it's done."

She paused, looking up at me with cautious eyes.

"Dominik… I'm scared. Really, *really* scared. My entire life just changed in a single day."

"Aspen, your life already wasn't your own. You knew you wouldn't have a place once the tour was done anyway. This is now being done on your terms."

I could see the gears turning in her head as she accepted that truth.

"Are you sure? Like 100% fully sure that you want to do this?" she questioned me.

"Yes, of course I am. There's no way I'd let you go without being right by your side."

"I can't believe I'm doing this. I can't believe I'm going back to my hometown. My little brother hasn't even seen me in over two years, and I haven't seen my mother in that long either. I'm so scared of what they'll think of me coming back."

I tried to slow down her anxious thoughts, resting my hand on her shoulder.

"And that's okay. It's part of the process, Aspen. No one just up and changes their entire life without some fear about it. We can get through this."

"*Together*, we can do this," she interjected. "I can't do this on my own."

"You could. I fully believe if I never showed up you would've done this all on your own. But I'd much rather be a part of it."

"Okay," Aspen said, blowing out a breath. "I'm going to do it. I'm going to go for it. I'll let Elissa know that we're leaving tonight and grab our bags from the bus, and then I'm going back home."

My heart swelled with joy as I watched her confidently take control, and my smile grew wider than ever before.

"I'm so proud of you," I smiled, kissing her lips gently.

"Thank you," she said quietly, her nose touching mine as she leaned into me.

And I think for the first time, she actually believed me.

Chapter Twenty-One

ASPEN

DOMINIK WAS A MAN OF HIS WORD.

Within an hour he'd discreetly thrown the plans together with Elissa, which thankfully she signed off on, and found a flight that would leave the same night.

She may have been under the guise that this was just a small break, and I would be back with Lyle soon as a shiny, happy couple but she was quite mistaken with that whole idea.

I wanted nothing to do with him after how he betrayed me.

While I had been plenty in the wrong myself with how I entertained Dominik for so long as someone in a relationship, Lyle was physically intimate with other women right under my nose. I still could hardly think about it without my stomach turning.

But there was much else to worry about now. Dominik and I had gone back to the bus while the concert was being set up and quietly re-packed our bags, though they had barely been touched with us only just coming back to tour.

I'd said my goodbyes to Harlow, who was heartbroken that we'd be leaving, but I promised I'd stay in touch with her as I figured all this out.

I simply couldn't regret this decision. As confused and lost as I felt, there was a gnawing feeling in my stomach that this had to happen. That somehow, someway this was always how it was meant to be. I didn't want more time to overthink it, or to question if this was really the right thing for me.

And once Dominik had given me the flight details, it set the plan in stone, and I went ahead and found an Uber that could take us to the airport.

There was no going back.

After being at the airport for a few hours, I was so ready to leave that I didn't even care if we'd be flying in the middle of the night, or that the flight would take four hours. I wasn't even a good flier, and yet I was fully ready to take the dreaded flight home if it meant I was done with this and away from Lyle.

My mind was still on overdrive, flipping through every scenario of what my family would think of me coming home.

But the way Dominik had comforted me was unlike anything I'd ever received before in my life. He was actively encouraging me, making me confident enough to take a leap like this only with his words. I still found it hard to believe that I met someone like him in this lifetime.

He'd handled the details of his contract over the phone and was very adamant about me not hearing any of it. I'd wanted to know what the penalty was and if he'd still get his last payout, which he did tell me would hit his bank account within the next week.

But any other details, he wouldn't let me in on.

I was glad of course that he'd still be receiving his last paycheck, but I hated that I had to care about it. I was never someone that normally cared about money and couldn't bear the thought that I would have to rely on someone else temporarily. But I had hardly anything to my name, let alone a bank account full of savings.

It hadn't occurred to me how much of a disadvantage I was setting myself up for when I blindly followed Lyle on his tour without any money or assets that I fully owned, but I sure realized it now.

I was 21, had no education beyond high school, and would have to find a job that could support me enough to get on my feet, in the blink of an eye. As sweet as Dominik was to offer to support me, I didn't want to be indebted to anyone for longer than necessary. I didn't want our relationship to feel transactional before it ever really began.

And yet despite all the worrying and unknowns, with Dominik by my side, my mind was settled.

Even with how I'd just ended things with Lyle, all my heart wanted was Dominik.

And now I had him.

It was like my body had a mind of its own, always wanting to be against or touching Dominik in some way now that we could be together.

Not like *that*. Like I could never get enough of him, even with him being right next to me.

We'd been unable to act on our feelings for so long that the freedom to do it now without any hesitation was borderline addicting to me.

Finally boarding the plane at midnight, Dominik and I had found our seats amongst a sea of other passengers and found some empty space for our luggage. He had taken my suitcase and pushed it into the overhead bin, in which his sweatshirt raised up and I was left looking at his gorgeous bare torso.

But it was short-lived as he put his last bag in and sat down in the aisle seat.

We squished together in our economy seats with me in the middle and an elderly woman by the window. Despite the lack of space, we settled in and made the best of it for the long flight ahead.

The night sky did ease my usual flight anxiety, and I thought

I might actually be able to sleep some on the flight. I'd intertwined my arm with Dominik's, curling up on his shoulder.

He'd kissed my forehead lightly, though he was focused intently on his phone and whatever falling out he was left with from his security company.

The guilt was enough to eat me alive, but Dominik had continuously tried to soothe me and reassure me that he was fine with the decision.

I just hated myself for uprooting his life like this.

I dozed for most of the flight. By the time I got into a deeper sleep, the landing announcement jolted me awake.

I rubbed my tired eyes and made my way out of Dominik's grasp. He was asleep himself, though he hadn't woken with the announcement.

I lightly nudged his shoulder, and he blinked his eyes slowly, waking up.

"We're about to land," I whispered to him.

He nodded his head, and he tried to shut his eyes again and sleep for a few more minutes, but I was dying not knowing what was going on.

"Will you tell me what was going on when we first boarded? You were texting like crazy."

He opened his eyes slightly and then shut them again. "Don't worry about it, everything's fine."

"Please?" I asked him again.

He sighed and fully sat up in his seat.

"I was texting Koen. The security company isn't happy because the new contract was in the midst of being processed today. There was a lot of inner workings to the deal I guess between them and the record label, so they just were being assholes about it."

"Dominik! That is exactly what I didn't want to happen.

Look, you could still go back and work for Elissa and them full time—”

“No. I have no desire to ever go back working for that team again. They will do just fine on their own.”

Passengers started moving around more as we prepared to land, and I angrily shifted in my seat. I was not going to let this go.

“Are they really just mad that they’ll have to draw up a new contract? Or is there something more that you’re not telling me?”

“It’s complicated, Aspen. I don’t want you worrying about anything.”

I was trying to keep my voice low but his need to shelter me was only hurting me from knowing what was going on.

“I’m serious. Did the company drop you or something?”

He refused to make eye contact with me. “Aspen, please stop asking.”

“Oh my god, they did. You broke the contract, so they fired you.”

I rubbed my hand over my face in disbelief, trying to find something to calm me down so I didn’t burst into tears.

I didn’t know how much more the universe could throw at me. Now neither of us had a job and we were minutes away from landing in a small city that already didn’t have much to offer.

Dominik didn’t respond but looked slightly dejected. I was sure this wasn’t the outcome he’d been expecting.

“I’m sorry, Dominik.”

“Well, it is what it is. I’d been with them for five years, so I thought that they’d have no problem just finding me a new client, but I guess I wasn’t being very realistic,” he sighed. “We’ll figure something else out. That’s what I do.”

As much as I wanted to believe him, it felt like everything was truly falling apart now. We’d have whatever Dominik had saved from working these past few months and his last paycheck, and that was everything we had to live off of.

The regret of leaving the tour was starting to creep in already and it had been less than twenty-four hours.

Eventually, the plane touched down after some mild turbulence, and we sat on the runway for a few minutes before we were able to start exiting the plane.

Dominik, being the gentleman that he was, helped the elderly woman who'd been sitting beside me and retrieved her luggage. She was very thankful, and Dominik made sure she got off the airplane safely. I'd trailed behind them like a lost puppy, torn on saying anything that would start an argument between us.

The truth was that I felt like all my hope was gone.

This was absolute rock bottom, and the fact that I was the cause of that for Dominik too just made me want to die.

The airport we'd arrived at was very small, but so was the town I grew up in.

On our way out, the sign hanging above the escalator caught my eye. 'Dayton, Tennessee' spelled out in big letters evoked a true sadness in me that I couldn't find the words to explain.

I had been so sure when I left this town that I was never going to come back. Lyle's career would take off and we'd get married and have some wonderful famous lifestyle.

The reality was much more depressing, and I felt ashamed for having to return this way.

Exiting through the airport's squeaky glass doors, we waited on the curb for the Uber to pick us up.

Dominik finally caved and rubbed my back gently, being the first one to talk. "It's going to be okay, Aspen. I know it will."

"I wish I had your kind of optimism," I mumbled.

"I've been through a lot of shit, Aspen. If I didn't have some kind of hope to keep me going, I would have been dead or in prison a long time ago."

My hands found their way to his chest as I leaned into him

and remembered that he was there with me. And that was so much more than I could ask for.

Recalling what he'd told me before about what it was like for him growing up, I figured it was as good a time as any to try and learn more. Considering how much of an asshole I'd been the last time he'd tried to open up to me, I didn't want to push it.

"Will you tell me about it sometime? Your past?"

"Yes. As long as you tell me more about yours. I don't know what I'm about to walk into otherwise."

I realized then that I was slightly setting him up for failure by just dumping him in front of my family with no real expectations. There were certain things he had to understand about why I left and that my relationship with my family was… tumultuous.

We went to a nearby hotel. It was the best we could do until I had the chance to talk to my mother and see about a temporary situation.

Although I had a feeling it wouldn't be a very warm welcome.

It was at the cusp of five in the morning, and I was desperate to get some real sleep. Dozing on and off on the plane only held me over temporarily and I needed some uninterrupted quality sleep.

We arrived at the hotel as the sun rose, gladly choosing a single king bed this time.

Receiving our key card, we tiredly found the elevator and just tried to get to our room as quickly as we could.

The sun was already rising, and I didn't want to sleep through the entire day.

Reaching our small room, I hurled my luggage to the corner of the room and began unmaking the bed. I didn't care about my hair, or my makeup, or anything else except getting some sleep.

Dominik had no objections and settled into bed with me as I reached my arm over his body and made light circles on his torso with my fingertips.

At this moment everything felt at peace, and there was a stillness that I hadn't yet taken a second to enjoy.

I kissed him deeply, a long and needed kiss, and sunk back into the bed. There was so much left unsaid, so many fears that I couldn't get rid of that were killing me.

But all I knew for certain was that I couldn't have gotten to this point without Dominik. And I was so glad he was there.

Chapter Twenty-Two

ASPEN

"P**EN, WAKE UP.**"

A hand jostled my shoulder and stirred me awake. Of course, Dominik was awake and ready for the day.

"Is that what you're calling me now?" I grumbled, voice thick with sleep.

"I still think Red is a better fit, but I know it's what you're used to."

"What time is it?" I groaned, still refusing to wake up completely.

"Late. It's about 1:00 in the afternoon."

I let out a massive sigh, and tried not to dwell on the fact that I was still incredibly tired so late in the day. Whatever sleep I'd managed to get had simply not been enough.

But being draped across Dominik all night certainly had helped. There was nothing like the comfort I found in his embrace.

"Are you hungry? There's some food downstairs I could grab."

"Not yet. I'm still half asleep."

I rolled over and started to fall back asleep again, wanting to be whisked away from my reality.

"Come on, Aspen. We've got to get the day going," Dominik said, trying to drag me out of bed.

"No," I moaned, hiding my face in the pillow.

"I know you're still worried about everything. Your brain goes a mile a minute despite how much you try to hide it."

I sat up in bed and gave him a blank stare.

"Things are not great right now, Dominik. Besides the fact that I feel like an absolute pathetic loser and a failure, I have to confront my *mother*."

He sat down on the bed and rested his hand on my thigh.

"I understand that it's a lot right now. I just don't want you to go down a black hole," he said worriedly. "You can tell me what happened with her."

I brushed my wild hair out of my face and refused to make eye contact with him. I was embarrassed enough as it was.

"She really wasn't that bad when I was younger. But then my father passed away when I was fourteen and she was very resentful about it. She worked two jobs to try and support us after his death, but she was always angry."

Dominik touched my face gently and tried to get me to look at him.

"You can keep going," he whispered softly.

I woefully met his eyes and took a deep breath.

"I think it appeared to her that I wasn't grateful, but I was. I knew she was sacrificing everything to give us a decent life. But her kids had fallen through the cracks in the process, and she drank to cope with her grief."

Dominik rubbed my back gently, and I felt safe enough to keep going.

"There was no one else to do it, so I raised my brother. I was the one who woke my brother up for school and packed his lunch and made sure he did his homework."

Tears welled up in my eyes despite urging myself not to cry. I just couldn't recount my past without wanting to run and hide.

"I basically became a parent to him at fourteen. I essentially took on my dad's role and it wasn't very fun. I became very bitter as I grew older and saw everyone else having normal teenage fun. I couldn't do any of that with having to take care of Myles all the time," I sniffled.

"Myles? That's your brother?"

"Yes. He's probably grown so much since the last time I saw him. I don't know if he'll even understand why I left," I said sadly.

"You make a lot of assumptions, Aspen. Maybe he will understand, maybe he'll thank you for what you gave up in order to raise him. You don't know until you hear it for yourself."

"How are you so good at that?" I laughed, pushing the tears off my cheeks.

"At what?"

"At giving me advice! Always being so insightful and smart and logical."

"It took me a while, but I learned from my own mistakes basically. Things weren't always easy for me, and my life wasn't all that great," he replied.

I pulled myself closer to him, and our hands found each other, locking into place.

"You told me some before, but I wasn't very receptive. And I'm really sorry about that. Would you be willing to tell me more now?"

He gave me a half smile, and kissed the top of my hand, wordlessly accepting my apology.

"Well, I was the child of immigrants. My parents only spoke Greek and had trouble finding jobs once they moved to the U.S. They wanted me to experience more than I would've in Greece but didn't know how to give me that."

"What do you mean?"

"They just didn't understand the American lifestyle. They thought events like Prom and school football games were stupid, so I never went to anything like that. I had to get a job at sixteen to support the family and have worked ever since."

That's interesting. For some reason I never imagined him as Prom King or quarterback anyway, but it made me sad that he never got the chance to experience it.

"Did you get your scar from one of your jobs back then?"

"No. I'd mentioned I grew up in a rough neighborhood. People were willing to do anything to get their hands on drugs. Even if it meant preying on those that were younger."

I clenched his hand in shock, my breath stuttering in my throat. "Someone hurt you for drugs?"

"The guy jumped me and tried to take my money. It was what was going to pay our electric bill that month so I wouldn't let him have it without a fight. Of course, I didn't see that he had a pocketknife on him though and he sliced through my hand and arm when I defended myself."

My eyes automatically went down to his arm where the scar, now healed and white, led down to his hand. It broke my heart.

"I'm so sorry you experienced that Dominik. That sounds really terrifying, especially to have dealt with so young. I can't imagine what that must've been like. Is that why you got into security?"

He blew out a long stream of air, likely to try not to get emotional about his past. "Partially. I knew college wasn't an option given the money situation, so I started training hard at the gym. Building muscle, growing my stamina. It took me a while, but I made my life what I wanted it to be."

"It paid off. I mean, you look incredible."

He smirked at that. "Well of course I do."

I jokingly shoved his shoulder and figured we might as well

confront the elephant in the room. "So, the question now is, what are we doing next?"

"It's up to you. Do you want to stay here for long?" he asked genuinely.

"Not necessarily. It's my hometown of course, but it never felt quite right. I'd rather just stay here until we're on our feet and then figure things out."

"So, you fully want to pursue this? Us?"

"Of course, I do. I want to build a new life for us, together. Plus, I have all my eggs in this one basket, and that basket is you," I joked.

"I want you to be mine, Aspen."

He looked into my eyes so intensely, I knew he was putting it all on the table.

"And I am yours."

"*Officially,*" he said more strongly.

"As in girlfriend? You want me to be your girlfriend?" I asked nervously.

"Yes. I quite like the sound of that," he grinned.

I didn't care about labels all that much in actuality, and I wasn't quite sure why he wanted one so badly. I was ready to start my life with him either way, but I would agree to it if it made him happy. He'd done enough for my own happiness.

"If that's what you want, then it's what I want. As long as you don't think we're moving too fast. Although it's kind of late for that," I chuckled awkwardly.

"Aspen I've had to pretend for months that I felt nothing for you. I had to watch you from afar and pretend that it wasn't killing me inside. We could expedite this at the speed of light, and it still wouldn't be fast enough to make up for all the missed time."

"I just hope I don't disappoint you then. I don't want you to finally see how I really am in a relationship and want to back out. I know I'm a lot sometimes and can be difficult and stubborn—"

"Stop, Aspen. That's your fear talking," he said softly, stroking my hair. "Your personality is what drew me to you. Your wit, and your sarcasm, and yes, how stubborn you are too."

I stared into his deep blue eyes, absolutely mesmerized at his ability to understand me and know why I'd be hesitant.

"You really are so sure about this."

"I am, and I have no hesitations about it. I know who you are on the inside and got damn lucky that you're just as beautiful on the outside too. All I want now is a chance for us to be together."

He leaned over and gave me a soft kiss, and it made the world calm for a minute.

"That's what I want too. I mean I still feel like my head is spinning half the time, but I've never felt more at ease than with you by my side. Do you know what that's like for someone with anxiety?"

"I don't. But fuck does it make me happy to hear you say that."

"It means a lot, Dominik. More than you'll ever know."

He kissed me more intensely this time, and I hungrily met his lips, feeling closer to him than ever before. His hand smoothed over my thigh and crept up my waist as he closed in on me.

I glanced down at his slow, steady movements, my heart pounding in my chest. His eyes met mine and although I had resisted him before, I knew where things were going.

And there was no reason to control myself anymore.

"I won't tell you to stop this time," I whispered.

"Then don't."

Chapter Twenty-Three

ASPEN

ITH HIS INTENTIONS MADE LOUD AND CLEAR, I eagerly met his mouth, my insides ignited. He pushed me back onto the bed as I felt my heartbeat in my ears, my stomach in knots at the pure passion radiating from him.

Lips trailing down my neck, he sucked at my collarbone and moved one hand between my parted thighs, meeting my tongue for another wild kiss.

Breaking the kiss long enough to take a breath, I tore my shirt off, letting my breasts be fully exposed.

The air conditioning's chill left goosebumps down my skin; my nipples now pebbled.

Dominik's eyes were everywhere, unable to land on just one place as he took in my naked upper body.

"So beautiful."

He left small kisses down the tops of my shoulders, treating me so delicately and making me feel the most cherished I'd ever felt. His teeth grazed the tender flesh surrounding my nipples and I audibly gasped when his tongue darted out and stole a taste.

My hands instinctively clutched onto his hair, imbedding themselves into his curls.

"Perfect. So perfect, every part of you."

I'd never had a man praise me like he was, and it drove me

absolutely mad. Growing more restless, I hastily pulled my shorts and panties down, anxious to finally have him inside me.

Seeing how he wanted to savor the moment, and I wanted to have more action, we agreed on a happy medium.

His hands found their way to my inner thighs, slowly caressing the skin there before coming closer to my pussy. His fingers traced the slick folds, every inch of me soaking wet and waiting for him to do something.

"Please, Dominik," I begged, his featherlight touches clouding my mind.

He still watched me intently, loving how desperate I was for him and how effortlessly my body moved against him.

Finally giving in, his middle finger entered me slowly, gliding with ease at how wet I was. It did little to satiate the intense desire I was feeling, and I rolled my hips, desperate for more.

"I need more, Dominik. I need you inside me."

"Soon enough. Patience, Aspen."

His voice was low and strained, as if this was just as torturous for him.

He skillfully added another finger, curling both inside of me as he began to pick up his pace. His tongue unexpectedly began teasing my clit, sending a jolt of electricity down my spine. The combination of the two started a new sensation to begin weaving its way throughout my body, the jumble of nerves in my abdomen tightening.

"I'm—I'm going to come!"

It was less of a warning and more of an act of desperation, as he licked and pumped his fingers in me at an even more rapid pace, bringing me to my climax.

"Fuck, Dominik!"

The orgasm tore through me furiously, the air having escaped my lungs as I desperately tried to come back down to Earth.

Dominik was all too enamored by the effect he had on me, proud of having made me into a heaving, gasping puddle.

But we were far from done.

Unbuttoning his pants, he pulled them down quickly and shamelessly stroked himself. He reached into his wallet for a condom and rolled it on, as I waited for him still positioned at the end of the bed.

Better safe than sorry.

Bracing myself, I could feel him aligning his body to mine before sliding into me. Fingertips digging into my flesh, he held my hips in place as he took one long stroke and let out a loud groan. He sucked in a fast breath, as his slow entrance elicited a desperate whimper from me too.

"Fuck," he muttered. Gripping my hips for stability, he pulled out and started gaining a rhythm as he moved in time with me.

I felt every last inch of him inside, biting back moans as he stretched me out.

The heat pulsated between us as each thrust was nearly more plentiful than the last.

I was hanging on for dear life, with another orgasm already following the last one as the pressure steadily built within me.

"You feel so good," I managed to choke out through my moans, feeling my body about to reach its peak.

"Fuck yes. That's my girl."

A string of curses came from his mouth as his hands explored every inch of my body, grabbing, pulling, pinching. His mouth equally wanted action, kissing my neck and breasts before he buried his face into my shoulder.

I'd never come close to having this kind of Earth-shattering sex before and now that I knew what Dominik was capable of, there was no way I'd ever be able to stop.

My hair was stuck to my chest, my whole body covered in

sweat, and I was sure my cheeks were flushed. And yet I'd never felt more beautiful than I did when with him.

The pressure in my abdomen was about to explode, seconds from a blissful oblivion.

I opened my eyes to look at Dominik and felt another wave of pleasure crash through me as I saw a man who was everything and more to me. His hair had fallen in front of his eyes, and he leaned his head back in pleasure, close to his own release.

His guard was completely down, and so was mine. There was simply no measure that existed that could explain the closeness I felt to him now. I could physically feel how much he cared about me, regardless of whether the words were said.

On the edge of bliss, his thrusts continued to wrack my body, the most wonderful feeling creeping up and threading its way through me.

"Yes, yes Dominik!"

My muscles contracted, and my body was sent into another mind-blowing orgasm. Shaking, a high-pitched moan flooded the room as I gave myself over to the pleasure.

"Fuck, Aspen."

Dominik chased my orgasm, on the verge of his own climax. He reached it soon after, grunting my name as a low, deep groan was expelled over and over.

We both were panting, practically on another planet with the type of high we were feeling. After a minute, I carefully removed myself from him and he laid down onto the bed beside me.

Crawling to him, I buried my head into his large chest as I tried to catch my breath and let myself feel every emotion that was clawing its way through me.

Feelings of love. Of pleasure. A kind of connection unparallel to anything I'd ever experienced before.

Dominik's hand came around my face to stroke my hair, his breathing slowing.

A silence fell over us both, but it was comfortable. It was like we both knew how each other felt without words needing to be said. And whether or not he was feeling as scarily strong as I was, things had never felt more right.

I turned on my side and kissed him softly, ruffling his hair that had gotten all sweaty.

"So, you want to come shower with me or what?" I asked, breaking our silence. A smile crept on my face as he turned over to me and ruffled my hair right back.

His smile made the sun's rays look dim. "Most definitely."

Dominik followed me into the bathroom as I turned the shower water on.

I was then met with large arms wrapped around my naked body as he peppered me in kisses all over my face and neck.

"What are you doing?" I asked through a fit of laughter.

"Making it clear how insanely happy you make me."

I turned around and leaned into him, relief washing over me that he wasn't regretting anything that had led him to this point. Even with my guilt, I knew he was the only person that could make my world this bright.

And I didn't want to apologize for it anymore.

"You make me happier. Everything was absolutely perfect," I whispered, standing on my tiptoes to loop my arms around his neck.

I stole another long kiss, unable to control myself with just how happy I was to be with him.

He seemed to be content with that as I stepped into the large, tiled shower with him on my heels. The warm water pressure beating down my body was much needed after how exhausted I was.

The sex was amazing. But thoroughly exhausting.

As I began washing my body, Dominik's eyes fell to the droplets of water cascading down my breasts, and he was yet again hungry with desire. I just laughed silently to myself as I continued on.

"That was incredible you know," he said after a minute, as I washed all the soap off my body.

I could've tried to hide how satisfying it was to hear that, but he deserved some praise for how absolutely mind-blowing my orgasms were. They absolutely could not be topped.

"*You* were incredible," I said with a smirk, turning around to see his tall soapy self. As he rinsed off, his muscles flexed, and his hair was slicked back in a way I'd never seen before.

All I could do was stand there like an idiot, becoming hornier by the minute with how amazing he looked. The water streaming down his broad shoulders, the lustful glances he kept throwing at me.

If this was the way it was going to be from here on out, we sure had a lot more in store for the night.

Chapter Twenty-Four

ASPEN

FTER HAVING MY DESIRES FULLY SATED, *MORE THAN once,* I had never felt closer to Dominik. It was more than just sex, it was… something else entirely. I didn't want to assume the feeling because of my fear, but it was dangerously close to one I'd only thought I'd felt before.

I hadn't imagined it would happen so quickly, but the sheer bliss I felt was unable to be contained. I was honestly happy I'd be meeting my mother again in such a good headspace.

I had promised myself I was going to try, *really* try, to stay calm when seeing her.

Finding her phone number had been hard. I hadn't kept it from when I originally left home and ended up having to find her on Facebook. It was almost pathetic until I reminded myself why I left again. And that I was better off without her.

And yet despite knowing that, I still ached for her approval. For her to be proud of where I was in life and apologize for once for what she did to me.

Although I doubted that day would truly ever come.

I'd texted her that morning, nervous as all hell that she wouldn't even want to see me. But to my surprise, she'd agreed, even saying that she'd make sure Myles was home, so I'd be able to see him too.

I'd left out the small fact that someone was with me but

knowing her it likely wouldn't change anything. Maybe putting on a better front for him, but that was a reach.

By the time we'd pulled up to my old house, my nerves were shot. I was sweaty and clammy, my throat parched, and I was sure I was going to crap myself before I even walked through the door.

But there was a hand on my arm the entire time. Softly comforting me and reminding me that he was there. I found it quite amazing that Dominik somehow always knew the right way to get through to me, but he had proven to me that he was always watching.

I really wondered how I got so lucky.

Taking a deep breath and shaking out my nerves, I straightened my shoulders and got out of the car.

As we got closer to the front door, the urge to retreat was very strong. I hadn't imagined what being back at the house would trigger for me. All I wanted was to run away, to not be reminded of what my childhood was like.

"I'm right here," a soft voice whispered by the shell of my ear.

Dominik's reassurance gave me the strength to knock on the door at the exact time I told my mother I'd be there.

As soon as the door swung open, I was frozen in place.

Two years had gone by. And in those two years, my mother had been destroyed.

Wrinkles covered her skin, the lining of her eyes a soft purple hue. She looked worn and weathered in a way I'd never seen before. Her years of drinking had finally caught up to her.

"Hello, Mom," I smiled, trying to ignore her shocking new look.

"Penny," she said curtly. "And who would you be?"

Dominik never missed a beat and outstretched his hand.

"Dominik Kostopoulos, Mrs. Reddick."

Kostopoulos?

She eyed him up and down in a rather repulsive fashion, snatching his hand.

"Well, aren't you handsome? You must be, what, 6 foot 3?" she asked coquettishly. "And you can just call me Larissa, dear."

I cleared my throat aggressively. "Can we come in, Mom?"

She held the door open a hair wider, and I shook my head, forcing my way through.

I had to take a deep breath once inside, absolutely in shock at what I was seeing.

The house was in shambles.

Beyond the obvious trash that scattered the floors, and filthy wallpaper that was peeling, there was so much damage.

Pieces of cheap countertop chipped off in the kitchen, the hardwood floors scratched and stained. And my poor grandmother's floral high-backed chair had been destroyed, with a large split down the middle cushion.

"Oh, come on, Penny let's hear it," my mother snapped, catching my expression.

Egging me on, like always.

"I wasn't going to say anything, Mother," I said calmly, reining myself back in. "Can you tell me where Myles is?"

"Myles! Your sister is here!" she yelled loudly, making me wince.

Dominik's hand snaked around my back, and I was thankful for his touch. It kept me grounded when everything else inside me was screaming.

"Penny? You're here?" Myles said in disbelief.

I was astounded at how different he looked. He'd grown into his teenage looks, now towering over me and had cut his chestnut-colored hair short.

He came up and hugged me with such force that I felt every moment we'd missed in the past two years.

"I thought Mom told you I was coming? I've missed you so much, Myles," I smiled, trying to hold back tears.

"No, she hadn't told me. You look so different. Look at your hair!" he laughed, twirling one of the scarlet strands between his fingers.

"And you're not Lyle," he said bluntly, staring at Dominik.

"No, I'm not. I'm Dominik, it's nice to meet you, Myles."

He'd politely shaken Dominik's hand but was very wary of him.

"Lyle and I are no longer together," I announced. I hoped they wouldn't press the matter, although that wasn't normally how my mother rolled.

"That's a shame, Penny. He's on the radio all the time now, even on TV. I'd assumed you were living the high life now, neglecting your poor mother and only sibling in the process," she said while grabbing a cigarette from a nearby carton.

"No, Mother, that really wasn't the case. We had our differences, and he is following his new career. It's best if we just leave it at that."

"Oh Penny, don't act like that. You could've had a ring on your finger if you just sucked it up," my mother barked, grabbing a lighter for her cigarette. "No offense to you, honey."

Dominik tensed his jaw but had learned a long time ago how to handle people like my mother.

"That's okay Mrs. Reddick. He wasn't a very good fit for Aspen anyhow. We're quite happy together."

"Ugh, you call her by her real name? Her father named her that, God knows why. Just shorten it for Christ's sake."

Ouch.

If there was one thing my mother was good at, it was always making sure she jabbed at me every chance she got. As if I was somehow to blame for the downfall of her life.

"Aspen is a lovely name, for a lovely woman," he replied shortly.

Dominik wore a tight-faced smile, but he was ready to battle her head-on. My mother did little to hide that she knew she'd met her match.

"Well, isn't that sweet. And tell me then, Dominik, what exactly do you do for a living?"

"Provide. Protect. More than you ever did, I'm sure."

Fuck.

"Excuse me, I don't think you know who you're talking to. I changed my entire life to raise Penny!"

"You tell yourself that so you can sleep at night."

"Enough!" I snapped at them.

Dominik's cheeks were red, and he breathed out heavily, completely fired up in a way I'd never seen before.

"Dominik, please wait outside," I asked him sternly.

His lip twitched, and he was clearly ready to go a few more rounds with her but he backed down for my sake.

"Fine. I'll be outside," he said, holding a stare down with my mother until he left.

"What a keeper you've got there, Penny. You really left Lyle for him?" she scoffed.

"Mother, please stop trying to talk about things you don't understand! Lyle and I had to split, and it is okay! *I'm* okay, that's life!"

"You ruined your chance at having a good life! You could've had it all, and you threw it away for what? For him?"

"I love him!"

The words flew out and I shocked even myself with how passionately I'd said it. I had yet to completely come to terms with my feelings, but once out into the world, it felt right.

I managed to regain my ground with a few calming breaths and kept my hands at my side. There would be no fight from me.

"Yes, okay, I love him. And I intend for him to be a part of my life for a long time. If you cannot accept that then I might as well leave now."

"Stop the theatrics. Just go on," she groaned, waving her cigarette around.

"I wanted to make amends with you. We're staying in Dayton for the time being for us to figure out what's next and I wanted to be able to spend time with you and Myles."

"You're moving back here? Really? Well, isn't that just something," she muttered.

"Yes, for the time being. Look I'm trying really hard here to forgive you, Mom."

"For what! For doing my best to raise you as a single parent? I'm not perfect, Penny, but I did my damn best!"

"No, you didn't!" I scoffed. "I had to raise Myles all by myself, Mom! Do you know what it's like to be a teenager and watch everyone else live their lives but be stuck at home with a kid to watch?"

Her eyes narrowed to slits, the anger only building as she realized I wasn't going to back down this time.

"Of course, you don't. You got drunk the second your ass touched that couch when you got home from work. I'm guessing you still do the same old thing, don't you Mom? Just now it's Myles having to live through it."

"Don't you dare talk to me that way, you ungrateful child! Myles is a good boy, no thanks to you."

"No thanks to me? The reason he's even in one piece is because I spent all of high school raising him! He was practically mine!"

"Don't use that tone with me anymore! I won't tolerate your disrespect in my home!"

"It's *grandmother's* home, you bitch! And she was a better mother than you'll ever be!"

My mother slapped me across my face, sending me stumbling.

Gulping down the pain, and hatred, and tears, I straightened my back.

Don't let her see you cry.

"You will never be my mother. I came here to make amends, but I see you aren't capable of that. I will not hesitate to call Child Protective Services to protect Myles. So, I suggest you sober up before he is taken out of here and you're in prison."

I didn't give her time to respond and silently went back to my brother's bedroom, finding him crouched in his closet like he always used to do when my mother and I would fight. As much as I'd tried to control my anger, I was pushed too far. And now I regretted it.

"Hey bud, I'm sorry about that."

"It's just like old times," he sighed, tucking his knees close to his chest.

"You would tell me if mom wasn't being good to you, right? If you're being neglected?"

"I make do, Penny. It's how I survive."

The words cut through me, piercing my heart.

He was experiencing the same life I did. But at a much younger age.

And I couldn't bear knowing that I'd left him this fate. By going out and trying to live a life for myself, I subjected him to this life. This awful, terrible life with the woman who had the audacity to call herself our mother.

"Okay, Myles, I'm giving you my phone number. You text me and we'll find somewhere to meet outside of all this. Don't tell mom where you're going, okay? I'm staying in town for a little while with Dominik so we can see each other."

"Okay, I guess. But won't Mom find out?"

"It'll be our secret. Dominik is a bodyguard for some really cool famous people, so he has some experience with protecting. You'll be safe when you're with us, okay?"

"If you say so. I missed you a lot, Penny," he sighed, hugging me. "And you'll always be the one who raised me."

I was at peace hearing him acknowledge that.

It made all those years of struggle and heartache worth it. But I couldn't give up on him now. Not when I'd finally given him a glimpse of hope and getting out of the hell hole my mother was raising him in.

"I'll see you soon. Just do your best to stay out of her hair. We'll figure something out."

He smiled at me, and my heart grew even more full if that was even possible.

"Love you, Penny."

I hugged him one last time, and then made a beeline for the front door. I didn't stop, I didn't look around, and kept my eyes only on what was in front of me.

Just like Dominik had taught me.

I opened the car door harshly, slamming it shut.

"Let's get out of here."

Chapter Twenty-Five

ASPEN

"**P**LEASE TALK TO ME ASPEN."

Dominik had been asking me for hours once back at the hotel to say something, *anything* about what happened after he left.

But I was frozen. Still stuck between wanting to set fire to that godforsaken house, and wanting to cry myself a river that my mother was still so cruel.

It was as if the two years had never even happened with how quickly I went back to that dark place. I hadn't realized that she still had such an effect on me, and I hated that she did.

Because now I was taking it out on Dominik when he was the only person to ever understand me or try to defend me against her.

I just felt so numb by the time we got back to the hotel. Tossing up every possible outcome of Myles' life, and what would happen if I resumed responsibility for him. Thoughts that I shouldn't have entertained with my life so unstable.

Especially with Dominik now a part of things. I couldn't just consider myself anymore, and although it felt prisoning at first, I didn't at all regret this.

Because seeing Dominik next to me every day brought me more joy than I ever imagined.

He looked at me with such concern in his eyes as he brought my hand to his chest.

"You know I'm with you every step of the way. I'm not going to judge you for whatever happened between you and your mom."

With my hand by his heart, I had to mentally pause before replying.

It's safe. He won't hurt you.

"My mom and I fought again like always. I told her I wanted to make amends and she's just not capable of that. It reached a breaking point and she hit me."

"She what?" His tone was dark, dangerous.

"She slapped me, okay? I told her that my grandmother was a better mother than she ever was, and that I was the one who raised Myles."

"Aspen…" he said slowly, rolling his wrists to prevent them from turning into fists. "Tell me that you did something in response. Tell me that you stuck up for yourself before I drive back there."

"I…took the high road."

"There is no high road in this scenario, Aspen. Not for me."

I knew he meant well, and I'd be lying if I said it didn't feel good to have someone sticking up for me for once. But it was so much more complex than that.

"I went and found my brother hiding in his closet like he did in elementary school when my mother and I would fight. I didn't need to scare him anymore."

Dominik pinched the bridge of his nose and shook his head.

"Well, I don't know if I can be mad at you for that. I'm sure Myles needed you at that moment, and I'm glad you went and comforted him."

"I'm just really worried about him. I mean you saw the house. It was an absolute mess."

"That's not my place to comment on where your family lives.

I understand things are tough right now for them and I certainly didn't grow up in a palace, so I get it."

Such a gentleman. He wouldn't say it, but it was a pathetic excuse for a home.

"It's more than just that though, it's all of it," I sighed. "I told her that I would call CPS if I found out she was neglecting him. Myles wouldn't tell me it straight, but I'm pretty sure she's doing the same shit she did with me. Drinking until she passes out on the couch, yelling at him, not making sure he has what he needs for school."

I ran my hand over my face, my stress levels increasing just thinking about what he was having to experience every day. "And look, if that's the case, it means he's also trying to cook for both of them at fourteen years old, likely on whatever little cash our mom didn't spend on booze. He's too young for all this."

"Oh, Aspen. I'm so sorry."

He wrapped me in a tight hug, and I melted into his embrace, feeling like the world had stopped caving in on me for a minute.

"I don't know what to do. Two years ago, when I left them, I was just so anxious to get out that I didn't even care about what I'd be subjecting Myles to. It's my fault he's dealing with this now."

"Don't say that. It's not your fault that your mom is an alcoholic that neglects her kids. You couldn't have stayed there forever, Aspen."

"But look at the mess I left behind," I cried, my voice cracking as a tear slid down my cheek.

"We can figure this out together. If you want to take Myles out of this situation, then I'll do what I can to help support you. But it doesn't look like it'll be easy. I'm sure your mom will fight it every step of the way."

I shook my head, absolutely not about to pull him into this disaster that was my family life.

"I can't ask that of you. We haven't even had a chance to really be together, Dominik. I can't let you take on all my baggage like this."

"I'm in it for the long haul, Aspen. You really think I care about what other people think? Because I don't. I don't care about how long we've actually been together, or anything else. You're here, and you're mine. That is all I care about."

I melted at his words, giving him my heart in his hands. It was like we were both still dancing around those three words despite knowing that I had never felt this way about anyone before. Not even with Lyle.

He wouldn't let go of me the whole night. Pressing soft kisses to my cheek where a red hue still glowed, leaving a hand on my thigh or my back just to assure me he was still there.

I had never been more grateful before to have met him. To have someone there that provided me that kind of comfort amongst my hurricane of negative thoughts, to be with me every step of the way. It was something I tried every day not to take for granted.

The next morning, I woke up still attached to his side and ran my hand over his bare chest. I always loved that he slept shirtless, and he did too considering I rarely kept my hands to myself.

But I had to get up, seeing that the time on the blinking analog clock already said nine.

I pulled myself out of bed and got my shit together. As easy as it would have been to fall back into the depths of depression, I had to start trying to get my life together. Especially if I wanted any chance of helping Myles.

Leaving Dominik still sleeping peacefully, I took a quick shower to distract my thoughts and put together a casual outfit.

Quietly sliding my laptop out of my bag to not wake him, I started browsing for job openings in town. I looked at anything I could get without a college degree that could help us qualify and make first and last for an apartment.

Dominik had put away a lot in savings, but I was in no way going to rely on him for everything, nor expect him to pay for an entire apartment for us.

If I was going to do this, then I wanted to do it the right way.

I found a few, slightly awful job listings that would be fine to get me by for the time being. They were minimum wage cashier or food service jobs, but I wasn't in a position to be picky. I was limited in the radius I could look in since I didn't have a car either. Yet another hindrance for us.

"Good morning," Dominik said huskily, his voice still deep with sleep.

"Morning, baby," I called over to him.

He walked over to the plush hotel chair I was sitting in, wrapping his bare arms around me.

"Baby? What an upgrade. I feel pretty special now," he joked, kissing my cheek.

"Well, I figured this far along, it's only fair. I can't call you Dom if you don't call me Pen. Has to be equal," I giggled. "Although I'm interested now in what Kostopoulos could possibly mean. Is your last name not actually Kostas?

"After hearing your mother's remarks about your name, I will happily only call you Aspen. And yes, it is, it's just very long," he joked, sitting down next to me. "I'd also much prefer any pet name to Dom. The boys called me that a lot."

I turned myself toward him, and asked him genuinely, "Do you miss them? Koen and everyone else on your team?"

"Not really. They were mostly just my coworkers. Koen and I have stayed good acquaintances, and he understands my situation. Plus, he's kept me updated on the tour still so it's nice to have someone on the inside."

"Wait really? Why wouldn't you say that you're still getting info from him?"

He shrugged his shoulders, getting up and grabbing a clean shirt from his luggage.

"It's not a big deal. My job was to protect you then, and it's still to protect you now. You don't need to know about some of the stuff going on, okay?"

"No. No way am I taking that for an answer. Spill it."

He sighed heavily, appearing apprehensive about revealing this to me.

"Elissa is still convinced you're coming back. Christian is talking to the press now about anything not in his NDA, likely because of that whole charade when he got fired. And apparently, it's bad enough that Clara flew in to talk to Elissa about damage control considering Lyle's reputation is on the line."

I paused, quite surprised that Christian would take that route in going against Lyle. I hadn't heard anything about it either, which made me feel pretty out of touch in comparison to Dominik.

"Wow, that's a lot. Christian must be really upset to have pulled a move like that. I'm not happy about things either, but I'm not spiteful enough to want Lyle to fail."

I didn't think so, at least.

"Koen told me so I could prepare you before you saw this somewhere else, I just hadn't wanted to say anything yet after everything with your mother," he said wincing. "But Christian is apparently trying to spread rumors about Lyle cheating on you."

"What? He knew?"

"Yes. I…think there were quite a few people that knew."

Okay, I was aware that Koen and the bus driver knew, given

that they were usually with Lyle or had seen him with someone. But who else could have known?

"What does quite a few mean?"

"From my understanding… everyone but Harlow pretty much. I'm sorry."

Everyone? Oh my god.

"That many people knew and didn't tell me? The whole security team knew too?"

"I…"

"Spit it out, Dominik! How long did you know?"

"Yes, we all knew. I found out right after I joined the tour. Lyle more or less confessed to me."

"And you really didn't think to tell me that for months? Did you cover for him?"

"No! Of course not. But I didn't know you then like I do now. It wasn't my place to drop that kind of bomb on you."

"That's a sorry excuse, Dominik. You really knew for that long and still looked me in the face every day acting like everything was fine? Even for you, that's just cruel."

I hastily gathered my phone and purse, shoving my shoes on my feet.

"Aspen, I'm sorry, I made a mistake!"

"Yes, Dominik. You did."

I slammed the hotel room door shut behind me, racing outside so I could catch my breath and have a moment away from him.

I was so conflicted, feeling a mixture of emotions. The fact that everyone on that goddamn tour bus knew what was going on but me, and still looked me in the face like nothing was wrong… it made me furious.

They'd seen girls come in and out, maybe even escorted them there. And yet no one ever had the courage to come and tell me.

For months.

Dominik knowing so early on felt like a knife through my heart.

It wasn't about the fact that he didn't know me that well, or thought he was overstepping. It was about him not doing the right thing. Him not telling me sooner once we got closer and started to form a kind of friendship.

But frankly it shouldn't have even mattered if he'd just met me that day. I thought he was the kind of man who'd never let that shit fly, or at least would've given me some kind of hint so I'd figure it out myself.

And yet instead I had to wait for months before someone would say something.

I just felt so stupid. Stupid for believing in Lyle, that the fame wouldn't get to his head. Stupid for prancing around the tour bus like a complete idiot and sleeping in a bed he brought another girl in.

But mostly, stupid for lashing out at Dominik.

While I knew some of my anger toward him was unfair and who I really was upset with was Lyle, I just hated that he knew for so long. No one wants to feel like an idiot when it comes to their relationship, and he basically let me walk around with it written on my forehead.

My gripes with him about the situation could wait for later though. I needed to figure out what the actual hell I was going to do with Christian trying to speak out to the press.

The whole time I didn't think he was the spy, but now I was convinced he'd had some kind of ulterior plan while he'd been with us. Or at least had taken note of any kind of dirt possible to use for later.

If Christian was going to drop this news to the world, Lyle would be in seriously hot water. And *I* would be the collateral. I didn't want to be known for that, or to have my face plastered all over bogus news sites. Wanting to live in peace and start a new chapter for myself didn't coincide with being tomorrow's news story.

I wanted it gone.

For the story to be destroyed and buried and for whoever knew about it to be paid under the table not to run it. But I didn't have those capabilities.

Scrolling through my phone, I found Clara's contact and dialed the number with shaky hands.

"Aspen? Is that you, love?"

"It's me, Clara. Listen, we've got to talk."

And by the end of the conversation, I'd booked a plane ticket to L.A. to meet with her and the record label directly.

My life felt back in my hands for once as I took the reins on the situation.

There was no way I was going down without a fight.

Chapter Twenty-Six

ASPEN

I HURRIED BACK TO THE HOTEL ROOM TO PACK A QUICK BAG I could bring with me.

I almost had whiplash from all the moving around different states recently, but I couldn't just let this story hit the front covers without trying to do something about it.

Returning to the room, I had planned to just ignore Dominik and get my things together without having to face him, but he was already waiting for me.

"Where did you go?"

"I just went downstairs for a few minutes. I needed to clear my head," I said casually as I started grabbing some spare clothes to pack.

"No. You don't get to storm away from me anymore without hearing what I have to say," he demanded.

I stopped throwing my clothes back in my duffel bag and turned around to face him.

"Alright, talk," I said, crossing my arms over my chest.

"There are a thousand reasons why I didn't tell you. I didn't want to be the one who broke your heart. I didn't want to see you fall apart and have been the one that caused it. I had just met you and already was infatuated."

The angry tears that had brimmed in my eyes were slowly changing into something else.

"You don't understand how hard I fell for you, Aspen. I had blocked women from my thoughts for years, solely focused on my work and making it through each day. But then there you were. Annoying and angsty yet undeniably beautiful."

As a stray tear fell from my eye, a laugh escaped.

"I could tell. You stared at me like a creep for a while, so it wasn't that big of a secret," I joked as my anger began to wane slightly.

"I couldn't help it. You were like a drug to me, and to have you so close all the time and not be able to touch you was torture. But let me make one thing clear," he said, bringing his hand to cup my cheek. "I do not regret what happened. Because if I would've told you that early on, we never would have had that time together. We wouldn't be here right now, and I can't stand to think about that."

"I…hadn't looked at it like that," I sighed. "And I am so happy to have met you, despite the circumstances. I was just so hurt. It's hard enough to know you were being cheated on for months and not feel like a total idiot, but then to add on the knowledge that everyone else knew?"

"And I'm sorry I hurt you, I really am. But I can't take you walking away from me again like that. I'm always here to talk it out. You just have to communicate with me."

I wrapped my arms around him tightly, nestling my head in the crook of his shoulder.

"I'm sorry. It was just my first reaction to all the pain I felt, and I'm not used to taking another person's feelings into account when I react the way I do. That wasn't fair of me to do."

He released me for a second but looked me directly in the eye.

"You haven't been in a good enough relationship before to have had the chance to create healthy boundaries or meaningful communication. I don't hold it against you. I just want you to understand that you don't have to run away from me. I'm right here, Aspen."

'I'm going to work on it. I promise," I said, kissing him lightly. "And no more secrets either. Like the last name. I would've loved to have known that before my mother did."

"Ah yes, that would be valid. It's just not something I'm forthcoming about."

"But why? Kostopoulos is a nice name. I quite like the sound of it. It's very—"

"Greek? Long?"

"Very *you*," I interjected.

"Well, we're all supposed to use variations of names for security anyway. Just in case something happens. I never really bothered to explain to anyone that it wasn't my real name, but I suppose I could adapt it again," he joked.

I smiled at that. "Speaking of no more secrets, I guess I have nothing to hide anymore. I took matters into my own hands while I was out there. I sort of called Clara when I was out there and… I have a meeting now with the record label in L.A. I'm trying to get the story squashed before it hits the news."

"So, Clara just went and bought another plane ticket for you? No hesitation?"

"Wait, you aren't mad at me?"

"No, because I'm coming with you."

I sighed, shaking my head. "Dominik, you can't do that. I have to fight this on my own."

"It can be your battle to win. But I will be right by your side. I told you before, anywhere you go, I'll follow."

"But…I can't help but feel guilty. We've only been here in town a week and now we're having to go again. I just want to settle down for a while."

He grabbed my waist, and pulled me close to his chest, comforting me.

"So do I. But I have a feeling you won't be able to if you just let this go. You want to be out of the limelight and these pricks just want another story. It can't go on like this."

"This is such a hot mess. I wanted to cut ties with that world for good," I whined.

"I know. But maybe this will finally give you closure. So, we can move on with our lives and leave this world in the past. If this story is buried, there is nothing else left to connect you to Lyle."

"I'm sorry for dragging you through this. I'm ready to move on with my life. With *you*," I emphasized, threading my fingers through his large ones.

"Well lucky for you, traveling is what I do. I'll call Clara to figure out what flight she put you on. If she won't let me get a ticket, I'll book one myself."

"I can't believe I'm doing this, but I'm ready to end this. Let's get ready to check out, I guess. It's certainly not how I planned on this day going, but life just always works out that way for me."

He kissed my cheek, and stroked my hair softly, which made me feel a lot better about things.

"We'll be back, okay? And we can still try and work on your brother and helping him out when we return. This is just temporary."

"I know, it's just bringing back those feelings of when I first left," I sighed. "But I think I should have time to stop by the house in Calabasas and pack up what I left there. It wasn't much, but I'd like to have everything out of there for good."

"You got it. I'll call us an Uber now to take us over there, and we can end this."

Clara begrudgingly agreed to get Dominik on the same flight to accompany me. But she was not very happy about it. Whether she'd tell me directly or not, I was very aware that me leaving Lyle had thrown off her own plans.

Thankfully the flight wasn't very full, and Dominik was completely unphased by traveling again so soon. I still got sweaty palms when we ascended and hated the feeling of the pressure changing.

The only difference was that I had someone now to be my rock. He didn't question when I'd grip onto his arm suddenly or close my eyes and have to take slow breaths to calm myself down.

I also was completely in my head about how I'd reacted earlier to the whole cheating thing. It was such an instinctual feeling to run away, and I hadn't even tried to talk things out with him.

But I was still learning. I hadn't been with someone who actually fought for me and tried to work things out instead of giving me the silent treatment.

And instead of trying to beat myself up over it, I tried to change my thinking on it instead. I actually worked on giving myself some grace and trying to learn from my mistakes. Who knew I was capable of such a thing?

By the time we touched down at LAX, I was so ready to get it over with and start a new life with Dominik.

I didn't want to be there any longer than necessary and to keep things as clean as possible. No messy feelings, no arguments. Just simple and to the point.

Clara was waiting for us when we got past baggage claim.

"Pen! I missed you so much sweetheart," she said, hugging my neck.

"And you must be Dominik. I see now why Pen is with you," she joked, looking him up and down.

"Glad you two have finally met. But please tell me you have a car to take us out of here. This airport is like hell on Earth," I groaned.

"You got it, babe."

We'd gone from the Eastern time zone to the Pacific which left us with a three-hour time difference. It was only two in the afternoon despite having left quite a long time ago which felt weird in my head.

A black Escalade rolled up outside the glass sliding doors as the bright and sunny California sky welcomed us.

"Alright guys so the meeting is at four, and the lawyer I work with will be there too. Now there'll be a few key players there from the label, and they are not to be underestimated. Denise is the head of Public Relations and she'll be really important to win over. John is the one who handles all the dealing between companies and Robert is the owner of the label who is one tough cookie."

"Okay, that sounds pretty bad. How will I convince them to kill the story?"

"We're going to sell the hell out of why they shouldn't. What you know, what you'd be willing to go on air and say to defend yourself. This is some legal stuff now sweetheart, and they *will* fight dirty."

I buckled my seatbelt and looked over at her confused.

"But I don't actually want to do that?"

"Of course, but we have to make it seem like you will. We have to play hard and prove to them that we can't be walked over. I'll be there to say anything you need me to, and the lawyer Jasmine will have your back too."

"Thank you, I really appreciate it, Clara."

"Not a problem. Lyle will also, uh, be there as well," she said partially under her breath.

"What?"

"Oh, trust me I tried to get him to stay back. But he took the one day break the tour had and flew here overnight. He wasn't kidding."

That was the only thing I was banking on to not make this

meeting completely awful. It seemed everything would be out of the bag once I showed up with Dominik.

"Oh my god, this is a nightmare," I groaned. "Why is he coming!"

"I can't say why or what side he'll be on. He hardly told me anything. We just have to hope for the best."

She went to look back at her iPad but paused for a second.

"Will you be coming Dominik?"

"Yes ma'am. For Aspen."

"Well, isn't that cute," she said sarcastically. "It might help us. Might not. But this will surely be interesting."

Chapter Twenty-Seven

ASPEN

I WAS COMPLETELY ON EDGE BY THE TIME THE MEETING rolled around.

Dominik tried his best to calm my nerves, but I was a mess. My anxiety was at an all-time high and knowing Lyle was going to be there just made it that much worse.

"Alright Aspen, are you ready?" Clara asked over the shoulder of her seat in the Escalade that came and picked us up.

I shot Dominik a nervous glance and swallowed the lump in my throat.

"As ready as I'll ever be."

I ran my hands over my black skirt that reached my knees, having grabbed the only semi-professional looking clothes I had when we went to the new hotel.

I'd certainly be glad when we didn't have to keep switching hotels.

As we approached the large multi-story building, my nerves heightened even more. I hadn't been to the label since Lyle signed his first record deal.

Stepping out of the SUV, Dominik rubbed his hand over my back reassuringly as Clara led us up the stairs and through the front door.

Piled high with large windows and a shiny exterior, the building seemed even larger once inside. Only the best furnishings in each waiting area, and a stream of platinum and gold records on the walls from all the artists they represented.

We were shuffled to the sitting area and told we had to wait for everyone to arrive.

"I don't know if I can do this," I murmured, my clammy fingers a tight grip on the edge of my skirt.

"Yes, you can. This is what we came here to do, and we're going to settle it once and for all. I'll be right here the whole time," Dominik reassured me.

"I promise it'll be over before you know it. I'm on your side and will defend you every step of the way. I even have an angle I can use for Dominik to help us out." Clara tried to comfort me, although it didn't help so much.

"Okay, okay, that's good," I said shakily.

I clenched my knees together to ease my nerves as my stomach churned. Dominik kept a hand on my back as an attempt to soothe me. Too bad I couldn't really be soothed.

After a few minutes, the large front doors opened and the lawyer, Jasmine walked in.

She was quite attractive, a petite frame on gorgeous Louboutin's that gave her a few extra inches.

"Hello, you must be Aspen," she smiled, shaking my hand.

"Yes, and this is my boyfriend Dominik. Thank you so much for coming today." She shook Dominik's hand, and I caught him smirking at being introduced as my boyfriend for the first time as we sat back down.

Lyle walked in soon after, although I hardly recognized him. Sporting some new fancy jacket, a ridiculously expensive watch that caught the light, and his hair gelled back to appear somewhat more professional.

Gross.

He spotted us immediately, taking his sunglasses off and sliding them down his gray acid washed t-shirt.

"Aspen, Clara," he said curtly acknowledging us.

His eyes wandered to where Dominik's hand now possessively gripped my thigh.

"Well, well and I see you brought your boy toy with you. Interesting, the kind of game you're playing, Pen."

"There is no game here," Dominik replied darkly.

"Didn't address you. And it wouldn't matter anyway. Two can play at this game," Lyle grinned.

Dominik's grip on me only tightened as Lyle practically undressed me with his eyes. I refused to make eye contact, but then something clicked for him, and he addressed me directly.

"Aspen, I need to talk to you. Privately."

I looked around nervously, not wanting to betray Dominik who was in clear protection mode. But if it was something related to the story, then I needed to know. I glanced over at Clara, who was consulting with Jasmine, and she nodded her head.

"I'll just be a minute," I whispered to Dominik as I eased myself out of his grip.

The hurt in his eyes made me want to die.

Lyle was all too pleased with himself, thinking he'd got a leg up on him.

He led me back to one of the secluded hallways in the back of the building.

"What's going on, Pen? Why're we doing all this? Come back on tour with me, and we can work everything out."

He tried to grip my neck and bring me closer to him, but I was quick to remove his hand.

"*No.* Maybe I didn't make it clear enough but when I walked out that day, I was leaving you for good. I don't want anything to do with you, Lyle."

"Baby, you don't mean that. I love you, more than anything. I want us to be together again," he pleaded, once more trying to kiss me.

I dodged him again but was growing more agitated.

"No, I do mean it. I'm going to get my stuff from the house and then you will never see me again."

"Fuck that. Are you doing this because of Dominik? He's a total fucking loser, Aspen. He can't give you a fraction of what I can. You could be taken care of for the rest of your life; we could be a family."

His voice graveled with desperation, and I had enough of his games.

"I don't want that, and I don't want you. You cheated on me, Lyle! Who knows how many times, and you don't even feel sorry for it."

"Baby, that's just how this world is. I am sorry, and I do regret it. Because being without you has been awful on tour. Elissa and Harlow always give me dirty looks and they see me differently now. We can still work this out."

He attempted to grab my waist, but there was no way in hell I was letting that happen.

That was the last time he tried to put his hands on me, as I forcibly removed them this time and pushed his arms down at his sides.

"That's not how this world works, and the old Lyle never would've done something like that. And Dominik surely wouldn't either. He can give me as good a life as anyone else. You need to get up off your high horse and have a fucking reality check."

"Oh, come on! He doesn't even have a job, Aspen! And he doesn't love you the way I do."

"Wait, how do you know that? Oh my god, are you why he got fired from the company?"

"I know people in high places. And anyone can be bought out. I got rid of him and finally Koen too, the fucking backstabber he was."

I scoffed but felt the final nail in the coffin go in at his admittance of how he fucked with their livelihoods.

"You are so much worse than I ever thought. I can't believe who you've become. You're not the Lyle I first met. The fame went to your head, and I hope for your sake you come back down to Earth one day. Because if this story runs, you're ruined."

"No, you are. I'll see you inside, Aspen. Go get your dog, who I'm sure is already playing sit. You're a fucking liar and just as much to blame. I'm sure you fucked him as soon as you could."

"Don't forget that I know your secrets, Lyle. And unlike you, I don't immediately betray the person I'm with just because I feel attraction to someone else. Although now I certainly wish I had. If you would've paid attention for just a second, you would've seen what was actually going on, but your head was up your ass instead. I'll see you inside."

I stormed away before he could get the last word in.

I walked back to the waiting area and Dominik immediately got up when he saw me.

"Everything okay?"

"It'll be fine, Lyle is just a dick. I really want this over with," I groaned, completely flustered from my run-in with him.

"It will be soon enough. Lyle needs to be put in his place, damn it."

"Yes, he does but not by you. I don't want you getting involved with him," I tried to counter.

"We'll see about that. If he tries to fuck you over in this meeting, then we'll have a real problem."

Before I could disagree with him again, a tall man came out from a hallway and motioned us over.

"Show time," Clara whispered to me.

Breathing in and out slowly, I followed Clara, Jasmine, and the unknown man to a large conference room where other executives were already waiting. Lyle was cutting up with one of them already as he tried to intimidate us. Great.

We sat around a large mahogany table as the man who led us in then sat at the head.

"Clara, very good to see you as always. Jasmine, you look ravishing," the man said with a phony smile stretched across his face.

He then situated his gaze on me and Dominik who was very possessively leaned over my side.

"You must be Aspen. Very pleased to meet you," he beamed, stretching his hand across the table for me to shake.

"Yes, very nice to meet you as well sir."

"And that leaves you, Mr. Kostas. I've heard much about you."

He didn't attempt to shake Dominik's hand.

"Likewise," he said with zero emotion on his face.

Whether Dominik realized it or not, he'd gone completely into protection mode.

"I'm Robert Newman. That's Denise Pritchard, John Forthright, and of course you already know Lyle," he introduced, motioning to each executive by us. "Let's get this started, shall we?"

Of course, he was Robert. Only the owner of the label would know how to work a table like he was.

"Robert, you know we wouldn't be here if we didn't see it as absolutely necessary. Aspen here is still reeling from these revelations," Clara said motioning to me.

"Is that so? You don't seem that upset to me," he commented while looking at the man draped across my arm.

"That is not what this discussion is about," I gritted out.

"Exactly. This is about having Aspen's image being defaced and toyed with to help Lyle's ratings. I don't think this will pay off in the way you think," Jasmine explained.

"Nonsense. Any publicity is good publicity, especially

when Lyle can pull the victim card just as easily. We have no reason to not go forth with these articles running," Denise said condescendingly.

She might as well had her nose upturned with the way she so callously spoke about destroying my life.

"Clara hun, I get what you're trying to do but the deals have already been set up. We can't change that now just because Miss Reddick might be affected by this," the ghastly old man John said.

"Might be affected? No, that's some kind of joke. My entire life will be ruined if this happens. I've already tried as best as I could to stay out of the media, and yet look at how well it worked out," I said motioning to my face.

"Yes, I recall that's why Mr. Kostas and his team was hired. Some fan incident at one of the shows?"

"It wasn't just some 'fan incident.' I have a scar across my chin now from the violence that night, and a fan intentionally causing me to fall. I had to go to the hospital and get stitches, and am now left with this," I punctuated, pointing at my chin. "So, that is an understatement."

"Huh," he said, examining my face. "I didn't notice that at first. Well, we provided the team to try and assist with that nonetheless."

He turned his eyes to Dominik who fiercely met his gaze.

"I'm still not seeing the issue here," Denise said with an annoyance in her tone.

"Denise let's be clear here. This is a 21-year-old woman who's trying to figure her life out right now. She's decided to live a normal life away from the spotlight, and this will only drag her right back into it. I'm sure there is another way we can positively promote Lyle's image in the media. Right, Lyle?" Jasmine asked him.

Lyle, who had been completely silent and shooting daggers at Dominik, tore his eyes away from us and turned to Jasmine.

"Sure, we could do something else. But this just seems so much more fun," he smirked.

"Lyle, stop being childish. We're already trying to turn this story to your benefit. If you didn't have the team you did, I'm sure the outcome would be very different," John said, staring him down.

He bit his tongue from saying anything else and shifted in his seat.

"And again, John and Denise, I know that you guys work very hard to ensure Lyle has the best image possible. But Aspen does not belong in your narrative," Jasmine said.

Her and Clara were taking turns working them but were still met with much resistance.

"Alright then, say we get the stories buried. How can we make sure that Miss Reddick stays permanently out of the media and won't talk like Christian?"

"We can do contracts drawn up by Jasmine, or—" Clara started.

"No. There is no way you'll ever know if I'll speak or not. I know enough about Lyle and his life before the fame that could destroy him. I'm sure any one of your rival media sites would happily run with my story."

Robert raised his head, staring me up and down. I doubted he believed I had it in me.

"Oh, please. Honey, no one would touch your story with a ten-foot pole with nothing to back it up," Denise laughed.

"You seem very sure of yourself. I have photos of Lyle at a party in only his underwear, wasted beyond belief. Him in a strip club for his 18th birthday that an old friend gave me. A video of him saying controversial things that could most certainly do more damage than I ever could."

I watched closely as the executives all started to grow

worried, attempting not to show it by shifting their weight and position.

Lyle had no idea all the things I kept from him when we were together. I guess in a way I had secured my own future by doing so, although I hadn't planned on that being the case.

Dominik patted my thigh reassuringly, as we both knew we had them now.

Lyle was breathing so heavily across the table, I thought he was going to explode.

"I see now, Miss Reddick. I believe we can work something out then," Robert said begrudgingly.

"Certainly. We can do a private deal with the deletion of said materials on Aspen's devices in exchange for the story not to be run," Denise claimed, now playing nice.

"No. If you want me gone for good, I want a financial deal too."

John choked back a laugh. "Come on, the deletion of the story is enough. Don't get greedy now."

Jasmine saw the angle I was pulling and ran with it.

"John, you can cancel your deals with the news sites and still make a couple million. So will the rest of you. Aspen's just asking for a small cut as a thank you for her silence and allowance for you to go through her devices and ensure Lyle's image is maintained."

Robert cleared his throat. "And what exactly qualifies as a small cut, Jasmine?"

There wasn't really a specific amount I had in mind when I'd blurted that out. I had made it all up as I went along so I trusted Jasmine as a lawyer to know what was reasonable enough.

"One million."

I choked on my own breath. She couldn't be serious.

"That's ridiculous, Jasmine, come on now. We can come to a fair agreement, I'm sure," Robert tried to reason with her.

"Fine, two million then. You'll get a two for one deal and have Aspen's compliance as well as a Non-Disclosure Agreement from Dominik."

Dominik chuckled to himself. I knew he liked the sound of that.

"Alright, Aspen I can try to understand but the bodyguard too? What could he possibly know?"

"Oh, you know, just the names of every girl he fucked on tour. It's a running list actually. Koen, the bodyguard who has been up Lyle's ass for the past couple months, gladly helped me out with putting the list together. I'm sure it being out into the world wouldn't be a good look for Mr. Hawthorne," Dominik smirked.

Oh shit.

Whether or not Dominik just pulled that out of his ass didn't matter.

The executives were now thoroughly rattled.

"You're your own worst enemy, you know that?" John whispered at Lyle through gritted teeth.

Robert contemplated this information for a minute, though I didn't know if he already had an answer ready or not.

"Alright fine, you've got a deal. Get together the contracts for tomorrow, Jasmine. Dominik, get this 'Koen' here since he's now involved in this mess too."

Success.

"And after tomorrow, I will never see or hear a trace of the two of you again. Are we clear?"

"Crystal," I smiled.

Chapter Twenty-Eight

ASPEN

SUCCESS HAD NEVER FELT SWEETER.

Walking out of the building hand and hand with Dominik, I couldn't have been more pleased with how things went down. I felt like a weight had finally been lifted off my shoulders and that I could move on with my life.

With a healthy amount of money to help us out.

I surely hadn't planned on having that much money be a part of the deal, but once Jasmine brought up the two million, it set our deal in stone.

"So, is what you said about the list true? That Koen helped make it?" I asked Dominik at the bottom of the steep cement stairs to the building.

"Not really. It was a bit of an exaggeration, but I did have a few names stored in my brain. Koen is the one who really has it all written down," he said casually. "I'm sorry I didn't have time to tell you before. Is that okay?"

"I don't care," I laughed. "It's Lyle's downfall, not mine. Just further proves to me that he really is a piece of shit. I have no idea why he thought he could get me back today after all that."

"He *what*?"

Shit. I didn't want to bring that up, knowing how Dominik would react. I guess the cat was out of the bag now.

"When he pulled me aside, he wanted me to drop everything

and get back together with him. Tried to sell me on this idea of marrying him and whatever other bullshit. I told him I wanted to get my stuff from the house and never see him again."

"That fucker," he yelled. "I'm going to kill him."

Sure enough, Lyle was walking out of the building at the same time. Bad timing on his part.

Dominik raced back up the stairs, pushing Lyle's chest harshly.

"The fuck is wrong with you? Trying to put hands on her, pulling that shit when she's with me?"

"Calm down, you got what you wanted. What're you going to do, pull a gun on me?" Lyle said cockily.

"No, but I can do this."

Dominik raised his fist and slammed it into Lyle's cheek, knocking him back.

"That's for everything you put Aspen through. I hope you have a terrible life. You deserve it."

His nose dripping blood from the impact, Lyle wiped his nose with the back of his hand and shook his head.

"Money can't fix what you two have. You'll never make it. Enjoy my leftovers, asshole."

There was so much venom in his tone that I almost flinched.

"That's where you're wrong. But thankfully, you'll never get to find out," Dominik said calmly.

He walked back down the stairs, meeting me at the landing.

"Sorry you had to see that. I just couldn't help it."

"Don't be. It was deserved," I smiled, giving Dominik a long kiss.

"Let's get your stuff from the house tomorrow. Tonight, we can go out to dinner and celebrate," he suggested.

"That sounds perfect."

He wrapped his arms securely around me, and as I enveloped

him in a tight hug, I had a perfect view of Lyle. I looked back at him still shaken, and silently said goodbye to him.

There was an understanding. A pain in his eyes as he saw me attached to Dominik.

And while a small piece of me mourned him and the relationship we had; it was over long before I ever met Dominik.

This was the way it was supposed to end.

Clara had given us the name of a very upscale restaurant near Beverly Hills that was absolutely beautiful.

The sultry and dimly lit interior was even more gorgeous than I could've dreamed of. I looked around for a minute trying to take it all in, as I'd only ever wished to be taken out somewhere this romantic.

There was a small intimate booth nestled into a quiet corner with a lit ivory candle and crystal wine glasses already set up. I was still trying to soak it all in as we were seated. The ambience, the dim lighting, and low jazz music. Even the white linen tablecloth just *felt* expensive.

Across the table, Dominik couldn't have looked any more handsome and dashing. His dark gray suit fit him like a glove. It was like a scene out of the Great Gatsby.

I had worn an emerald green dress that hugged my body with a sweetheart neckline. It was one of the only nice articles of clothing I owned, and the women that surrounded me still made me feel like it was inadequate.

But it was quickly forgotten.

I was filled to the brim with so much love and joy with the outcome of everything, and having Dominik with me was the cherry on top.

Dominik ordered a fancy bottle of red wine for us, and I couldn't help but smile from ear to ear.

"You know this is our first real date," I giggled.

"I suppose that's true. I guess I never really thought about it that way."

The waiter came back and popped the wine bottle, pouring us a hearty amount in each glass.

"You look amazing, Aspen."

I shyly tucked a piece of hair around my face. "Thank you. Now that we're millionaires, I guess the sky's the limit," I teased.

A wide grin stretched across his tan face.

"Millionaires, huh? Isn't that a wild thought."

We both raised our glasses to toast.

"Cheers to us and starting a new adventure together."

"Cheers to you, Aspen," he smiled, pausing for a second. "I love you."

Dominik said it as if it was any other phrase. My heart dropped to my stomach, wondering if I'd actually just heard him say that.

The way he so casually said it, the pure adoration in his eyes. I was in shock.

Yet, despite how sudden it was, I couldn't have imagined a more perfect moment. Or a more perfect human to be sharing it with.

"And I love you. There is so much more I could say, but I can't string the words together eloquently enough to explain just how glad I am to have you in my life," I said from my heart.

He kissed the knuckle of my hand and I felt everything finally falling into place at last.

"So, after tomorrow that's it, we'll be done with this chapter for good. Question is, what's next?"

"Well money isn't exactly an issue now. We have enough to not have to go back to my hometown, but I can't just leave my brother in that situation," I winced, thinking about how awful their lives were back home.

"I understand that. We can still go back temporarily if you want, just to try and figure out our next steps. At least we can finally move in somewhere."

"Hotel life is getting really old. I'll be glad when I don't have to live out of suitcases anymore."

The waiter came back and took our order. We were going big on this meal.

"I guess I'm not sure what I want to do after this. When I first left home, I was just so desperate to get out, I wasn't able to have a plan. Now that I can, I don't know what to do."

"The options are limitless. You can do anything you set your mind to," he beamed.

"Oh stop, that's cheesy," I laughed.

"But it's true. I don't doubt for a second that once you figure it out, you'll be unstoppable. I'm just glad to be along for the ride."

"And what about you? Koen has been kicked off the tour as well, so I don't know how that affects his standing at the company. Maybe the two of you could find a new security job together?"

"That would be interesting. I don't know how I feel about going back though."

The food runner sat down a platter of steaming hot shrimp on the table that looked absolutely delectable.

"You haven't mentioned that yet to me. You don't want to go back to security?"

I grabbed one of the shrimp and dipped into the spicy dipping sauce, the flavors bursting on my tongue as I savored the taste.

Shit, this food was good.

"It's not that necessarily. I just hate always being on call, waiting for the next god-awful celebrity or politician to guard. If I found a new agency and got placed in L.A. or somewhere similar, that wouldn't be fair to you. And I don't even think I'd want to do that."

"So don't."

"Well, look at you now," he smirked.

"I'm serious. If you don't want to go back, you have the money now to choose something else. I know going into security meant a lot to you after how you grew up, but who's to say you have to leave it completely?"

"Well, there's only so many opportunities and agencies in the U.S. Most of them have a monopoly too. Usually once a certain field starts working with an agency, they don't switch after that. Word of mouth and whatever."

"You could always shake things up. Start a new agency with Koen, be your own boss. You would have a different perspective with clients since you've worked within all the different fields. You could keep a wide range of bodyguards that fit clients' different needs."

"That's... not a bad idea. How would I convince new guys to join the agency though? The incentive Koen and I had was the pay, which was massive."

I thought about it for a second, taking a sip of the red wine that was likely more expensive than I could even fathom.

"Well Koen is a military veteran, right? What if you tried to recruit other veterans. Like Army dogs or Navy SEALS that come back to civilian life?"

He laughed to himself, considering the idea.

"You know all the answers today. Koen might actually like that idea. I'll have to run it all by him but that sounds like a real plan."

"Life is what you make it, baby. I'll support you in whatever you want to do. If you really want to make it happen, I'll be right here the whole time."

"So, are you finally admitting you're in for the long haul?"

"Of course, I am. I plan on having the last name of Kostopoulus one day, so I'd say so."

There was no hiding the smile on his face.

"Give me a year. Then we can see about that."

The rest of dinner was quite enjoyable, and my heart warmed every time I got to see just how happy Dominik was. I felt much happiness myself, so much that I hadn't been able to experience in so long.

We were right there at the end of closing this chapter. All we had to do was tie up the loose ends.

Chapter Twenty-Nine

ASPEN

Early the next morning, Dominik and I had a car brought over so we could go to the mansion in Calabasas that Lyle and I used to share, however brief that was.

Dominik had refused to let me go alone, hyper aware of Lyle's previous comments and the fact that he wouldn't be able to protect me if he wasn't there.

I may have played a bit of a game pretending I wanted to go by myself, but it was all in good fun. Besides, two sets of hands were better than one when it came to packing.

We had to wait at the call box for Lyle's housekeeper to open the steel gate for us.

Luckily, Lyle had taken the comments to heart the previous day and was purposefully gone from the house so I could clean it out without him there.

"This is where you lived?" Dominik asked in astonishment.

Rolling up to the square, blocky modern house was quite the wonder.

It was massive, the property spanning over an acre and was fit with decorative garden topiaries, a koi fishpond, and a large stone fountain in the middle.

It was about as over the top as it could get.

"It was only for two months. I never even got to enjoy it before the tour started."

Thanking the same driver Clara had loaned us, who I was sure was plenty curious, we hopped out of the car, and I grabbed the lone gold key from my purse to unlock the door.

I'd imagined Lyle would've put some super modern electronic keypad on by now, but when you're on tour for months on end, there's only so much you can do.

As I turned the key in and opened the large modern door, I was greeted by his housekeeper, who only nodded at me before turning and going back to another room somewhere else in the house.

"So how much of this is actually yours?" Dominik asked while looking around at the stark white walls and ultra-modern furniture that looked like it came out of some home designing TV Network.

"Bits and pieces. I'm definitely going to take some of my frames down," I cringed, while looking in the living room at the picture frames that still stood on the fireplace mantle. "But besides that, and grabbing my clothes from the bedroom, that's about it."

"I understand. Let's go see it."

There were more twists and turns to get to the bedroom than necessary, but there were six bedrooms in the house, and just as many bathrooms, so it was a bit of a maze.

Entering my former bedroom, that I really only spent a handful of nights in, I felt clarity. I thought I might have felt upset or depressed coming back to the room that Lyle and I had spent happy days in once upon a time, but I felt nothing.

The room still looked exactly the same. A giant king size bed, and a plush white headboard leaned up against the wall. Some ridiculously expensive black nightstands by the side of the bed that I'm sure Lyle paid an interior designer to select, despite how unattractive they were.

But that wasn't what we were there for.

Opening up the suitcase that I had brought, I started going through the clothing drawers and just sweeping them out handfuls at a time and neatly stacking all the clothes back in the suitcase.

Dominik tackled the bathroom and took control of picking up any knickknacks of mine or random items like a hairbrush or makeup mirror that he knew I would want to bring with me.

It wasn't about the fact that I could afford to replace all of this in the blink of an eye with the money from the contracts with the record label, it was about completely erasing any trace of me from this life.

I wanted it to look like I had never lived here or stepped foot in this house.

And with how stark and clean the house looked, I wasn't that far off as it was.

"Alright I think I've gotten everything from the counters in there," he said, dropping a bag on the other side of the suitcase. "Do you want me to go and get your products from the bathroom drawers? Knowing you, I'm sure you still have some here with your night routine."

"Sure, go ahead. There shouldn't be much in there, but I would like it back. And whatever makeup I had in there too."

He gave a thumbs up at my response and went into the bathroom while I finished cleaning out the last few drawers that held random things like bathing suits and socks.

It was nice to finally have a full wardrobe again, having lived with only a certain amount of clothes the whole time we were on tour and living hotel life. It sounded ridiculous, but I was dreaming of the day that Dominik and I could move in together, and I would finally have a closet and a set of drawers to put my clothes in instead of the current lifestyle we were living.

"Hey Aspen?"

"Yeah?" I yelled back.

"I don't know how to say this, but I'm not sure what of this is yours."

Furrowing my brows in confusion, I got up off the floor and went into the bathroom where he was.

Looking at the open drawer, I realized that there were a bunch of new makeup products that didn't seem to be mine. They were brands I didn't use, in shades that I didn't wear.

As much as I wanted to feel upset and heartbroken that every day seemed to reveal some new revelation in regard to Lyle's cheating, I wasn't surprised at this point.

"Just forget about it. I'm not even sure myself. The skin care products are definitely mine so let's just pack that and my hair products and be done."

"Why are you acting so calm about it?"

"Because there's nothing else I can do at this point. I've given all my energy to it since I found out and I don't see the sense anymore. I doubt I'll ever truly know how many girls he screwed but I'm okay with that. I'm guessing that these belong to whatever chick he was screwing when he went to record that song during my birthday."

"I'm sorry. You know I would never do that to you, right?"

I gave him a tiny smile, so grateful that he was still trying to reassure me of his intentions, even though he had no reason to do so.

"Of course, I do. It may still take me some time to get over what happened, considering I was in the dark about it for so long. But I've never felt as safe and reassured as I do with you. I believe you when you say that you want a future with me. And I know that you wouldn't hurt me."

"I wouldn't dream of it. I just want you to know that I'm always here to remind you I'm not like him, even if you have some kind of unrealistic fear. I know how your brain works and your irrationality. That it can sometimes get the best of you, but I will do my best to respond in a way that works for you."

"You are something else you know that Dominik Kostopoulos?"

We shared a passionate kiss and I felt myself at ease again with his reassurance.

"Okay, it looks like we're just about done. Let's go ahead and get everything together and then I'll double-check to make sure I have everything."

"You got it."

I looked back over the bedroom, all the drawers in the night-stand to make sure that there was absolutely nothing I was forgetting. There was still a nagging piece of me saying that I was forgetting something. I finally gave up and left the bedroom and moved onto the rest of the house.

I cringed walking by the music room that held the guitars that Lyle loved so dearly, including the one that he started with. That acoustic guitar was everything and more to him.

But it was time to move on.

The final and last place I had to retrieve anything from was the wood mantle above the fireplace. I was the one that put up all the picture frames and tried to bring some life into the house. I had printed out each picture of us together from birthdays to holidays to special gigs that he played while we were together. Each picture represented a time in my life when I thought I had it all.

But I never did. It was all a lie. And being with Dominik made me realize that I never saw just how much I was missing out on by giving up my life for his and sacrificing my own dreams to make his happen. I lost a piece of myself. A piece of my late teens and early 20s that I couldn't get back.

And I couldn't go back in time and change things. But I could choose how I moved forward from here, and I was choosing to move on with someone that loved me fearlessly, and without condition.

I gathered the picture frames and stacked them up in my arms. Dominik was waiting for me by the door frame as I looked again at each one and recalled the memories for the last time. I then took the pictures and dumped them in the trash.

If the housekeeper took out the trash before Lyle got home and he never saw them again, it honestly wouldn't matter. It was for me.

That was the last piece of us here, and the last tie connecting us together. And now it was gone.

"Are you ready to head back?"

I looked around at the mansion one last time. Even though it never felt like home, it felt like a dream come true of the life that we always envisioned for ourselves. The one that I dreamed of for so many years when I was stuck under my mother's wrath, and in the tiny house that scarred me.

But dreams change, and this was one I was ready to be done with.

"Yes. Let's go home."

Home was always where Dominik was. As much as I complained about awful hotel rooms and never feeling like I had somewhere to call my own, just being able to sleep beside him was enough comfort for me.

It brought back the memories of being stuck on the tour bus and feeling trapped with no way out, wishing that I could be next to him without the prying eyes of those around us.

I enjoyed reminiscing about how much we annoyed each other. When we first met it was like a moth to flame and while most of my annoyance came from battling my ever-growing feelings, I had never fallen harder for someone. He figured me out in just a few days of being there. He saw beyond the walls, and facade that I had built like an iron guard around myself and saw just how deeply unhappy I was.

No one else did.

And while I missed those on tour like Harlow and the occasional company of Elissa, they never truly understood just how much I was wanting.

Now curled up next to Dominik, lying naked beside each other, if I could've told myself just how happy I could be I wouldn't have believed it.

We accept the kind of love we think we deserve.

A notion that I'd always heard of, but never understood until it was me. Unknowingly having accepted a conditional and untruthful love, convincing myself that it was fine.

If only I knew then what I knew now.

There were many things that I was worried about for the future as I laid awake that night. Many questions to be had of where we would end up or how I could continue enjoying my life, knowing that my brother and mother were still left in such a mess.

But I chose to give myself grace and enjoyed the moment for what it was.

That night, when I snuggled in close to him and laid my head on his beating heart, I felt a calmness that laid my worries at ease.

Chapter Thirty

ASPEN

AFTER A HEAVENLY NIGHT'S SLEEP, WE WOKE UP TO THE shrill tone of my iPhone's alarm at an early seven o'clock. We had to be back at the record label by eight to start the proceedings.

Koen would meet us there and would have his deal put together separately, although he'd surely give us all the details later.

Now being held up to my end of the bargain, I had to bring my phone and laptop to be thoroughly investigated. I knew there wasn't anything else on there of any interest, so I didn't mind handing everything over.

I had even done the honor of putting each photo and video into a special folder for them to have all in one place. They would know for sure that I wasn't bluffing after they saw how hideous Lyle acted in those times, when it was easy to just pin it on him being a young boy.

It always catches up to you at some point.

"You ready for today?" Dominik asked as he started getting ready.

"Definitely. We have a late flight back to Dayton so the sooner we get done, the better."

"And we're still in agreement? Three months in Dayton?"

"Yep. After that the sky's the limit."

He pressed a quick kiss to my cheek and went to brush his teeth while I started doing my hair.

I tried to make it a sleek ponytail to show some professionalism, taking a large scoop of gel and plopping it on my scalp. I used a comb to push my hair back as I tied it tight in the back.

My hair had faded so much from the lovely red shade it once was. Now it was a muddy auburn color, dancing between the two shades, after not having Harlow around to color it for so long.

"Hey Dominik?"

"Hm?"

"How would you feel about me dying my hair back to its natural color?"

He dried his mouth off with a hand towel and looked at my hair thoughtfully.

"I think if that's what you want to do, then I'm sure you'll look perfect. You're amazing already, but I'd be lying if I said I wasn't a little curious to see you as a brunette."

I could work with that. "I'll see if I can find someone in Dayton to dye it back. I'll miss the red, but I'll definitely be glad to be done with the upkeep for it."

"You have no idea how beautiful I thought you looked that day Harlow dyed your hair when we were still on tour. I remember it perfectly."

"Really?"

"Yes. It was the first time I'd seen you smile and laugh so freely. I was just so captivated by you. I couldn't believe you were so perfect and in front of me," he laughed. "But you looked like you wanted to kill me as soon as I walked in."

The memories came flooding in and I could recall clear as day him standing in the doorway, acting all brooding and cocky.

"I remember that day. You'd gone off on your whole tangent about groupies and I was pretty mad at you. I didn't like thinking about you with anyone else and I felt conflicted enough as it was. You really put my emotions through the ringer."

"Maybe so but we wouldn't be here otherwise. And besides, I was always yours. It just took you a little longer to realize it."

I jokingly shoved his shoulder, but he leaned in for a kiss anyhow, and I gladly obliged.

"Well time's ticking. Let's make sure we have everything and then head over."

I smoothed the pink chiffon blouse and tucked it into my neat pencil skirt. I looked pretty damn good for someone who was about to get a million dollars.

Dominik looked as delicious as ever. Watching him thread the buttons up on his white shirt in the mirror made me just about drool. It was like I had hit puberty all over again being around him so much. I was aroused by even his smallest movements.

Which he'd picked up on and now purposefully teased me with. But with a man as hot as he was, it was almost impossible to stop.

We'd banged our way through every surface in the hotel room, christening every spot since arriving in L.A. I felt sorry for the poor soul cleaning the room after we left.

But it was hard to stop. I'd likely initiate it again as soon as we got back.

Sliding my laptop and phone into my purse, I checked myself over again one more time before ringing Clara and letting her know we were ready.

The same black Escalade pulled up and drove us over to the building. We arrived right on time, and I leaned over to the driver before stepping out of the car.

"Thank you, sir. If this is the last time, we see you then thanks for your service and discretion."

The bald man cracked a bit of a smile.

"You wouldn't believe what I know. These lips are locked

though," he joked, miming the movements of locking his lips and throwing the imaginary key over his back.

I could only imagine the amount of dirt he had on everyone the label worked with. Chauffeuring had its own perks, I'm sure.

Dominik outstretched his hand for me to take as he helped me out of the car and we went back up those ugly block stairs, and into the building.

"Hey guys, how're you doing today?" Jasmine asked with a smile.

"Good, ready to get this over with. How're you?"

"Not bad. Clara sent her regards, but she's tied up with work right now. Trust me when I say I'm glad I don't have her job."

"Reddick, Kostas, we're ready to see you now."

The woman gestured for us to come in and we were led into the same conference room we were in previously. Robert, the owner of the label, was seated at the head of the table with presumably his lawyer to the right.

I thought we might see the two other executives that we had to deal with the day before, but they were nowhere to be found. It was likely for the best so we could wrap things up as quickly as possible without any fuss. Dominik and I surely weren't going to put up a fight. We were going to do what we had promised.

"Good morning. This is our lawyer who will watch over the proceedings, as well as collect the material from your items, Aspen. As long as everything goes to plan, we should be done within the hour. Are we clear?"

"Yes. Let's go ahead and start."

"Aspen, you will take the longest, so let's get yours out of the way. Do you have all the material on your current electronic devices that was mentioned to us yesterday?"

"Yes, I do. I even sorted into its own folder. Just so you'd know I wasn't kidding. If you want to search through the entire thing, go ahead, but this is the only place these items are. There are no other hard drives, or electronic devices containing this material."

I took the items out of my bag and placed them in front of me, unlocking each.

"We have to be able to verify that," the lawyer said without a hint of emotion in his voice.

"Be my guest. Everything I own is in my hotel room. I've cleaned all my belongings out of Lyle's house."

"We'll be checking that just to be sure. A forensic search may be necessary to ensure these items truly aren't anywhere else," he said while pushing his glasses up over his nose.

"Okay. Like I said before, you guys can do what you want. I'll comply with whatever."

"And why exactly are you so agreeable? Is there an ulterior motive?"

This lawyer was really getting on my nerves. He was just supposed to oversee the proceedings, not interrogate me.

"No, I just want this done as quickly as possible. I have no reason to try and drag things out any further. I will provide whatever you ask for."

The lawyer didn't seem to like that answer but it was clear that he was betting against me. Whether it's because of the amount of money being exchanged, or just the fact that he was having to go over the proceedings at all.

I wasn't intimidated though.

The lawyer started going through my devices to retrieve the files as we waited silently for him to flip through them all.

Robert, being the curious man that he was, looked through every single picture and video, not only to look at the damage, but also ensure that I was not lying about it. His face twisted when he heard all the vile things that Lyle drunkenly talked about in that video that I had buried in my phone from over a year ago.

Dominik hadn't heard it before but with the video playing

at full volume from my phone, we all had to listen to his slurring atrocities. He was lucky enough that night that I just blamed it on him being absolutely wasted and didn't leave him then and there.

Although now, I certainly wish I would've had better morals.

After viewing the materials thoroughly and seeing that I had provided what I said, it seemed like they were tossing up whether or not they needed to actually go through everything else.

"I see that you have everything laid out here. As long as we have an understanding that this is everything and there's no need to search any further, I will return your items to you," the lawyer said.

"Trust me, all I want is a normal life after this. I have no other reason to try and tear down Lyle's career."

The lawyer methodically deleted each photo and video.

"Yes, well since these images have been deleted, we have two contracts to sign. One is for having released all the images to us willingly in exchange for the sum of five hundred thousand dollars, and an NDA for the same amount."

On cue, Jasmine retrieved the contracts from her briefcase, and slid them over to the other lawyer to read over.

Once glad with all the nonsense legal jargon he read on the pages, he slid my contracts across the table to me, and I was given a pen to begin signing with. Although some of the words were confusing, I didn't really care at this point and was confident that Jasmine had drawn up a contract that would protect me.

"The Non-Disclosure Agreement states that you will under no circumstances discuss these materials with friends, family or the media and there is no expiration date to this agreement. It is in perpetuity, for the sum of five hundred thousand dollars. The other contract states that you have willingly given the electronic material to our label, for the sum of five hundred thousand dollars. If you accept these terms, please sign your name."

Jasmine pointed to every place I needed to initial or sign my name as I went through each page carefully and considerately. Even though my legal knowledge was not great, I did try and glance at the wording every now and then just in case.

Dominik sat patiently by my side, watching them like a hawk. He was still waiting to sign his own contract as a comfortable silence fell over the room. It took a few minutes as I continued to fill out paper after paper, but I was fine with it.

I never knew that something as simple as a pen on paper could mean a whole new life for myself.

As I finished the last signature, the tension in my shoulders released.

The lawyer assured me that I would get copies of both for my own personal records. I slid them back to him and gave a look at Jasmine to make sure she knew that I would definitely be wanting those copies.

"Alright, besides that, I guess we're done with you. The news stories have been killed courtesy of PR and will not be run. I hope you appreciate my kindness in stopping them and remember that in case you ever get any future ideas. I hope this is the last run in I have with you, Miss Reddick," Robert said, shuffling the papers together.

"Oh, it will be. Thank you."

"Moving onto you, since you did not provide us with your actual legal last name, we had to dig and find it Mr. Kostopoulos," Robert said accusingly as he glared at Dominik.

"It's all the same anyway, just give me the contract and I'll sign it."

"Not quite yet. We want to corroborate the list you give us with the one Koen gives us. I want every last detail to make sure that each woman is investigated thoroughly about their involvement with Mr. Hawthorne."

"Oh, right I forgot about that. Crazy what one little list could do to ruin his entire career."

Robert didn't laugh at that although I was having to actively restrain myself at how carelessly Dominik talked about it.

Unlocking his phone, Dominik found the list he'd worked on the night before with Koen of the full names and approximate ages of every woman that he knew of who had slept with Lyle since joining the tour. What used to be a knife in my heart, was now only a pin prick as I viewed the staggering list he presented to them.

The lawyer, and Robert, both made copies of this list and pulled out some previous NDA's that I had assumed were made with some women, or at least the ones that they knew of, to confirm the list.

Robert looked visibly annoyed.

"I see Lyle got around more than I thought. Thank you for providing this list, Dominik. It will be very helpful in making sure that each one of these ladies do not have a reason to talk. I'm sure John will have fun telling him to keep his dick in his pants again."

"Not likely," I scoffed.

Once they pulled out the previous files and saw that the names matched some of the previous NDA files, Jasmine pulled out the contract and the lawyer glanced at it to make sure it was fine. Then it was sent over to Dominik.

"This contract states that you will never disclose this information to family, friends, or the media for the sum of one million dollars. The Non-Disclosure Agreement does not have an expiration date and is in effect for perpetuity. If you agree with everything I have stated, then please sign your name."

Right on cue, Dominik started initialing and signing his name on every spot without hesitation. He hardly glanced at each section, having no care as to what the fine print stated.

With each of our contracts fully signed, the lawyer shuffled the papers in his hands and gave us a demeaning look.

"Alright well I think that covers it. You will each have a check made out in your name for the sums listed on the contracts. That means, Aspen you will receive two checks," Robert clarified to me.

"If you have any difficulty, I'm sure you can let Jasmine know who will then tell me. Otherwise, I believe this ends our meeting and our proceedings. Good luck with your lives but I truly hope to never hear your names again. Goodbye."

We each politely shook his hand before we were left alone with Jasmine.

Although I wanted to celebrate and jump around, I tried to remain professional before Jasmine excused herself.

Once we were alone together, I let out a massive sigh and no longer tried to hold back how happy I was.

"That went smoother than I expected. It was quick and easy and honestly, I feel like I finally have a giant weight lifted off my shoulders," I said excitedly.

"Robert's the kind of guy that doesn't like anything messy. You learn about how men like him operate the longer you're in the business and it's clear to me he would've probably paid us even more if it meant we were out of his hair," Dominik laughed. "But yes, it's finally over."

"Damn. Do you think I should've asked for another million?" I joked.

"You very well could've. Although he put on the front yesterday like they couldn't afford it, they have millions they could've afforded us. Though now, given that they're having to pay off each woman Lyle slept with, I'm sure their money will be running a little low."

We both openly laughed at that, although I felt a tinge of sadness for those poor women now involved in this mess.

"It's for the best. Maybe having his management see everything will finally show Lyle that he needs to look at his life and what he's doing and figure out who he wants to really be. Because this person is truly just someone I don't know," I sighed.

"You live and you learn. It's something he'll just have to figure out on his own. It makes me happy though to see you being kind and still wishing the best for him. I'm proud of you."

"I just realized that I have no other reason to wish ill of him. I met you along the way, and that is what I'm truly grateful for."

We shared a deep kiss, and I looked lovingly into those cerulean eyes of his, ecstatic to see what our new life would hold.

"This means we're finally done now with LA. Are you ready to go back home?" he asked.

"More than ready. I can't wait to start our new life together."

And with that, we walked out of the room hand in hand, and I felt like I'd finally found my place in this world with Dominik by my side.

Epilogue

THE SOUND OF A SEAGULL PASSING OVERHEAD SHOOK me from my daydream as the sunset made its way through the sky.

The incoming tide kissed the edge of the shoreline as I approached it, the waves calmer now as the sun went down. The cold, salty air combed through my hair as I breathed in its comforting scent, birds landing on the shore around me.

My toes sunk into the damp sand as a frigid wave touched them, sending a shiver through me.

The water had gotten colder as the seasons changed, but it was always pretty warm. Thank you, Florida.

Dominik and I bought a small beach cottage at New Smyrna Beach about six months prior.

A popular Florida beach that hosted a lot of unique locals, there was always something happening in the charming town.

Neither of us had ever lived at the beach, or initially found the location to be all that interesting as our winter hideaway.

But once we found our gorgeous beach cottage nestled along the coast, it felt like the perfect place for us.

Our main house was located in Georgia. A perfect blend between being close to my mother and brother, and a decent drive to our beach home. Dominik's family had even moved to Georgia to be close to us, as they rekindled their relationship.

It was still hard to fathom that we were lucky enough to own two homes. Modest homes, but nonetheless, still amazing to own.

Coming back up the shore and to our deck, I washed my sandy feet off in our outside shower before heading inside.

"Hey baby," I smiled, stopping in the kitchen to give Dominik a quick kiss and ruffling his now long curls. I rounded the corner into the living room where the antique record player hummed out the tune *'Breathe'* by Pink Floyd as it spun circles.

Dominik was busy getting dinner ready for the night, which just so happened to be some fresh fish he'd caught that day. He loved getting to relax and fish on our boat, even having a cold beer sometimes when I'd join him. But the boat always made me nauseous, so he often went out there on his own just to clear his mind for a while.

"Hey, how was the sunset? Water feel okay?" he asked as I sat down on the couch.

"It was great. I can't wait to come back in the summer when it's really warm out. Winter at the beach is pretty cool but I know the summers here will be amazing. Don't you think, Myles?"

Myles, who'd just about outgrown Dominik by now, had visited us for the week during his school's winter break.

I was so happy whenever he got to visit. By some miracle, our mother had chosen to go to rehab after my encounter with her a while back, and she slowly got sober.

Things were still hard sometimes, and she struggled every day with her sobriety. But she had decided to make the effort to get better for Myles's sake. And that was something I honestly never saw coming.

I was so grateful to be able to spend time with Myles when our mother let him stay with us. Dominik had fit so easily into the family, having made amends with my mother and playing a large part in keeping her sober by offering her steady work.

Myles looked up to him a lot, although I knew he'd never tell him. Dominik always had a keen eye though and picked up on it himself.

It was little things he'd try to do to help Myles out when needed, and he always made sure he wasn't overstepping.

But wow did it make my heart swell.

"Summers will be really cool here. It's so fun to have a vacation house. Plus, with the business taking off, you never know what you guys could get after this. Maybe a mountain house is next?" Myles joked, sitting across from me in our *repaired* grandmother's chair.

We all laughed, but as the one who kept track of the new security business' finances, he wasn't that far off.

With Dominik and Koen entering business together, they had a very unique outlook and plan of recruiting new bodyguards that did extremely well.

There were many veterans coming out of the armed forces who felt lost once in civilian life again. Koen had a way with them that helped them understand how to put their training to new use.

And Dominik was largely involved in the training recruits would go through once they joined. The mental and physical sides of it before sending them through appropriate firearm training.

I'd never seen him so happy as he was getting to take all his years of knowledge and teach new members himself. Plus, he always looked damn good during the physical training sessions, which I got to benefit from.

And what was I doing?

Well, I was still figuring things out. I'd taken some time to try and see what my passion was in life and what called to me. And while I hadn't found it yet, I had all the time in the world.

For now, I was happy to support Dominik in his business and work on the back end of things to keep it running smoothly.

I wouldn't mind taking care of our kids at some point though.

I wondered at times if that would be my passion. Raising a family, having a few miniatures of us running around, and creating a healthy environment for them to live in like the one I never got.

While the timing wasn't right yet, I knew once I had a ring on my finger, I would start imploring Dominik on expediting things. And that day would be here before I knew it, since we finally felt settled down enough now to move to the next step.

My current life though was one I was grateful for, and I didn't take it for granted.

"Alright guys, dinner will be ready soon. Do you want to watch some football while we wait, Myles?" Dominik asked as he finished the major parts of dinner.

"Oh yeah!"

They both sat down on the couch, flipping on the TV as I casually joined them in the nearby recliner.

I had no interest in football, and I honestly didn't think Dominik did either. But seeing them bond was always really special to me.

The news channel automatically popped up after the TV turned on and I unexpectedly saw a picture of Lyle flashing on the screen.

"Popstar Lyle Hawthorne is now seeing one of the worst nosedives in music history as his rankings have tanked significantly following the release of his recent album. After a string of controversies, the world turned its back on him and these my friends, are the repercussions."

We all watched in awe, no one expecting Lyle to be gracing the evening news with that kind of unfortunate outcome.

"Wow. Well, I guess I saw that coming," Dominik said with a laugh as he moved on and switched to the sports channel.

"No kidding. What a loser," Myles laughed.

I hadn't thought of Lyle in a very long time but was unsurprised that karma came for him in the end. While this likely meant that his career was over, I enjoyed knowing that he had such a fitting end.

With a world as toxic as that one, I was certainly glad I'd never had to step foot back in that lifestyle.

When I closed the door to that chapter of my life, I locked it and threw away the key.

They all seemed completely unbothered by his surprise interruption though, enjoying the game without a care. I didn't care about it all that much myself, but found my mind settled with the knowledge of what happened to him after I left.

And I realized then that everything had panned out exactly the way it was supposed to be.

My family was happy, I had a successful life with the person I loved, and most importantly, I had Dominik.

Fate had a mind of its own and nothing was ever as it seemed to be.

Falling and busting my chin open may not have been apart of my plans all that time ago, but I unknowingly changed the outcome of my life.

Whoever that girl was, I now thank. Because she was the reason I found Dominik.

And as I watched Myles and Dominik laugh together and watch the silly sports game, I closed my eyes and gave a silent thank you to the universe.

I was free.

Author Note

What an incredible journey.

I never imagined I would be able to pursue my dreams, but that is what this book is to me. My wildest, most far-fetched dream that is now a reality. When I wrote my first book about a puppy in the third grade, I read it to my grandparents in my parent's living room. It was such a dream for me to be a writer, but I let that dream go as adulthood loomed.

To have achieved a fully completed, published novel is massive for me, and I could not be prouder. A huge thank you to my family who has supported me since day one and listened to me talk about this book forever. I also want to thank everyone on social media who has been rooting for me and so supportive of this little book of mine.

This has been the most wonderful start to my career, and I cannot wait to see where we go from here!

Thank you for reading, I am so grateful to each and every reader! If you liked this book, please consider leaving a review on GoodReads or Amazon! It would mean so much to this small indie author!

Acknowledgements

I want to personally thank everyone who helped make this book possible!

My beta readers, Courtney, Lameez, Michelle, and my sister Alexa who gave me so much feedback and support.

My amazing editor, Dani Galliaro, who was such a joy to work with, and provided the best expertise.

My lovely book cover designer, Jules, who crafted the most beautiful cover and saw it through with me until we got it just right.

And my incredible formatter, Stacey Blake, who created the perfect formatting you see now!

There are so many people who helped make this book possible and I truly cannot put into words how much I appreciate each and every one of you. This book means the world to me, and it wouldn't be here without everyone's support.

About the Author

Francesca Forbes is a romance writer living in Orlando, Florida. Dabbling in different romantic sub-genres, she crafts protective yet lovable male characters, and relatable female characters. She enjoys reading, vanilla lattes, and all things Disney in her free time when not with her beloved dog Sage.

Check out these socials to keep up with Francesca's next release.

Instagram: @authorfrancescaforbes
TikTok: @authorfrancescaforbes
Website: francescaforbes.com